Praise for

shannon stacey

"This is the perfect contemporary romance!"
—*RT Book Reviews* on *Undeniably Yours*

"Sexy, sassy and immensely satisfying."
—*Fresh Fiction* on *Undeniably Yours*

"Shannon Stacey's books deliver exactly what we need
in contemporary romances....
I feel safe that every time I pick up a Stacey book
I'm going to read something funny, sexy and loving."
—Jane Litte of *Dear Author* on *All He Ever Needed*

"I'm madly in love with the Kowalskis!"
—*New York Times* bestselling author Nalini Singh

D1052858

HILLSBORO PUBLIC LIBRARIES
Hillsboro, OR
Member of Washington County
COOPERATIVE LIBRARY SERVICES

**Also available from
Shannon Stacey
and Harlequin HQN**

Exclusively Yours
Undeniably Yours
Yours to Keep
All He Ever Needed
Be Mine (anthology with Jennifer Crusie
and Victoria Dahl)
All He Ever Desired

**Also available from
Shannon Stacey
and Carina Press**

Holiday Sparks
Mistletoe and Margaritas
Slow Summer Kisses

shannon stacey

all he ever
dreamed

HARLEQUIN® HQN

HILLSBORO PUBLIC LIBRARIES
Hillsboro, OR
Member of Washington County
COOPERATIVE LIBRARY SERVICES

If you purchased this book without a cover you should be aware that this book is stolen property. It was reported as "unsold and destroyed" to the publisher, and neither the author nor the publisher has received any payment for this "stripped book."

Recycling programs for this product may not exist in your area.

ISBN-13: 978-0-373-77758-7

ALL HE EVER DREAMED

Copyright © 2013 by Shannon Stacey

All rights reserved. Except for use in any review, the reproduction or utilization of this work in whole or in part in any form by any electronic, mechanical or other means, now known or hereafter invented, including xerography, photocopying and recording, or in any information storage or retrieval system, is forbidden without the written permission of the publisher, Harlequin HQN, 225 Duncan Mill Road, Don Mills, Ontario M3B 3K9, Canada.

This is a work of fiction. Names, characters, places and incidents are either the product of the author's imagination or are used fictitiously, and any resemblance to actual persons, living or dead, business establishments, events or locales is entirely coincidental.

This edition published by arrangement with Harlequin Books S.A.

For questions and comments about the quality of this book, please contact us at CustomerService@Harlequin.com.

® and TM are trademarks of Harlequin Enterprises Limited or its corporate affiliates. Trademarks indicated with ® are registered in the United States Patent and Trademark Office, the Canadian Trade Marks Office and in other countries.

Printed in U.S.A.

TM www.Harlequin.com

This one's for Jess. Your enthusiasm and support mean the world to me, and I hope your Prince Charming is waiting right around the next corner.

And for Sharon Muha. Thank you for having my back.

all he ever
dreamed

CHAPTER ONE

JOSH KOWALSKI'S LIFE could be summed up in just a few words—thirty years' worth of itches he couldn't quite scratch.

He itched to get out of Whitford, Maine, and away from the Northern Star Lodge. He itched for adventure and travel and a job he'd chosen, rather than one chosen for him before he was even born. He itched to find the woman who'd make him want to forsake all others until death do they part. There was no medicated powder to cure those kinds of itches, either. All he could do was bide his time, and that had gotten harder with every passing year.

This year, though, things were looking up. Josh grabbed a six-pack out of the fridge and bumped the door closed with his hip since he was clutching a bag of stolen baked goods in his other hand. Breaking his leg back in July had sucked. But his brothers coming home to help out at the lodge, giving him the chance to let them know he resented being left holding the bag just because he was the youngest, had been his big break.

"You heading out?"

He almost dropped his beer. In her sheepskin-lined-suede winter slippers, Rosie was almost silent as she moved around the lodge. "Yeah. Half hour until kickoff."

Rose Davis had been the housekeeper at the lodge for as long as he could remember, but when Josh's mother died when he was only five, she'd become much more than that. She was as close to a mother as he could have. That meant, of course, that he was thirty years old and essentially still lived with mom. No wonder he had such a hard time scratching that need-a-woman itch.

"If you—" She broke into a coughing fit and Josh frowned. A bad cold had gone around Whitford a while back and Rose had ended up with pneumonia. She'd bounced back pretty well, but he didn't like the sound of that cough. "If you see Katie, tell her I said hi."

"Maybe I should stay home."

She scoffed and waved her hand. "I'm going to curl up with my knitting and the *Criminal Minds* marathon. The last thing I want to listen to is you screaming and swearing at the television in the other room."

"You had pneumonia, Rosie. If you don't take care of yourself, you'll end up back in bed."

"Is that my banana bread in your bag?"

"You're trying to change the subject."

"You're stealing my banana bread."

"You told me you wanted to lose a few pounds, so really I'm doing this for you." He was busted, but he didn't even break a sweat as she raised an eyebrow at him. "Even though you're perfect the way you are, I just want you to be happy. Eating this banana bread won't make you happy, but it'll make my friends—including your daughter—very, very happy."

Rose laughed, but it quickly deteriorated into another bout of coughing. Josh didn't like it, but it passed fairly quickly and she waved away the concern she must have seen on his face. "You think you're a charmer, Joshua Kowalski, but I've had your number since you were four years old and told me you peed on the back of the toilet so I'd always have something to clean and your parents would keep paying me. You were doing *that* for my sake, too."

"See? I'm always thinking of you, Rosie."

She shook her head and made a shooing motion with her hand. "Go. Take the banana bread. And I bet you put a dent in the cookie jar, too."

Busted again. He'd dumped at least a dozen oatmeal raisin cookies into a baggy to supplement the loaf of banana bread. Usually a guy didn't bring baked goods to watch a game with his buddies, but nobody in Whitford could resist goodies from Rose's kitchen. He preferred chocolate chip cookies himself, but Katie liked oatmeal raisin and, if he was going to steal her mother's cookies for her, at least they would be her favorite.

"You have your cell phone in your pocket?" he asked before he opened the back door.

She nodded, patting the pocket of the thick cardigan she was wearing. "I'll call you if I need you."

"Promise?"

"I'm fine, Josh." She gave him a tender look and his heart squeezed when he thought about how sick she'd been at the beginning of November. It had scared the crap out of him and he didn't want a repeat of that anytime soon. She'd been well enough to celebrate Thanksgiving at the new home of his brother Mitch and his wife, but he was constantly worried she was pushing too hard. It had been ten days since then, which meant almost a month since she'd gotten sick, but he still worried every time she coughed.

"You'll call me if you need anything at all?"

"I promise. Now, go, so I can make my tea and get back to my show."

He went because the sooner he left, the sooner Rosie would curl up with her tea, knitting and her show. But, as he climbed into his truck and fired up the engine, he wondered what was going to happen when the Northern Star opened for the season in a couple of weeks. If Rose hadn't bounced back to her usual self by then, he was in trouble.

The easy answer was to hire one of the teenage girls in town to help out around the place for a while. They'd done that in the past occasionally, but for the past few years they hadn't been able to spare the money. They already had a record number of bookings this year, thanks to the woman who handled all the internet stuff for Mitch's company. She had revamped the lodge's website and gotten them on Facebook and such, but every dollar they paid extra help was a dollar less in the profit column. Profits were the key to Josh's freedom, so he'd wash the bedding and scrub the toilets and make the beds himself if he had to.

But he'd worry about that tomorrow. Weekdays were for work, but today was for football, friends and food. Sometimes he was convinced those few hours each Sunday when he could sneak away from the home and business that had consumed his life for as long as he could remember—although when the snow was really good, he couldn't get away even on Sundays—were the only things that had kept him from just saying "screw it" and walking away.

So he'd drink beer, eat stolen banana bread and yell at the television. Katie would give him a hard time and he'd end up making some stupid bet with her. Hopefully, the Patriots would win and the good mood would carry him through Monday.

But when he parked his truck alongside the few that were already in the yard, Josh didn't see Katie's Jeep. She never missed Sunday games at Max's house, and a glance at the clock told him it was almost time for the kickoff, and the Pats were playing the early game.

With all the germs the people of Whitford had been spreading around the past couple of months, maybe she was sick. The thought dampened his enthusiasm a little. He liked hanging with Katie and he'd even risked the wrath of Rosie to steal oatmeal raisin cookies for her.

He told himself he'd give her a call if she didn't show or text by the end of the first quarter, just to see if she was sick. Watching football without Katie wouldn't be quite the same.

KATIE DAVIS WEDGED her ancient but much-loved Jeep Wrangler between two pickups and grabbed the grocery bag of munchies off the passenger seat. She was running late, but one didn't show up at Max Crawford's house empty-handed, so she'd run into the market for some junk food. Fran had been in the mood to talk, of course, so paying for a couple bags of chips and three tubs of dip had taken almost fifteen minutes.

The big white truck with Northern Star Lodge on the sides was hard to miss, so she knew Josh was already inside. He made it to Max's whenever he could, but it was still nice to have the advance warning. She'd become quite the actress over the years of hiding how she really felt about her best buddy, but she still needed a few seconds to take a deep breath before going onstage.

The stage, in this case, being Max Crawford's living room. He lived alone, loved every sport but golf and tennis, and had the biggest television in Whitford. Nobody was quite sure what he did for a living—something to do with the high-tech security system in his basement, which had Rosie convinced he'd be the inspiration for a future episode of her beloved *Criminal Minds*. But as long as he had the games in HDTV, and three battered leather sofas, nobody asked too many questions.

Max was in the kitchen when she went in the side door. He was a tall, blond, really built, sports-loving hottie who did absolutely nothing for her. And she'd tried. No matter how often she looked at his handsome face and made a mental catalog of all the reasons he'd be so right for her, however, her body refused to cough up so much as a hiccup in her pulse. Nothing.

"Hey, Katie. Wasn't sure you were going to make it."

"Fran was feeling sociable."

"Ah." Max took the bag from her and peeked inside. "Yes! Nobody else brought dip. You saved the chips."

She rolled her eyes and left him with the bag so

she could go to his gigantic fridge for a soda. "Bet somebody already stole my corner."

One of the comfy leather sofas was a sectional and Katie's favorite spot was the corner. She could pull Max's Bruins throw blanket off the back and make herself a nest. Even though they all generally sat in the same place, she wouldn't put it past somebody to take advantage of her being late to steal the prime couch real estate.

"Like Josh would let anybody take your spot."

Katie froze in the act of pulling up the tab on her soda. What was that supposed to mean? The can hissed as she finished opening it so she could wet her mouth. "He doesn't care where anybody sits as long as he can see the screen."

"Maybe not 'anybody,' but he cares where *you* sit."

She snorted, making a show of how stupid she found that observation. No matter how much she wanted it to be true, the last thing she needed was to be a topic of conversation for the guys.

"I don't think he even knows it," Max continued, "but he definitely puts out a vibe."

"What vibe?"

"The *Katie sits near me* vibe."

"I don't know what you've been smoking, but you might want to cut back." Katie had been waiting for Josh to put out that kind of vibe for most of her life—and she'd just skipped celebrating her thirty-third birthday—so if there was one, she wouldn't have missed it.

It wasn't as though she'd been sitting in some tower her entire existence, pining away for her oblivious prince. She'd dated. She'd even had a few serious relationships, but, in the end, none of them were Josh. No, if there was a vibe, she would have felt it.

"Everybody in this town knows you're his girl but him." Max didn't seem to notice the heat she could feel lighting up her cheeks like a stoplight. "You should…I dunno. Wear some lipstick and put some of that crap on your eyes."

"Makeup? I don't think so."

"Men notice that stuff."

"I have worn makeup before, you know." Not often, but for the occasional funeral or wedding. "He didn't do any kind of cartoon double-take and walk into a wall."

"Maybe you need more."

"I'm not doing my face up like a clown to get him to notice me, Max. This is me and this is always going to be me, so if I don't do it for him like this, then I don't do it for him at all."

"He just needs a nudge."

"I've known him my whole life. The only thing that nudges Josh Kowalski is a softball bat upside the head."

"And yet your soft, nurturing nature hasn't

drawn him in yet. I'm shocked." Max dumped the entire bag of chips into a cheap plastic bowl.

"Bite me, Max." She took the bowl and the dip and walked into the huge living room. When he'd moved to town and bought the place, Max had removed some walls and let the space absorb what had been a formal dining room.

She glanced toward the sectional and found that, as Max had predicted, the corner was still empty. And Josh smiled at her when she walked over to claim it, setting the chips and dip on the coffee table. That damn smile had always made her feel like a giddy teenage girl, but she had years of practice hiding that giddy girl from the world.

"Thought maybe that junk of yours finally shit the bed," he said when she'd dropped into the corner.

"Leave my Jeep alone, Kowalski. She's outlasted three of your pickups."

"Because I know when to put a vehicle out to pasture." He leaned forward to grab a slice of what looked like her mother's banana bread off the table and turned his attention to the big screen, where the pregame chatter was wrapping up.

"Hi, guys," she said to the room at large, and she got some hellos and a "Hey, Katie" back. Gavin Crenshaw, who cooked at the Trailside Diner, was there with his dad, Mike. Butch Benoit, whose wife, Fran, had made her late, was sitting in the recliner.

He was the oldest guy, so he got the prime leather real estate. It was a light crowd this week. Usually there were a few more guys, but it was the first weekend of December and she knew the town well enough to know there were a lot of Christmas lights being hung in lieu of watching football.

Since her spot in the corner put Katie just slightly behind Josh, she was able to watch him through the corner of her eye. She was pretty sure Max was wrong about Josh putting out any kind of vibe where she was concerned, but even the possibility was enough to make her heart beat a little faster.

He looked better, she decided. Some of the tension had left his expression over the past several months, and more of his usual charm shone in his blue eyes. Even though her mother never said much, Katie knew Josh well enough to see the strain the past few years had put on him. He'd been unhappy and had started drinking enough that she'd half-jokingly given him a hard time once in a while. But then he'd broken his leg, his brothers had come home to Whitford to help and they'd all devoted themselves to getting the Northern Star back on its feet.

Katie had mixed feelings about that. She'd practically grown up at the lodge, so she didn't want to see it go under. And it had been her mother's home since Katie went off to college and it didn't make sense for Rose to have her own place anymore. They were turning things around, which was good. Whether they hired a manager or sold the place, she knew her mom would be taken care of.

But, in either scenario, the endgame was Josh leaving Whitford. As the youngest, he'd seen his older brothers and sister all go off to live their own lives and, by the time it was his turn, he'd been unable to leave his dad to run the place alone. Then Frank had passed away and everybody had just assumed Josh would go on taking care of business. He wanted out and the day was coming when he'd get his wish. Katie didn't want to think about that.

Josh pulled off his Patriots ball cap and pushed his dark hair back before settling the hat back on his head. He'd need a trim soon, she thought, and she had mixed feelings about that, too. On one hand, she knew what it felt like to run her fingers through his hair. On the other…she knew what it felt like to run her fingers through his hair. It could be excruciating, touching him like that—especially when he made that little moaning sound if she washed his hair before cutting it—but she couldn't deny herself the pleasure. Plus, there was nowhere else to go but the beauty parlor, and sending Josh there would be too cruel a thing to do to her best friend.

"What the hell are you doing?" Josh yelled, sitting forward on the couch as if he could physically intimidate the television into taking back whatever had set him off. His voice was almost drowned out by the other guys shouting, and Katie realized she'd been so busy mooning over the side of Josh's head, she'd missed the kickoff. Damn.

She grabbed a handful of chips and forced herself to focus on the replay. If she got caught making googly-eyes at Josh in this crowd, she'd never hear the end of it.

AFTER ALMOST FUMBLING the ball during the first kickoff return, the Patriots got their act together and Josh relaxed against the superior cushions of Max's couch, wishing he could afford furniture like this for the lodge. Someday he was going to get a straight answer from the guy about what he did for a living. It wasn't easy to keep a secret in Whitford, but Max Crawford managed.

But if anybody would know, it would be Fran. And if Fran knew, Rosie would know, which would mean Katie might know.

When Max went into the kitchen at the start of halftime, Josh slapped Katie's leg. "Hey, does Rose know what Max does to earn couch and television money?"

He'd kept his voice low, so she had to lean closer to him to answer him in the same tone. "Nobody knows. It's no secret he doesn't go anywhere on a regular basis, so I guess he works in his basement."

"It's quite a lock he's got on the door." Had a security keypad and everything.

"So nobody can find the bodies."

Josh snorted and shook his head. "It's weird that he's lived here, what…five years? And nobody knows what he does?"

"Has anybody actually asked him outright? I haven't."

She usually got her information the normal way—from Fran, her mom or from keeping her ears open and her mouth closed while the old bucks chatted in the barbershop. But Josh didn't get out quite as much, and Fran didn't share gossip with him as much as she did with other women.

"I did once," he said. "He changed the subject and didn't even try to make it smooth."

"I bet I can find out before you do."

That perked him up and he turned his body so he was fully facing her. "Whaddya got, Davis?"

"If I find out how he makes his money before you do, I'll cut your hair free for six months."

He snorted. "Lame. Winner washes the other's vehicle once a month for a year."

She hesitated, but he'd expected that. It was a half-hour drive to the car wash and twelve bucks down the drain, but Katie never backed down from a bet. "Car wash when it's cold, but hand wash and wax from May through August?"

"Done." He stuck out his hand, then pulled it back before she could shake it. "Wait. I have a condition."

"Admitting it's the first step."

"Funny, smart-ass. The condition is no using feminine wiles."

She laughed, which made everybody in the room stop talking for a few seconds. Katie had a great laugh. "Feminine wiles? What are you, eighty?"

"Call it whatever you want, but no flirting or making kissy faces or letting him look down your shirt to get information out of him."

"How do you see that going, exactly? 'Hey, Max, if you tell me what your job is, I'll let you see my boobs'? You're a moron."

"That's the deal."

"Fine." She shook on it.

Josh loved a good challenge. Gathering up their empties and a couple of used paper plates off the table, he headed for the kitchen to restock.

Max was leaning against the counter, cell phone to his ear, and Josh shoved the stuff into the garbage can as quietly as he could. Then he opened the fridge, looking for a couple bottles of water.

"I promised you it would be there before Christmas, and it will be," Max was telling whoever was on the other end of the line. "I'll shoot you an email when I ship it out, okay?"

Josh didn't try to pretend he wasn't eavesdropping as Max ended his call. He really had no choice but to overhear, since they were the only two people in the kitchen. "Christmas present?"

"Yup." Max snapped his phone back into its holster.

"Family?"

"Nope."

"Something for work?" It was a natural segue into the conversation he wanted to have.

"When are you and Katie finally going to hook up?"

Josh's head whipped around. That wasn't the conversation he wanted to have. "What the hell are you talking about? Why would I hook up with Katie? She's…Katie."

Max shrugged. "Just seems as if you two would be good together."

"We are good together. That's why she's my best friend. Hell, we practically grew up together, so that would be weird, man."

Max shrugged again, then grabbed a soda off the counter. "Shame. You guys are a great couple."

He brushed by and was out of the kitchen before Josh could think of a response. What was he supposed to say to that? Katie was like one of the guys and they'd known each other their whole lives. If they were going to be a great couple, it probably would have come up before.

Halfway back to the couch, he realized Max had managed to evade answering the question about whether his phone call was work related. And he'd done it by deliberately blowing Josh's mind with the concept of hooking up with Katie. It was a slick move on Crawford's part, Josh had to admit.

During a lull in the third-quarter action, Josh pulled out his phone to make sure he hadn't missed any calls. Butch and Mike had disagreed on a referee's iffy call and the volume level had been pretty intense for a few minutes. There was nothing, so he had to assume Rosie was still watching television. It was tempting to call and check on her, but she wouldn't take kindly to that. Or to being woken up if she'd nodded off.

"Waiting for the 1-800-Loser hotline to call you back?" Katie asked, sticking her toe out from under Max's blanket to poke at Josh.

"Yeah. I told them I was worried about you." He shoved the phone back into his pocket. "Have you talked to your mom lately?"

She frowned. "A couple of days ago. Why? What's wrong?"

"Nothing, probably. Did anybody ever say how long her cough might linger after the pneumonia?"

"A little while, I guess, but it should be getting a lot better by now. Is it bad?"

He tilted his head and shrugged a shoulder. "I don't know. She seems to be coughing a lot, but she says she's fine."

"She said she was fine last time, too, right up until she passed out. I think she was even saying it as she hit the floor."

"If it gets any worse, or doesn't get any better, you should talk her into a follow-up appointment." He felt bad when he saw how the concern scrunched up her face. Rosie said she was fine, and he was certainly no doctor. "I'll keep an eye on her. It's probably just left over from having pneumonia."

"You'll call me if you think there's anything wrong with her, right?"

"Of course. Unless I'm on the phone with the 1-800-Loser hotline. You getting help is really important."

She laughed and shoved at his hip with her foot before pulling it back under the blanket.

The other guys cheered and Josh turned back to the game, but Max caught his eye. Crawford jerked his head toward Katie and then made some goofy motion with his eyebrows. Josh gave him a what-the-hell look and then focused on the television.

Dude was losing his mind. He'd run with Katie for as long as he could remember, through good times and bad. He wasn't screwing up a lifelong friendship to get in her pants, even if she *was* into him. And she'd never given any sign she wanted him in her pants.

Yeah, Max Crawford was totally barking up the wrong tree.

CHAPTER TWO

AT WORK THE next morning, Katie snipped at what little remained of Dozer Dozynski's hair while pondering how best to get Max Crawford to tell her what the hell his job was. Assuming he wasn't a serial killer, what did he do in the basement that kept him busy, earned him money and required a security system? CIA? Computer hacker?

"How did you manage to sneak away from the hardware store on a Monday morning?" she asked when she realized her silence might come off as awkward, since there was nobody else Dozer could talk to.

"Lauren and my wife came in to drive me crazy looking at a million paint samples, so I told them to watch the store and ran as fast as I could."

Katie laughed. Lauren was his daughter and she was also recently engaged to Ryan Kowalski. Lauren and her teenage son, Nick, were in the process of preparing to move to Ryan's home in Brookline, Mass, and there had been a lot of talk about paint samples. The house was beautiful as far as form, function and resale value, but it was very bland. Lauren had declared her first act as the future Mrs. Kowalski would be to "unbeige the place."

"I stopped by Lauren's a few days ago," Katie said. "Looks like they're almost ready to make the move."

He nodded, but fortunately she saw that coming from experience and paused the snipping until he stopped moving his head. "Very soon. Nick will finish school here in a couple of weeks. They want to have a week to move in, and maybe he can familiarize himself with the neighborhood. Then they'll come spend Christmas week here so Nick can be with his father and the little ones while Ryan and Lauren finish getting her house ready to sell."

Katie moved to the other side of the chair, halfway done with the cut. "So Nick can start his new school with the new year, instead of starting and then having time off. Makes sense. How's Mrs. Dozynski taking it?"

"She's happy for our daughter, of course, but it will be hard for her. She doesn't drive and Lauren helped her a lot. Now she'll be nagging me even more to retire."

Katie hoped not, though she didn't say out loud. The hardware store ran on such a thin thread, Dozer didn't even have hired help anymore. The only way he could retire was to close it, which would be heartbreaking and inconvenient, or sell it. There wasn't much of a market for small-town hardware stores anymore. Not with the big-box stores springing up around them.

Before she could respond, the big black phone on the wall rang with a loud jangle. The thing was practically a relic, but she'd answered it when she was a little girl hanging around with her dad, and she couldn't bring herself to replace it with something less alarming. "Just a second, Dozer. Don't move."

The phone rarely rang. The shop's hours hadn't changed in at least thirty years, so the only time anybody bothered to call was during the winter, when somebody might check to see if she was there during a snowstorm. Since she lived upstairs, she usually was.

"Barbershop." She didn't bother identifying herself. There had only ever been one barber at a time in Whitford. First her dad, then the idiot who'd "run" the business for her mom after her dad died, and then Katie as soon as she met the licensing requirements.

"Hey, it's Josh."

The little zing she'd been feeling at the sound of his voice since her body had reached zinging age was chased by a pang of anxiety. He never called her at the shop. "What's up?"

"It's not a wicked emergency or anything, but I'm taking your mom to the hospital."

The pang of anxiety solidified into a knot of fear in her gut. "What's wrong?"

"Same as last time, more or less. The cough's gotten worse since yesterday and she's got a fever. She won't let me take her temperature, but it's pretty obvious."

"Is it bad enough for an ambulance?"

"No. She's arguing with me, actually. Says she just needs to have some tea and lie down for a while, but I can tell from looking at her she feels like she did when we took her in before."

Katie's fingers tightened around the old-fashioned phone receiver. "So you think she has pneumonia again?"

"I'm not a doctor but, like I said, seems to be the same symptoms that got her that diagnosis last month."

"Can you wait for me? I need maybe five minutes to finish this cut and then I'll hang the sign and lock up."

"Yeah. She's still trying to convince me she doesn't want to go, so we'll be here debating the point for a while yet."

"I'll be there as quick as I can."

She hung up and walked back to Dozer, but took a few seconds to calm herself before taking the scissors to his hair. The first bout with pneumonia had been scary enough, but her mom was a pretty healthy woman. Now if she had it again, it could be so much worse. Her immune system was still building itself back up and she hadn't fully regained her strength.

"Is Rose sick again?"

Katie shook off her dread and made sure her hands weren't shaking before lifting the scissors. "Maybe. Josh doesn't like the sound of her cough and he says she has a fever, so we're going to take her to the hospital to get checked."

"I can have Pat finish this if you want to go."

"I appreciate that, but I'm almost done." And she'd seen what Pat Dozynski had done to his hair when the hardware store was busy and he hadn't had a chance to get away while the barbershop was open.

Ten minutes later, Katie locked the door behind Dozer and used a dry-erase marker to write Gone Fishing on the bottom of the Closed sign before turning it around. She'd probably take less flack if she wrote Closed for Family Emergency, but that news would spread through Whitford like wildfire and concerned neighbors would descend upon them like torch-bearing villagers.

When she got to the lodge, she found her mom in the front room, still arguing with Josh.

"I'm fine," she said to Katie when she saw her come in, but then she broke into a coughing fit that took her breath away.

"If you're fine, the doctor will tell us you're fine

and send you home with us," she said. "Please, Mom. If Josh thinks you need to go, then I need you to go. For me."

Rose sighed dramatically. "Fine, but I'm going to change my clothes first."

Josh waited until she'd disappeared up the stairs to turn to Katie. "I don't think I'm overreacting. I could hear her coughing and hacking all night and she's wicked pale, except for her cheeks and around her collar, which are red."

"She's definitely sick. I just really hope it's not pneumonia again."

"How we doing this? One vehicle? Two?"

"You don't have to go, you know. I can drive her."

"I'm going. One vehicle or two?"

"Even though it kills me to say it, she'll be more comfortable in your truck." She ignored his smug grin. "And there's no sense in burning extra gas. I'll just ride with you guys, unless you don't want to stick around at the hospital."

"You know I'm going to stay."

She nodded, because she did know. All five of the Kowalski kids considered Rose almost like a mother and they loved her as much as Rose loved them. Josh wouldn't leave the hospital until he knew she was going to be okay.

Rose took her sweet time getting changed and, when she came down the stairs, she was lugging her big tote bag. Josh rushed up the last few stairs to take it from her. "Jesus, Rosie. You moving out?"

"You know how waiting rooms can be. I have my book and my knitting and a few other little things."

Katie's heart twisted as she looked at the heavy tote. There was more than a book, a skein of yarn and a few little things in there. Her mother was afraid she wouldn't be coming home from the hospital and she'd thrown the things she couldn't live without into the bag.

"I'll go start the truck and throw this in there," Josh said. He grabbed a set of keys off the side table and went out the door.

"I feel horrible," Rose said.

"Which is why you're going to the hospital."

"Hush, little miss smart-ass. I mean I feel horrible that you kids have to bother with this. It's an hour just to get there."

"So it's an hour drive. You took at least a year off my life when you passed out last month."

"Just let me double-check that everything's off in the kitchen."

Katie went to get her mom's coat out of the closet and then watched Rose check the stove burners and oven she had never once left on. She was obviously worn down and, maybe it was Katie's imagination, but she seemed to be looking worse by the minute.

There was a clinic the next town over, but the doctor was more the ear infection, stepped on a nail, need a physical kind of guy. Since Rose would almost certainly need chest X-rays and an IV, he'd only refer her to the hospital anyway, and charge her a hefty exam fee for the advice.

Josh stuck his head in the back door. "You ladies ready?"

Katie watched as Josh helped her mother climb up into the shotgun seat, and then she settled herself next to Rose's tote on the narrow bench that passed for a backseat. As tempting as it was to say to hell with the gas and follow in her Jeep, she wanted to keep an eye on her mom.

They hadn't gone very far down the road when Rose nodded off. Her face was flushed and her breathing raspy, and Katie's concern was reflected back at her from Josh's gaze in the rearview mirror.

ROSIE HAD PNEUMONIA again, and they weren't letting her go home. Josh sat in the waiting room, turning his cell phone over and over in his hands while he debated who to call first. Even though there wasn't much anybody could do, they all had to be informed that Rose was being admitted.

Mitch was someplace or another for work. He owned a controlled demolition company, which required a lot of travel, and he was pushing hard to wrap up a job so he could enjoy an extended holiday stay at home with his new wife. Ryan had left Whitford last night and gone back to Brookline for the workweek. He was still commuting back and forth until Lauren and Nick were ready to make the final move. His other brother, Sean, lived in New Hampshire, and Liz—the only girl—was even farther away, in New Mexico.

He'd call Paige, he decided. Mitch's wife could spread the word not only to the rest of the family, but around town, as well. And she'd do it without adding drama. Since she'd still be at the diner, he pulled up that number on his cell and waited for her to answer.

"Trailside Diner," she said a little breathlessly after four rings.

"Hey, it's Josh. Sorry to bother you at work."

There was silence on the line for a few seconds. "What's wrong? Did something happen?"

"Katie and I brought Rosie to the hospital this morning. She has pneumonia again and they're admitting her."

"Oh, God. What do you need? Do you need me to call people? Bring some things from the lodge for her?"

One of the many reasons he adored Paige— she didn't hesitate before offering to make a two-hour round-trip to help out the family. "I think she has everything she needs, but I was hoping maybe you could call everybody. After your shift ends, of course."

"Absolutely. What should I tell them? I mean… do they need to come home?"

"No," he reassured her. "It's not that bad. But it could be if they don't have her on the antibiotics and IV and shit. She's going to be okay and nobody needs to come home. I just don't want anybody finding out later Rosie was in the hospital and they didn't know."

"I'll take care of it. You're there now?"

"Yeah. Katie's with Rosie, getting her settled and everything. Once she's in her nice hospital jammies and tucked in, I'll go in again. Oh, and she has her cell phone, but they'll probably be fussing over her today, so tomorrow she might like to hear from people."

After he got off the phone with Paige, he leaned his head back against the wall, stretched his legs out and closed his eyes. He should have listened to his gut instead of Rosie and brought her to a doctor sooner. Maybe she wouldn't have had to be admitted to the hospital and stay for who knew how long.

And he had no idea how he was going to keep her corralled once she got out. With less than two weeks until the first guests of the season arrived at the lodge, the list of things to do was insane and quite of few of those things usually fell to Rosie. She was a stubborn woman and there was no way he could do everything and make sure she stayed in bed. As soon as he turned his back, she'd be running the vacuum or sneaking bedding down to the washer.

"The way the nurses keep walking back and forth, giving you the eye, I'm surprised you haven't been offered a bed yet."

Josh opened his eyes and grinned at Katie. "I'm holding out for the hot doctor who examined Rose down in Urgent Care."

"Pretty sure she was wearing a wedding ring."

He shrugged and pushed himself upright in the really uncomfortable chair. "So I'll be holding out awhile. How's your mom?"

"Worried about getting the lodge ready for guests."

Josh sighed and scrubbed his hands through his hair. "She can't feel too awful, then."

"I feel bad. They might have let her come home, but when they asked me if I thought she'd rest, I said probably not."

He threw one arm around her shoulders and gave her a squeeze. "It was the right thing to say, because she probably wouldn't."

"I offered to stay, but she said we should go back to Whitford and get on with things."

"Let's say goodbye, then, because the thought we're actually getting stuff done will comfort her a lot more than sitting around watching daytime television with her."

Katie shook her head. "She was actually nodding off when I left her. She said to tell you she'd call you tomorrow."

It didn't seem right to leave Rosie without at least a kiss on the cheek or something, but he'd heard how rough her night had been and he didn't want to wake her up if she was managing to sleep. "Probably with a list of things to get done."

"Of course."

He waited while Katie went to the nurse's station to double-check all the contact info they had, and then they went outside to find it had started snowing at some point. It wouldn't amount to anything, since it hadn't merited a mention on the morning news, but every little bit helped.

The snow cover wasn't quite as good as he'd hoped for, but the white stuff had been building up on the ground. Though there was hardly anything in town, in the woods and higher elevations there was enough for the groomer to pack down. Maybe every trail wouldn't be open for the fifteenth, but the gates would open and there would be enough riding to keep their guests happy. Unless they had some weird warm-up and rain and all the snow melted. But that was something to worry about when he was supposed to be sleeping, as usual.

"I'm glad there's snow this year," Katie said as they walked across the slick parking lot. "Working to get business back up and then not having trails to ride would suck."

"Got that right." He shoved his hand in his pocket and dug out his keys. *Suck* wasn't even a strong enough word for it. This season had to play out for him. Good snow, good business and a good opportunity to get the hell out of Whitford.

"So I was thinking," Katie said when they were on the main road, headed back to Whitford. "Mom's going to get released before the fifteenth."

"Yup. And she's going to drag her ass out of bed and make herself sick again trying to make sure everything's perfect for the first guests."

"I'm going to move in for a while."

Josh risked taking his eyes off the road to glance over at her, but she was looking out the side window and he couldn't see her face. "What about the shop?"

"It's Whitford. I'll cut back on the hours and put a sign up. If I'm open just in the morning or even just three mornings a week for a month or so, they'll adjust. Especially if it's for my mom."

He wondered about income, but she probably wouldn't have offered if she couldn't afford it. Her dad had owned the building, so there was no rent for either her apartment or the barbershop, and it wasn't as though she was paying utility bills for fancy tanning beds or anything.

"That would be great," he told her. "You can take Liz's room, since it's right next to hers. And right across from mine, so we'll both be able to hear her."

"You don't think it's stupid?"

"In the waiting room I was wondering how the hell I was supposed to do everything that needs to get done in the next two weeks and keep her from doing any of it at the same time. You staying at the lodge is a perfect solution. And, hell, it's almost as much your home as it is ours."

He saw her nod through the corner of his eye. "I'll put up a sign at the shop today about the temporary shop hours. And when we find out when she's coming home, I'll bring over some of my stuff."

"It's a plan, then." Plans were good and helped him sleep at night.

Having Katie live under the same roof, even temporarily, was the perfect solution to his problems.

The way Rose saw it, this was her best—and maybe final—shot at interfering in Josh's and Katie's lives without getting caught, and that meant it was her best shot at raising grandbabies at the Northern Star Lodge. But she had to play it smart, no matter how bad she felt or how fuzzy her head was.

When Katie had called to say good-night and see if there was anything she needed and had forgotten to bring, she also said she'd be moving into the lodge to help Josh and make sure Rose did nothing but recover. It was a perfect opportunity.

Having Josh and Katie living under the same roof might not be enough, though, because it was a big place and they were used to being around each other after years of being practically best friends. Rose would have to come up with ways to throw them together. If she could keep them tripping over each other, eventually the boy was going to get a clue and realize his feelings for Katie were a little less platonic than he'd always thought.

Getting the place ready for guests would mean working together occasionally, but it wouldn't be enough. Rose needed to come up with something that would require them to talk to each other and spend time in each other's company.

Something like planning the Christmas Eve party for the family. A lot of lodging establishments put on Christmas for their guests, because some families would take the holiday to go on that snow-mobiling trip together. But Frank and Sarah Kowalski had made the decision when she was pregnant with Mitch that, for Christmas Eve and Christmas Day, the Northern Star would be closed.

The family had decided over Thanksgiving they wanted to have a special get-together and, since Nick was spending Christmas Day with his dad, stepmom and younger brother and sister, the Kowalskis would celebrate the night before. And Rose wanted it to be special. It would be Paige's first Christmas as Mitch's wife and, though Ryan and Lauren wouldn't marry until summer, she and Nick were family, too.

If she knew the kids, they'd try to remove the so-called burden of the party from Rose. No doubt Paige would offer to host it, or they'd try to make it low-key. She didn't want that. She wanted something special.

And because Josh and Katie had no clue how to plan a holiday party—since Rose had always done it—they'd have to work together. Closely. And that kind of proximity, without sports or something else to focus on, would make the chemistry everybody else saw between them pop.

Even Josh wouldn't be able to miss it.

Her brilliant plan was pushed to the back of her mind when another coughing fit ruined the moment. She was so tired of coughing. Tired of feeling exhausted and weak and on-and-off feverish.

Once it had passed, she tried to make a comfortable nest out of the extra pillows they'd given her and fished around for the television control. She couldn't find *Criminal Minds,* but at any given moment one could always find a rerun from one of the *Law & Order* franchises, so she settled for that. She should probably knit, since she had several projects to finish before Christmas, but her arms felt as heavy as her eyelids and she closed her eyes instead.

Tomorrow she'd call Andy and let him in on the plan so he didn't accidentally work against her. If he made life easier for Josh, Josh might not turn to Katie for help.

She had a long history with Andy Miller, most of it spent with her refusing to speak to him. But the boys had hired him to do some work around the lodge over her objections, which had led to her forgiving him, and she'd actually come to consider him a really good friend over the past few months.

And with his help, she was going to make this a Christmas Eve party Josh and Katie would never forget.

CHAPTER THREE

JOSH PULLED INTO an empty spot in front of the barbershop and killed the engine.

Katie was on a stepladder, hanging Christmas lights around the big window. She must have been at it for a while because she'd stripped down to a sleeveless red shirt, and he spotted a fleece hoodie tossed onto a mound of garland at the base of the ladder.

That was Katie. For as long as he could remember, Rose had had to threaten Katie to get her to wear a coat, because she was never cold. And, while the temperature was hovering in the low forties, the sun was so warm he'd left his own sweatshirt at home since the long-sleeved henley was more than enough. Fortunately, it was forecast to be a very brief warm spell, because they couldn't afford to lose what snow they had.

He leaned against the tailgate of his truck and crossed his arms. "Need a hand?"

She looked over her shoulder and made a face. "This sucks."

"That's a festive attitude."

"Mom always does the decorating."

But she'd been sick and now she was in the hospital. "You could just skip it this year."

"I could." She climbed down the ladder and joined him on the tailgate. "But it would be the first year in the history of the Whitford Barbershop it's not decorated."

Sometimes Josh had to remind himself that, while Katie might be just one of the guys, every once in a while she'd do that complex woman thing where what was going on in her mind didn't make any sense. But this time he thought he might get it.

Earle Davis died when Katie was nineteen, the year after she graduated from high school. Even as a clueless sixteen-year-old kid, Josh had felt her pain. She and her dad had been close, and it had been painful to watch another man move in and run the shop for Rosie, who hadn't been willing to sell it outright. And when it became clear that guy was an idiot, Josh had watched Katie get through school and work her way through the licensing requirements so she could take it back.

In Katie's mind, the barbershop and her dad were all wrapped up together in an emotional ball and, especially with her mom sick, decorating the shop for Christmas had probably become the most important thing in the world.

"I didn't think it would take this long," Katie

said. "I was going to get this done and then go to the hospital and visit Mom."

"Why don't I give you a hand and then we can drive over together?" It was Thursday and, while he'd talked to Rosie on the phone, he hadn't seen her since they'd brought her in Monday.

She laughed. "Sure, now you show up to help. All that's left is to wrap the garland around the damn pole."

"Good, let's wrap the pole and grab some lunch before we hit the road."

They made quick work out of merrying up the place and then she grabbed her hoodie before jumping in his truck. She looked the barbershop over and nodded. "That's better."

It was definitely cheerful. She didn't plug in the lights when she wasn't going to be around, but the garland had plastic candy canes hung in it, and all kinds of Christmas vinyl cling decals were stuck to the massive pane of glass. "Ho ho ho. Let's go eat."

They went to the Trailside Diner, not only because it was really the only place to go, but because he hadn't seen Paige in a while. She lit up when she saw them walk through the door, her dark ponytail bouncing as she half jogged over to hug each of them.

"How's Rosie?"

"She's getting better," Katie said. "She's starting to get grumpy, which is a good sign."

"Oh, good. When is she coming home?"

Katie shrugged. "She's not sure yet."

"When I talked to her on the phone yesterday," Josh said, sliding into a booth, "she said her lungs weren't as clear as they wanted yet. And she still has no appetite."

Paige sighed. "Even though she's getting grumpy, it's best if she stays there, then. They won't let her vacuum or clean the ovens, at least."

"Katie's going to move into the lodge for a little while to make sure she's not cleaning our oven, either."

"Really?" Paige asked, but she arched an eyebrow and drew the word out, like *reeeeeeaaaaally*. He wasn't sure what that was about. The Northern Star was practically Katie's home. She didn't sleep there and she wasn't there every day, but she'd more or less grown up there.

"Yeah, really. What's Mitch up to?"

Paige glanced down at the rings on her left hand and smiled. "He's finishing up some advance work on a job in Southern California so when he comes home in a few days, he won't have to leave again until the middle of January. One more week and then he'll be home for a whole month."

"Be nice to have him around for a while," Katie said.

"I can't wait." After glancing around the diner, Paige pulled her order pad out of her apron pocket.

"You guys know what you want? Gavin whipped up some amazing baked mac-and-cheese for the dinner special last night and, trust me, it's even better reheated."

Gavin hoped to go to culinary school someday and Paige let him try out new recipes on the diner's customers, provided the ingredients weren't too expensive and tofu wasn't on the list. Josh had liked some dishes more than others, but taking a chance on the kid rarely steered him wrong.

"I'll give it a try," he said. "With a coffee."

"Ditto," Katie said.

When Paige brought their drinks and went to see to the other diners, Josh leaned forward. "So, I've been wanting to ask you something. It's probably personal, but…it's kind of relevant to me. Maybe."

Katie gave him a look he couldn't quite decipher, but after a few seconds, she shrugged. "Ask. I'll either answer or I won't, as usual."

"It's about Andy, actually." He saw her expression change. It was subtle—her mouth tightened and her eyes narrowed just a little—but it was obvious she knew more about Andy's story than she'd let on before. "What's the deal there?"

"The deal is that he pissed her off a long time ago, but she forgave him and now they're actually friends."

"Gee, I couldn't figure that out from the fact she didn't talk to him for like thirty years and then she forgave him and now she's knitting him a Christmas present."

"Then why'd you ask?"

His least favorite Katie Davis trait. If she didn't want to talk about something, she'd be a pain in the ass and annoy him to the point he didn't give a crap anymore. "Don't be a smart-ass. What did he do to piss her off?"

"Why don't you ask her?"

"Because I don't think she'll tell me."

"Then she probably doesn't want you to know." She took a long sip of coffee, looking at him over the rim.

"Come on. You know how much I love your mom, and the guy's in and out of my house all the freaking time now. It bugs the shit out of me not knowing."

"When I was little, Andy and my dad went on a sledding trip. They grabbed dinner at a bar and Andy chatted up a woman and got her to go back to the motel with them. She had a friend and my dad cheated on Mom. She blamed Andy."

He sat back against the booth. "Holy shit."

"Yeah. She told me blaming Andy made it easier to forgive Dad." She was turning her coffee mug around and around on the table, staring down into the swirling liquid. "I never knew. She didn't tell me until you and Mitch hired Andy to work at the lodge and I asked her straight out."

Josh felt a slow burn of anger, but it was pointless. Earle Davis had been dead fourteen years. "You okay with Andy being around, because if you're not—"

She held up her hand. "I'm fine. I mean, yeah, if Andy hadn't hooked up with that woman, Dad might never have cheated on Mom, but nobody held a gun to my dad's head. It was his decision. And Andy lost his best friend out of it because he and my dad stopped hanging out after that."

"I had no idea it was that bad. I always thought it was probably something stupid or funny, like him saying her meat loaf sucked or something, and they were both too stubborn to get over it."

"Nope. Not stupid or funny."

Paige showed up then with their meals, giving Josh a couple of minutes to digest what he'd heard. In a town like Whitford, the fact it wasn't common knowledge Earle had stepped out on his wife was nothing short of a miracle. And even if he could remember back that far, Josh probably never would have guessed Rosie's marriage had almost come undone. She was more a stiff upper lip in front of the kids and cry in the shower kind of woman.

"You let me know if you want to move the Christmas Eve party to my house," Paige said, stopping to refill their coffees.

Oh, damn. He kept forgetting about that stupid party. If he had his way, the whole thing would be cancelled. Or postponed until April or May, maybe. "She gave Thanksgiving over to you, but I don't see her giving up Christmas Eve at the lodge."

"Mom's a smart woman," Katie said. "She'll understand there's only so much we can do and she's sick and Paige has plenty of room for everybody. She'll be reasonable."

"WE'RE HAVING CHRISTMAS Eve at the Northern Star and that's the end of it."

Katie looked at her mother reclined against her pillows with her arms folded across her chest, and swore. But only in her mind, of course. She wondered what the chances were of flagging down a nurse and getting a sedative. For her, for her mom. Either worked.

"The Christmas Eve party isn't what's important," Josh said. "You getting better is all that matters."

"You listen to me. The party is important to me. I don't know if Sean will come and Liz probably won't be here, but Mitch and Ryan will and you four kids being home for the holidays matters to me. And it'll be Paige's first Christmas with us— her first with a real family of her own and I want it to be perfect."

Katie shook her head. "Because we *are* Paige's family now, she cares more about you than a party."

"I'm having a Christmas Eve party."

Katie knew that tone. There would be a party at the Northern Star on Christmas Eve. She sighed. "We'll take care of it."

Josh's eyebrows shot up. "You're going to throw a holiday party?"

"No, *we* are going to throw a holiday party."

His eyebrows dropped into a frown and he opened his mouth, but Rose beat him to it. "You two can do it, if you work together."

Katie was still trying to wrap her mind around the fact she'd be sleeping across the hall from Josh every night. She figured she'd survive it because he'd be working outside a lot, while she'd be taking care of her mom and doing housework. It was a big place. But planning a party together meant they'd have to talk. A lot.

Sure, they talked all the time. They talked about football and hockey and baseball. Basketball. The weather. Trucks. Griped about their love lives when either of them had one. Katie had long ago fallen into a rhythm of "guy talk" that kept her from accidentally letting on that she'd like a one-way ticket out of the friend zone.

Now they'd be playing house, and so much proximity was going to play hell on her nerves. The other night an image had popped into her mind of bumping into him in the hallway, his bare chest glistening from a hot shower and a small towel hanging low on his hips.

She wasn't sure if that would be the best or the worst thing ever, but she'd lost sleep thinking about it.

"You'll need to come up with a menu, of course," her mom said. "Hopefully, I'll feel up to baking a couple of pies, but you guys will have to take care of the rest. Josh, did you get the tree and the decorations up yet?"

"Uh…no."

"The doctor said I can probably go home Monday if I don't relapse at all, so I'll lie on the couch and supervise."

Katie had no doubt he'd spend the next several days busting his ass getting the lodge decorated before Sergeant Rosie was there to nitpick the process.

"I want music. Happy stuff," Rose continued. "And candles and…well, you two can figure it out. But I'll look over your lists, of course."

"Of course," Katie muttered. In the meantime, she'd also keep her own business going while helping Josh run his. Haircuts, washing bedsheets and feeding the whole family—or most of it—a holiday meal that met Rosie's standards. No problem.

They hung around for a while, but her mom eventually shooed them off. There were rumors of some bad weather coming in as the night wore on. She didn't want them driving in it, and she wanted to get her beauty sleep so she could go home Monday.

It was dark already and the temperature had

dropped pretty drastically but, unlike her Jeep, Josh's truck warmed up quickly and she felt herself getting sleepy.

"When are you planning on moving in?" Josh asked when they were on the main road, heading back to Whitford.

"I was thinking if Mom's getting released Monday, then probably Sunday. I can open the shop for a full day Saturday, then get settled at the lodge Sunday morning. That'll give me time to freshen up her room. Change the sheets and stuff."

"Sounds good."

"Unless you need help with the Christmas decorations. I assume you're going to get it done before she's home to supervise?"

He laughed, and the rich sound seemed to fill the enclosed space of the cab. "You got that right."

"Do you need a hand with it?"

"I think I'm all set. Probably." He shrugged. "I'll give a shout if I get too backed up."

"Good. Gives me time to stop by Max's and... be nosy."

He turned his head and, in the lights from the dash, she could see the scowl. "No wiles."

"I don't need to cheat, Kowalski."

"Maybe you should move into the lodge tomorrow so I can keep you busy. And keep an eye on you."

The shiver that tickled her spine had nothing to

do with the snowflakes falling outside the truck. She wouldn't mind him keeping her too busy to win their Max Crawford bet. But she suspected he was talking about dishwashers and furniture polish rather than tangled sheets.

"Nothing against Liz's room, but I'll sleep in my own bed as long as possible, thanks."

Growing up, Katie had always been jealous of Josh's sister. She'd hated leaving the Northern Star at the end of her mother's workday and every year, when she made a wish on her birthday candles, she'd wished to live at the lodge. When she outgrew birthday wishes, she daydreamed about Josh realizing he was madly in love with her and asking him to marry her. As his wife, she'd spend her days helping him run the Northern Star and her nights in his bed. When her dad died, though, she turned her focus to saving the barbershop, and her dreams of being Mrs. Kowalski faded into the constant low hum of attraction that wouldn't die.

She must have nodded off, because the next thing she knew, Josh was nudging her arm, her neck felt permanently kinked to the right, and they were parked outside the barbershop.

"Why didn't you wake me up?" she asked, trying to get her head back in an upright position. And she was pretty sure she had a seat belt mark across her face. "I was supposed to keep you company while you drove."

"Figured if you nodded off, you must need the sleep."

After taking her seat belt off, Katie scrubbed at her face, trying to shake off the grogginess. She hated napping. Those first few seconds when she wasn't in her bed and didn't know what time it was always disoriented her.

"Go eat something and get some sleep."

"Thanks for the ride," she said, opening the door to a blast of cold.

"Stay away from Max."

She might have argued the point with him, but it was too freaking cold to stand around having a pissing match. Instead she flipped him off as he drove away.

She'd just unlocked her door, which was next to the barbershop's door, and gone up the stairs to her apartment when her cell phone rang. The caller ID said it was Hailey Genest, the town's librarian. "Hello."

"Have you eaten yet?"

Katie flopped down in her battered recliner, which might have been as old as her Jeep, and sighed. She knew she had peanut butter and jelly, but she wasn't sure the last loaf of bread she'd bought hadn't become a science project already. "Not yet. Josh and I went to the hospital to see Mom and I literally just got home."

"How's Rosie?"

"Getting better. They seem pretty confident she'll come home Monday."

"Good news. Now, how about you meet me at the diner for supper."

"It's really freaking cold out there." It would take forever to warm up her Jeep.

"I heard you're moving in with Josh."

Katie laughed. "Technically, yes."

"Diner. Fifteen minutes. You know there's no sense in putting me off."

"Fine. But make it twenty."

KATIE WAVED TO Ava, the older woman who worked the two-to-close shift at the diner, and then to Gavin in the pass-through window before sliding into the booth Hailey had chosen. It didn't escape her notice they were sitting as far from the coffee counter as possible, which meant Hailey was expecting juicy details. She was going to be disappointed.

"I ordered us both hot chocolate," Hailey told her. "With extra whipped cream."

Hailey and Katie hadn't been very close as kids. Hailey was two years older than Mitch so, other than a notorious tumble with him in the back of her dad's new car, she hadn't socialized a lot with the Kowalski kids and Katie was almost always with them. As adults, though, they'd become good friends. They even looked a little alike, though Hailey was curvier and her blond hair was lighter.

"Hot chocolate sounds perfect," Katie said, and she almost got whipped cream on her nose when she leaned down to inhale it the second Ava set it in front of her.

"You girls know what you're having?"

"Do you have any of Gavin's macaroni-and-cheese left?" Hailey asked. "I've been hearing about it since last night."

"I think there are three servings left. You want to try it, Katie?"

"I had it for lunch and it lives up to the hype. I should be good, though. Maybe a grilled chicken salad."

Ava snorted. "Lettuce doesn't go with hot chocolate. Beef stew."

"Beef stew sounds even better."

Once Ava walked away, Hailey focused all her attention on Katie. "Okay, spill."

"It's not that big a deal. With the holidays coming and the first guests arriving at the lodge, there's no doubt my mom's going to fight taking it easy, so I'm going to stay at the lodge until she's totally better. A third bout of pneumonia is not a charm."

"This is your best shot. Just imagine bumping into him in the dark with you wearing nothing but scraps of black lace."

She'd imagined it all too often, albeit with slightly different details. "I don't own any scraps of black lace."

"You're kidding."

"Why would I wear lace scraps?"

"To feel sexy under your clothes."

That concept made no sense to Katie. "I like being comfortable under my clothes."

"Don't tell me. White cotton, right?"

"Don't ask if you don't want me to tell you. And there's nothing wrong with that."

"Of course not." Hailey rolled her eyes. "Just think, you can be a spinster like me."

Katie almost choked on a mouthful of hot chocolate. "Spinster? Seriously, does anybody even use that word anymore?"

"Spinsters do."

"You are not a spinster, Hailey."

"Even better, I'm a spinster librarian."

Katie shook her head. "I'm pretty sure spinsters have to be virgins."

"Oh, maybe. That would disqualify me, I guess."

Ava stopped by with their mac-and-cheese and beef stew, which ended the spinster conversation, even if Katie suspected it was only a temporary reprieve. She hadn't realized she was hungry until the smell of Gavin's stew hit her. Not even bothering with salt and pepper because he seasoned everything to perfection, Katie dug in.

"It's best for me if Josh isn't seduced by your comfy white cotton, you know," Hailey said after a few bites.

Katie frowned. Hailey knew Josh was off-limits to her, plus she'd never shown any interest in him, anyway. "What do you mean?"

"Paige married Mitch. Lauren's not only marrying Ryan, but she's moving away. I need you to be whatever spinsters who've had sex are called with me."

"You're forgetting something. Even if Josh temporarily succumbs to my irresistible white cotton, I'll still be a spinster who's had sex, because Josh is going to leave the second he can. I'll just have had sex more recently than you."

"Maybe when he realizes he's been a blind idiot all these years, he'll stay."

Katie shook her head, some of her appetite for the stew gone. "He won't. All he's ever dreamed about is leaving Whitford."

"Fine. Seduce him, use the hell out of him and then send the oversexed, possibly dehydrated husk of him out into the world."

"That's a little harsh," Katie said, but she laughed, anyway. "And if he hasn't noticed me by now, he's never going to."

"But—"

"Let's change the subject." Katie was tired of thinking about Josh and sex and white cotton. "Does Max Crawford use the library?"

Hailey blinked, obviously thrown off. "Uh, yeah. Sure."

"What kind of stuff does he read?"

That earned Katie a wagging finger and a *tsk-tsk* sound. "Sorry, love. I never date-stamp and tell."

"Dammit. I need to know what he does for a living."

"I heard he's a serial killer."

"You should go on a date with him."

Hailey stared at her for a few seconds, her eyes wide. "I'm just going to sit here while you replay that last bit of conversation in your head."

Katie did, and then she laughed. "You know Max isn't a serial killer. I'm at his house all the time."

"Alone?"

"No, but—"

"Have you ever been in his basement?"

"No, but—"

Hailey jabbed a finger at her. "See?"

"I've never been in your basement, either. Or Lauren's. Really, that would be weird. 'Hey there, wanna see my foundation?'"

"Good point."

"I have to find out what Max does for work before Josh does or I'll have to wash his stupid truck for a year." Katie gave her best smile. "I bet if you went on a date with Max, he'd tell you."

"If it was oral for a year, I might take that bullet for you, but washing vehicles? No."

"You're always complaining there are no good single guys in Whitford. Max is hot and he has a really great couch. You could have sex on it and cement your non-spinster status. You know, just in case there's a time limit on the had-sex thing."

"I hate sports," Hailey said, and Katie had to admit that could be a problem. "And he never talks to me when he's in the library. He's really…awkward."

"Really? I don't think he's awkward."

"Well, maybe if I was just one of the guys, wearing white cotton underwear while screaming obscenities at the television because some dude didn't throw a ball right, he wouldn't be awkward with me, either."

"I don't think he knows what kind of underwear we have on."

"The point is, I'm not banging Max Crawford in his torture chamber in the basement so you don't have to wash Josh's truck."

"When you put it like that, I guess it does sound a little out of bounds, favor-wise."

Hailey laughed. "Just a little. Why don't you go on a date with him? Find out what he does and make Josh jealous at the same time."

"I'm not allowed to use feminine wiles, as Josh called it."

"It's so cute he thinks you even know how to do that."

Katie managed to look offended. "Hey, I have feminine wiles."

Hailey downed the last of her hot chocolate and set down her mug with a thump. "Prove it. If you're wily enough to get Josh Kowalski into those white cotton panties, *I'll* wash his truck for a year."

CHAPTER FOUR

JOSH WAS EXHAUSTED. He'd spent more than a few nights praying for snow, but now he'd had enough. Because he'd wasted so much time on the damn Christmas decorations, he was behind on everything else. But trimming the tree while Rosie micromanaged from the couch sounded even worse than dealing with a foot of wet, heavy snow instead of getting the barn ready.

Part of their plan to spruce up the lodge included redoing the floor out there, because they allowed guests to park their snowmobiles in the barn. It kept them snow-free and it made people feel more secure than just pulling them into the yard. But, thanks to the renovations, there was building debris all over the damn place and he had to clean it up, so Mother Nature had kicked him in the balls by dropping double the white stuff they'd expected.

The plow made quick work of the driveway and cut a wide path to the barn, but thanks to the raised landscaping his mother had chosen to line the walkways many years ago, the sidewalks leading to the doors had to be done by snowblower.

He'd just fired it up when he saw Andy Miller's truck coming up the drive, and he could have cried in relief. He needed the help.

"Would've been here earlier," Andy said when he'd parked alongside Josh's truck, "but I had to stop and help a lady get her car out of the ditch."

"I didn't know you were coming. You do know it's Sunday, right?"

"Got nothing better to do. I called Rose this morning, but she forbade me from visiting because of the snow. Rather be here than sit on my ass in front of the TV all day."

"I can use the help." That was the understatement of the year. Not only was he dog tired, but his leg wasn't too happy about the cold. "When I called her last night, she was still waiting for the doctor to do his late rounds. Is she still scheduled to get out tomorrow?"

Andy nodded, pulling on his gloves. "That's the plan. She sounded good, but we're going to have to duct tape her down to keep her from overdoing it."

"Katie should be here any time with her stuff. She can do the duct taping."

"Yeah." Andy pointed to the snowblower. "Even just standing here I can see you're favoring that leg. Why don't you go do some desk work for a while and I'll take care of this."

"You sure you don't mind? I need to make a phone call and it might be smart to rest it for a few minutes before I start on that barn."

Andy waved him off and Josh went through the back door into the kitchen. He stepped out of his boots and threw his coat on the back of the chair since he'd be putting it back on. Then he pulled out his cell phone and scrolled through his contacts to Sean's number.

His brother, who was the middle of the five kids, answered on the third ring. "Hey, Josh, what's up?"

"You busy?"

"I can spare a few minutes. How's Rose?"

"Good enough so the doctors are releasing her back into the wild tomorrow."

"Two bouts of pneumonia and winter hasn't even really started yet," Sean said. "Maybe we should talk about hiring some help. A teenager or something."

"Katie's moving in for a while."

"Really?" Sean asked, but again with the *reeee-aaaally*.

"Why does everybody say it like that?"

Sean either had a funny cough or choked off a laugh. "No reason. What about the barbershop?"

Josh explained how she was cutting back to part-time hours temporarily and then filled him in a little more on Rosie's doctor's reports, before moving on to the real reason he'd called. "Are you and Emma coming for the Christmas Eve party or what?"

There were a few seconds of silence. "We're still talking about it, actually. But are you sure it's a good idea? I mean, Rosie shouldn't be worrying about feeding everybody and—"

"She's not. Katie and I are handling everything."

Sean laughed and Josh thought about hanging up on him. "So we'll be having chips, dip and a deli platter?"

"You're funny."

"So I called Mitch the other night and he said, based on the number of reservations coming in, the lodge should have a good season."

"We haven't had this many bookings in years," Josh admitted. "And the trails aren't even open yet. They always jump up once the guys in southern New England realize we're riding up here and they're not."

"At this rate, it won't be long before we have to all get together and discuss what we want to do."

"I know."

And it wouldn't be an easy discussion. They all owned the lodge together, so they'd all decide whether they were selling it or keeping it together. But the one thing they were all agreed on was the fact Josh had been left holding the bag and it was time he got to go have a life.

He wasn't sure how everybody felt about it. Of

course it wasn't easy to let go of the home you grew up in, but they all had homes of their own now. Sean, though, would probably be the most okay with selling. Even as a kid, he'd hated having strangers in his house and he'd never learned to be comfortable living in a snowmobile lodge. That was one of the reasons Josh suspected, when Sean had gotten out of the army, he'd gone to New Hampshire to visit Aunt Mary and Uncle Leo instead of coming home—he was afraid he'd get sucked into helping out at the Northern Star. It had worked out well for Sean, since that's where he'd met and fallen in love with Emma. But it didn't work out as well for Josh, who'd hoped to hand the lodge over to him for a while.

The primary concern for all of them, of course, was Rosie. No matter what they did with the lodge, they'd make sure she was taken care of. But Josh knew if they sold it and the new owners chose not to keep her on, it might break her heart.

Their other option was to hire a manager to run the place once the income could justify the expense. Even though Rosie essentially ran the place, she couldn't do it alone. And they certainly wouldn't leave her alone at the lodge to deal with guests who were primarily male.

"My lumber delivery's here," Sean said, breaking into Josh's thoughts. "Kiss Rosie for me and I'll let you know about the Christmas Eve party."

"Don't wait too long. Katie and I need to plan the menu."

Sean was still laughing when the call disconnected, and Josh flipped off his phone just on principle before sliding it back into his pocket.

He was going to enjoy rubbing everybody's face in it when he and Katie threw a party even Martha Whatshername would envy.

KATIE PARKED HER Jeep beside Andy's truck and took a deep breath. Cohabitation time.

It was no big deal, she told herself for the umpteenth time. The fact they'd be sleeping under the same roof for a while didn't change anything. They'd been friends for decades, so it wasn't as if things would be awkward or uncomfortable. They'd go on just as they always had.

She was still sitting there when Andy knocked on her window and made her jump.

"You okay?"

She opened her door, making him back up a bit. "I'm fine. Lost in thought, I guess."

"You need some help carrying stuff?"

"No thanks." She grabbed the duffel bag off the passenger seat and climbed out. "I travel light."

"It's good that you're able to stay for a while. Your mom's a stubborn woman, but having you here will help keep her in check."

"I guess you'd know as well as anybody how

stubborn she can be." Damn, she hadn't meant to say that.

"Guess so."

Well, since she'd brought it up, she might as well ask the question. "Andy, was he really sorry? My dad, I mean?"

His expression sobered, and she was almost sorry she'd asked. He was a handsome man, an older version of his son, Drew, but he looked older when he wasn't smiling. "Honey, I don't have words to describe how sorry he was. I know it's not easy finding out somebody you love made a mistake like that, especially after he's gone and you can't talk to him about it, but believe me, he loved your mother."

She shifted the duffel to her other hand and they walked toward the house together. "For what it's worth, I don't blame you like Mom did. Dad was responsible for what he did, not you."

"That's worth a lot, but if I could go back and not say hello to that woman, I would. Just asking them back to the motel disrespected your mother—and you—and that I'm sorry for."

"So you guys are really friendly now."

"I enjoy Rose's company. I think she feels the same."

She suspected that was all she was going to get out of Andy on the situation. He wasn't a man of many words. "Good. You can watch *Criminal*

Minds with her while Josh and I try to figure out how to throw a party."

That made him laugh. "Good luck with that. I'm gonna go finish snowblowing around the house."

Katie went in the back door and kicked her boots off next to Josh's. She was surprised to see his coat thrown over a chair, because it was one of her mother's pet peeves. But she wasn't home, so Katie peeled off her sweatshirt and tossed it over another chair.

Duffel in hand, she went into the living room and found Josh sprawled on the couch, eyes closed. He was very sexy when he sprawled.

She wasn't sure if he was asleep or not, but it wasn't as if she needed him to show her around. Before she headed for the stairs, though, she looked around, taking in the Christmas decorations. Josh had done a good job. So good, in fact, she'd never have guessed Rosie hadn't done it personally.

The tree dominated the corner of the room—tall, full and glistening with garland and ornaments—and it looked magnificent, even without the light strings plugged in. Because they liked to keep the decorations up the entire month of December, Josh and her mom had bought the artificial tree a few years back when a guest's allergies forced him to cut short his family's stay at the lodge.

Sarah Kowalski had loved Christmas trains, and one ran around the base of the tree. It was a cheap plastic set so guests' kids could play with it, but some of Sarah's treasured trains were on display around the room. Her favorite—a music box with a tiny train driving around and around a small town—was on the mantel of the fireplace, next to a photo of Frank and Sarah. There were electric candles in each window, of course, and candy cane garland wrapped all the way up the stair banister.

"I don't know how Rosie does it," Josh said, and Katie jumped. She'd almost forgotten he was in the room. "It seems like the weekend after Thanksgiving, I go out for a few hours and—*bam!*—it's Christmas when I get home. I've been working on this since Thursday and I just finished last night."

"It looks amazing. And I told you to call if you needed help."

"I had it under control."

It was too bad, she thought, looking around the room. It would have been fun to decorate together. Passing the garland around and around the tree. Watching Josh stretch to hang the balls high on the tree. Yeah, she might have enjoyed that.

"I guess I'll take my bag up," she said when it became obvious he didn't have too much else to say.

He grunted, but whether it was in response to her or because he was reaching for the television remote, she couldn't tell. She went up the stairs and down the hall to Liz's room. Josh's room was right across from it, but his door was closed. It was tempting to peek in, because she hadn't looked inside for years, but she forced herself to leave it alone.

It was dumb, anyway. As she'd told others, if Josh was ever going to see her as more than somebody to argue referee calls with, he would have done it by now. She was thirty-three and it was time to start seriously thinking about her future. None of the guys she'd dated had been able to take Josh's place as the most important guy in her life, and a few had even tried to make her choose. They'd lost, of course.

Now, sitting on the edge of Liz's bed, she wondered if Josh's leaving Whitford wouldn't be the best thing for everybody. It would certainly make him happy, but maybe it would also free her to find a guy who *did* want to settle down with her and make babies.

Just thinking about it made her heart hurt, though, so she shoved those thoughts aside and went to the room next door to strip her mom's bed. She was here to help with the lodge so her mom wouldn't relapse, and that's what she'd do. That was *all* she'd do.

As EAGER AS ROSE was to be home, the journey really—as Earle would have said—beat the snot out of her. By the time Josh, who insisted on holding her elbow whenever she was in motion, took her coat and practically pushed her onto the couch, she never wanted to move again.

The lodge looked beautiful though, she thought, taking in the holiday atmosphere. "Did you two decorate this together?"

"Josh did it," Katie told her. "I told him to call me if he needed help, but of course he didn't."

That wasn't part of the plan. She'd known when she'd asked if he'd gotten the tree up yet that he'd make sure it was done before she was released, but Rose had imagined him calling Katie to help him. They'd deck the halls, maybe watch a movie. Cuddle on the couch. That was her plan.

Clearly she'd underestimated Josh's stubborn streak when it came to not asking for help.

"I was thinking," she said. "I'd like for everybody to dress for Christmas Eve."

"Yeah, me, too." Josh snorted. "Running around naked with lit candles and hot gravy can be a bitch."

She pinned him with a look, but he only grinned at her. "I want everybody to dress up. Really make it a party."

Both kids groaned, but Katie got her objection out first. "You want our family party to be formal? Seriously?"

"I'm not talking tuxedos and pearls, or even ties. Just everybody looking nice so we can take pictures."

"Specify *nice*," Josh said.

"A shirt with buttons would be nice."

He grimaced. "With jeans?"

She considered that for a few seconds. Josh's wardrobe wasn't exactly well-rounded. As far as pants went, he owned sweats, jeans and a funeral suit. "As long as they're nice ones. No holes or raggedy hems."

The sound of a truck coming up the drive made her smile. It was Andy's. "If I can talk him into staying, you two can still go to Max's for *Monday Night Football*."

Josh shook his head. "Forget it. I didn't drive two hours round-trip to bring you home just to abandon you. You're stuck with us."

"I bet the Hallmark and Lifetime holiday movies have already started playing," she said with a sweet smile.

He shuddered. "Great. I'm going to go make you some tea."

Rose heard him talk to somebody in the kitchen and realized Andy must have come in the back door. The man was really making himself at home now. "How'd you sleep last night, Katie?"

"Good. Liz's bed is actually a lot more comfortable than mine." She laughed. "Maybe I'll just move in here permanently and drive the few minutes to the shop every day."

That was Rose's master plan. Her endgame, as FBI guys would say.

Before she could say anything else, Andy walked into the room, and she tried not to get all mushy inside at the way his face lit up when he saw her. "Hi, Andy."

"You up to some company?"

"Of course. The kids don't seem to want to watch Christmas chick movies with me." The flash of panic that crossed his expression made her smile. "Maybe we could play rummy."

"You should go to bed," Katie said.

"I've been in bed for a week and I'm bored. Lounging on the couch playing cards isn't going to do me in."

Her daughter sighed. "Fine. I'll be in the basement, sorting through boxes. Time to start putting together the toiletry baskets for the guest bathrooms."

Once she was gone, Rose shook her head. "They're both so damn stubborn."

"But you're *more* stubborn."

"That I am. The cards are in the drawer over there. What are we playing for?"

"Cookies?"

It was on the tip of her tongue to say *kisses,* but she didn't. It was silly, really, and she had no idea if he'd even considered kissing her. He was attentive and sweet and sometimes a little flirtatious, but he hadn't yet done anything she could interpret as putting a move on her.

"Cookies it is. First to five hundred gets a fresh-baked batch from the loser."

Andy laughed, and Rose reveled in the sound. It was so warm and husky, rather like the man. "Woman, you better hope like hell I win."

CHAPTER FIVE

JOSH WAS GOING to lose his mind. Or maybe he'd already lost it and that was why he couldn't think straight.

The first guests of the season were checking in in a few days and Rose was obsessed with this stupid family Christmas Eve party. Because she was one hundred percent in attentive-daughter mode, that meant Katie was bugging him about it. Constantly.

"We have to decide if we're having turkey or ham."

He tossed the paper plate from his lunch into the trash and crushed his soda can before throwing it into the can bin. It didn't do much to relieve the stress. "Which one can you cook better?"

Katie shrugged. "The turkey has a timer thing that pops up when the bird's perfectly done. Hams don't."

"Then make a turkey."

"I don't think a turkey will be enough."

As tempting as it was to beat his head against the doorjamb until he was blissfully unconscious, he dug deep for some patience. If Rosie thought he and Katie didn't have their shit together, she'd drag herself out of bed to make sure the family's holiday wasn't ruined. Rosie back in the hospital would definitely put a damper on things.

"Close to a dozen people, right?" She shrugged. "Maybe both, then. Pretty sure they put cooking directions on the ham wrappers."

"Jesus. A dozen people? Really?"

"You, me and Mom is three. Mitch and Paige. Ryan, Lauren and Nick. I know Mom invited Andy and, since Drew's newly almost-single as well as Mitch's best friend, he'll probably come with him."

"That's ten."

She glared at him. "I said close to a dozen. Ten is close to twelve. What about Sean and Emma? Did you call him yet?"

"Sean doesn't want to travel during the holidays, with Emma being pregnant and all."

"Is there something wrong?"

"Not with the baby, no. Him? Maybe. It's some kind of superstition thing. He says there's always a super-sad, tragic accident on the news Christmas Eve and being out on the roads with a pregnant wife is tempting fate."

She tapped a pen against the notepad she was making lists on. It was a habit that was really starting to drive him insane. "That's a little weird. I didn't think Sean was afraid of anything."

"And she's not even that far along yet. I hope he realizes if he wraps her totally in Bubble Wrap, she'll suffocate."

"How many pounds of potatoes should I make?"

"How the hell should I know? Check Google. Or, better yet, ask Rosie."

"We told her we'd take care of this."

Yes, they had, but he'd seriously underestimated the effect this nitpicky shit would have on his sanity. "I don't think telling you how many pounds of mashed potatoes ten people will eat will cause her to relapse. Or call Fran. Call Paige or Gavin. Just stop asking *me*."

"You're in a pretty crappy mood for somebody who didn't spend the morning scrubbing toilets and counting rolls of toilet paper."

"You offered. If you don't want to help, don't. I've done my share of toilet scrubbing over the years and I don't really give a shit."

"Hey," Katie said quietly.

He didn't want to hear any more. After shoving his feet into his boots, he opened the back door. Fresh, cold air would do him some good. Especially if it kept anybody from bugging him.

"Hey!"

He turned, halfway out the door. "What?"

Katie looked him in the eye, her face calm but very serious. "You're being an asshole."

He shoved his hand through his hair, then

stepped back into the kitchen so he could close the door. "Yeah."

"Tell me why."

"Because nothing's changed." The words he hadn't meant to say just kind of slipped out, but he wished they hadn't, because he didn't want to explain what they meant, even if he could.

Back during the summer, telling his brothers how he felt about the Northern Star had been a huge relief. And their understanding—their willingness to work toward freeing him from the obligation—had given him hope. But now, as the snow fell, it was more of the same thing he'd done every winter for as long as he could remember.

"But things *will* change, Josh. It probably feels as if you're doing the same old thing you've always done, but this year's different. You're not doing it alone and your whole family's working on making things change for you. But it's going to take some time. You know that."

He should have known Katie would know what he meant. Nobody got him like she did. "I know. It's just that this is always a stressful time for me, and with Rose being sick and this party and everything, I'm a little overwhelmed and I get back in that *stuck forever* mind-set."

She grinned, killing the tension just like that. "Stop being so stressed. You have me this time."

He laughed. "That would be helpful if you'd

spent more time as a kid cooking with your mom and Liz and less time changing the oil in the tractors with me and my dad."

"Shut up." She started tapping the pen again. "What are you going to do now?"

"I need to take a quick ride out through the woods. Getting snow and then a warm spell and then a heavy, wet snow means there are branches down. I want to make sure there's nothing that'll screw up the groomer going through. You?"

She sighed. "Mom made me sprinkle some freshener stuff on the guest mattresses. Now I have to go vacuum it all up."

"Have fun with that."

"I hate you."

On his way out, he said, "Oh, and don't forget it's your turn to make supper tonight."

He jerked the door closed just in time to hear the pen bounce off the window.

In the barn, he started his four-wheeler to let it warm up. It was cold enough that the wheels wouldn't dig up the snow too badly and he didn't want to use his sled until the trail was groomed, because getting stuck sucked. After gassing up the chain saw, he locked it into the bracket on his ATV and swapped his around-the-house work coat for his good snowmobile coat. A few hours of trail work would put his head right.

He was right about that. It helped put his head

right, but it wiped out his body so he ended up napping on the couch after dinner. He managed to sleep through whatever shows Rosie and Katie were watching and the news, which was how he found himself unable to sleep when he actually went to bed.

A little after midnight, he gave up and went down to the kitchen. Midnight snacks of the fresh-baked variety were sadly lacking, but he grabbed a couple of the brownies Katie had baked and set them on a napkin so he could grab some milk.

The first bite surprised him. Katie wasn't in the running for Queen of the Bake Fair, but they'd come out better than he'd expected. Better than store-bought, anyway. He decided a third would fill his belly enough to help him sleep, or at the very least keep him from lying in bed wishing he'd had a third brownie.

After rinsing his glass, he crumpled his napkin and shot it into the trash basket, Kevin Garnett–style.

"Two points."

Josh whirled, barely biting back a yelp of surprise. There, in the kitchen doorway, was Katie.

And, holy shit, Katie was…hot.

Not just hot, but smoking hot. Her hair was down, and she had on a white tank top and some flimsy shorts that looked a lot like boxers. And nothing else.

"Surprised the Celtics haven't called you yet," she said, and then she went to the fridge and started rummaging around.

Katie had a great ass.

Josh stood there, staring like an idiot. Had Katie always had a great ass? And her legs. Jesus, they went on forever, all long and toned and perfect for wrapping around...

He was losing his mind. This was Katie. His friend. His best buddy. His pal.

Except looking at his best buddy's ass shouldn't make him thankful he was wearing sweats because if he'd had on jeans, his dick would have busted out the zipper teeth trying to get at her.

Well, shit. Katie Davis was definitely not just one of the guys.

KATIE WAS LOOKING for something delicious and bad for her, but she'd already gorged on brownies earlier, so she settled for pulling out a pint of blueberries. With a little milk and a lot of sugar, it would satisfy the sweet tooth.

She grabbed the milk with her other hand and used her hip to bump the fridge door closed. When she turned to set them on the counter, she saw Josh staring at her. Or, more accurately, glaring at her. "What's wrong with you?"

"Put some damn clothes on. We don't run around half-naked here."

Katie looked down at her tank top and boxers. "Shirt. Shorts. Pretty much the opposite of naked."

"You're not wearing a…" He waved his hand in the direction of her chest, swore under his breath and stormed out.

Katie looked down again. Okay, so she wasn't wearing a bra. And, whether it was the chilled air from the fridge or the way Josh had looked at her, her nipples were taking full advantage of the lack of constraint.

"You've never seen nipples before?" she called after him.

It sounded as if he tripped on the stairs and he cursed again, but he didn't come back or answer the question.

The moment was sweeter than teaspoons of sugar heaped on blueberries. He may have been glaring at her and he may have snapped at her, but when Josh stormed past her, his sweats had been sporting a tent worthy of the cover of a Cabela's catalog.

She really hoped he didn't break anything tripping on the stairs like that.

Humming a Christmas carol under her breath, she made her snack and sat down at the table.

The holiday spirit slowly seeped away, though, as she picked at her blueberries. After all these years, Josh had to finally notice her when he was already planning his escape from the lodge and Whitford. And her.

Not that it mattered. A man noticing a woman's breasts wasn't exactly a life-changing event. But, hot damn, it had felt good.

After rinsing her bowl, Katie turned off the lights and made her way back upstairs. She paused just for a moment between Josh's door and hers, listening. No snoring, which meant he was still awake. And as she stood there, she heard the telltale rustle of tossing and turning.

Thoughts of Josh naked and tangled in sheets were put on hold when the sound of her mother coughing broke the silence. Katie tensed, but it sounded a lot less brutal than it had before. Once it passed, Katie went into her room and quietly closed her door.

Then she leaned back against it, letting the wood cool her skin. There was no way she was going to sleep tonight. She'd slowly been working toward letting go of her attraction to Josh. Not that she'd had a lot of success, but she'd been trying. Now it ran unchecked again, fired up by the way he'd looked at her.

It was still dark when her alarm signaled the end of tossing and turning. Because she didn't want to wake her mom, she crept down the stairs and used the shower in one of the guest bathrooms. She'd be cleaning them all before guests arrived, anyway.

Then she grabbed a yogurt and a banana and went out into the cold.

Rather than risk running into Josh again while she was still feeling warm and fuzzy from the resurgence of her Josh-based fantasies, she'd eat her breakfast at the shop before she opened it. She had one of those single-serve coffee brewers, too, for customers. Copious amounts of caffeine might help get her back on track.

Though it wasn't very likely, she hoped it would be busy. Anything that kept her mind off the way Josh had looked at her. She had a few hours away from him and she intended to spend them not thinking about him. Not much, anyway.

JOSH WOKE UP surprised he'd managed to sleep at all. Every time he closed his eyes, all he could see was Katie in that skimpy tank top and shorts, which had led to an erection that refused to die.

Since he wouldn't allow himself to jerk off to mental pictures of his friend, he'd suffered. A lot.

He screwed up making Rosie's tea and managed to splash it over his hand when he dumped it in the sink. Then he burned her English muffin. Managed to discard that one without injuring himself, but it wasn't a good start to the day.

Thankfully, Katie had gone to work, so he didn't have to face her yet. But Rosie was waiting for her breakfast.

He set the breakfast tray on the floor in the hall so he could crack her door open. She opened her eyes and smiled. "I'm up."

Managing to get the tray to her lap without dumping the whole thing seemed like a small victory, but he'd take what he could get.

"You need to go get a haircut," she said before he could make his escape.

Josh frowned and ran his hand over his head. "Not yet I don't."

"Yes, you do. It's already starting to grow out and once the lodge is officially open, you'll never get around to it, so you'll look like a shaggy mutt in the Christmas pictures."

Shaggy mutt was a little harsh. "There's plenty of time to get a trim before Christmas, Rosie. I'm not leaving you alone in the house."

"Andy's coming over in an hour or so. I'll be fine for that long, since I'm still in bed."

She was up to something, but he couldn't for the life of him think of what it was.

"You needed to go to the hardware store, anyway," she said. "I saw your list on the fridge. And, with everything you have to do, I just know you're going to end up looking mangy for the holiday."

"Shaggy. Mangy. Mutt. Maybe I should skip the hardware store and make myself a vet appointment." She didn't crack a smile. "Fine. If it makes you happy, I'll go get my hair cut so I won't look like a stray dog in your precious pictures."

"Can you stop at the library for me, too? And I need a few things from the market."

It was another twenty minutes before he was on the road, with the music cranked in an effort to drown out the chaos in his head. He had a million things to do, the woman who'd always helped him was lying in bed worrying about his freaking hair of all things, and in a few minutes Katie would be running her fingers through that hair.

There wasn't a sound system ever put in a vehicle capable of drowning out that thought. He couldn't even begin to count how many times she'd done it before, but it must have been at least a half-dozen times a year since she'd taken over the barbershop. This, however, was the first time he'd ever had to pause outside the door and take a few seconds to check his nerves.

There was a guy ahead of him, so Josh grabbed a magazine out of the rack and settled in a chair to wait his turn. It wasn't as if he could take a rain check, since Rosie would just be up his ass again about looking like a shaggy dog.

He didn't fish, though, so neither field nor stream was interesting enough to distract him from watching Katie work. She was a natural, chatting Mr. Harwin up about his model airplanes while making quick work of trimming his hair. Thankfully, she was wearing a traditional white coat over her clothes today, so he was spared a good view of her body. It was a welcome reprieve after last night, but he still closed his eyes so he couldn't see her at all.

Now that he'd become aware of the breasts and legs and really great ass, he was noticing other things. How expressive her eyes were. How often her hair was in a ponytail and how very much he'd like to see it down more often, as it was last night. It looked soft and he'd bet it would tickle sliding across his bare chest.

"Hey, Kowalski, you fall asleep?"

Oh, shit. He'd lost track of time and gotten lost in a hot little daydream about what came *after* her hair tickling his chest. Pushing himself out of the scooped plastic chair was no treat, and he took advantage of Katie turning her back to adjust the crotch of his jeans.

When she turned on the water in the sink, he shook his head. "Just a quick trim's fine."

"Shut up. You've always gotten the full treatment."

That was before, but it wasn't as if he could explain that to her without feeling even more awkward than he already did. Taking the magazine with him, he walked over and made himself as comfortable as he could in the wash chair.

"You want me to toss that magazine on the table?"

"No, I, uh…" It was staying right where it was—hiding his crotch like an eighth-grade math book. "I've got my thumb holding my place. I was reading an article."

"You being such an avid fisherman and all." He jumped a little when the spray of water hit his head and she jerked it away. "What? Too hot?"

"No, it's fine," he muttered.

It was less fine when her fingers plunged into his hair and it took everything he had not to moan. Then came the shampoo. Her fingers massaged his scalp, working the lather into his hair, and he shifted the magazine on his lap, making sure it was centered over the evidence of how very good it felt. It always had before, but this time was…different.

Everything was different now. Somehow, wanting to have sex with somebody you'd considered a friend your whole life shook things up. How was he supposed to enjoy football with her now? Hard to focus on third-down conversions when you were thinking about the breasts of the person sitting next to you. Maybe he could show up early and beat Butch to the recliner without anybody noticing.

She finally finished rinsing the soap out and, after rubbing and squeezing out the excess water, she told him to go sit in the chair. That was a little better because she draped him entirely in a huge cape. And at least he could sit up straight instead of being stretched out with a magazine in his lap.

The haircut itself didn't take long, because despite Rosie's nagging he hadn't really needed one yet. By the time she'd brushed the hair off his ears and neck and whipped the cape off, he'd managed to get control of his body, more or less. But when he reached for his wallet, she waved him off.

"We'll skip it while I'm eating your food and burning your electricity."

"I'm also making you work for the lodge without paying you."

"Josh, forget it. Where are you off to now?"

"I have a list. I think Rosie nagged me into cutting my hair just so I'd be in town to go to the library and the market for her."

"She nagged you? It wasn't even really time for a trim yet, so I was wondering why you were here."

"She convinced herself I'd get busy and look like a shaggy mutt in the party pictures. I agreed just to shut her up."

"Have fun, then."

Josh waved and made his escape. That had really sucked and he wasn't sure how the hell he was supposed to survive living with her now. He started his truck and pointed it toward the library. He'd get Rosie's books and groceries, and then he'd go home and deal with his newfound sexual frustration the way men had for centuries.

He was going to split the hell out of a pile of wood.

CHAPTER SIX

WHEN NOON CAME and she flipped the sign to Closed, Katie wasn't in any hurry to get back to the lodge.

Josh was acting weird and it was all her breasts' fault, dammit. Stupid nipples. Despite the unrequited lust on her part, one thing she and Josh had never been was awkward. The fact he'd had to keep a magazine across his lap while she'd washed his hair should have made her deliriously happy, but not if it came with weirdness.

Once the Jeep had warmed up enough to quit making the ominous sound she hadn't gotten around to diagnosing yet, she headed to the library and was grateful to see the parking lot was almost empty. In a place where silence reigned, having a discreet conversation wasn't always easy.

Luckily the few cars appeared to belong to the moms trying to corral their kids in the children's section, so nobody was within earshot of Hailey's desk. "Got a second?"

"Of course." Hailey set aside the new books she was covering in plastic while Katie stole one of the computer chairs and wheeled it over. "You look flustered."

"Apparently Josh does likes white cotton."

Hailey sucked in a breath, but clapped both hands over her mouth before the squeal could escape. Then she leaned forward so she could whisper. "Guess you have some feminine wiles, after all."

"If feminine wiles means white tank top with no bra, then yeah."

"Feminine wiles. Boobs. Same thing. So tell me *everything*."

"That is everything." Katie shrugged at her friend's disappointed look. "Sorry. He told me to put some clothes on and then stormed off."

"I was hoping for something a little more salacious."

Katie frowned. "Salacious?"

"Yeah. I hear it all the time about romance novels, so it must mean hot and scandalous and sexy and maybe a little bit dirty. I'm improving my vocabulary."

"Vocab building works best when you know the definition. But, anyway…no. It wasn't salacious. But he finally noticed me."

Hailey sighed and shook her head. "I hate to break this to you, but a man noticing a woman's nipples when she's wearing a white tank top without a bra isn't newsworthy."

"Maybe not in general, but he noticed *my* nipples. All these years I wasn't sure if he even knew I had breasts. And now he's acting funny."

"Define funny."

"He had to keep a magazine open across his lap while I washed his hair this morning."

Hailey's eyes widened. "Now we're talking. That's a little salacious. I think."

"We're in a library. Maybe one of us should look that word up."

"Later. Did he say anything?"

"Not really." Katie thought back. "He tried to get out of me washing his hair. Just wanted a quick trim to make Rosie get off his back, but I didn't listen because he always has me wash it."

Hailey smiled. "But this time he didn't, because you running your hands all through his hair was going to make that magazine pop up like a tent."

Katie's phone gave the text chime and Hailey made a big fuss out of shushing her. Rolling her eyes, Katie pulled up the message from Josh. U leave yet? When she texted back that she hadn't, she got an almost immediate response. Stop @ market.

She didn't bother asking him what was needed. Her mom no doubt had called Fran with a list, which she'd written down and would hand to Katie when she walked in the door.

"So what are you going to do?" Hailey asked after she tucked her phone back in her pocket.

"About what?"

"Seriously? About Josh."

Katie shrugged. "Nothing, I guess. Yeah, he noticed I have breasts. Big deal. And it's already awkward. I don't want to make it worse."

"It's going to stay awkward until you guys just give in and do it. It's the tension and the dancing around it that's going to be awkward."

It sounded as if the moms were herding the kids toward the desk now, so Katie wheeled the computer chair back to the desk. "I have to go."

"If you do anything salacious, you better call me."

Katie waved a goodbye and headed for the market as the kids dumped piles of picture books on the desk. Fran was knitting what looked like a sock when she went in, but she paused long enough to hand her a list scrawled on receipt tape.

Tea, milk, flour, butter, eggs and a Slim Jim. It looked as if her mom was going to attempt baking something soon and Josh had a craving for something spicy. She gathered up the items and took them back to the counter so Fran could ring them up and put them on the lodge's account, along with the candy bar she felt was a fair payment for her time.

"How's your mom feeling?" Fran asked. "She sounded a lot better on the phone, but she's one for putting on a stiff upper lip."

"She actually is doing better. If I wasn't around,

she'd probably try to get up and go on a cleaning binge to make up for lost time."

"Sometimes lying around can make a body feel worse."

"That might have worked on me after the first time she had pneumonia," Katie said. "But we're not letting her take any chances this time. She can putt around and make a batch of cookies if she's up to it, but she's not doing any of the heavy lifting."

"And Josh? How's he doing?"

"Good." After a few seconds of awkward silence, she realized Fran must be looking for more. "First guests arrive tomorrow, but I think almost everything's ready now."

Like Hailey, Katie got the impression Fran was looking for something a little more salacious, but she wasn't handing out intimate confidences to her mother's best friend. That was all she needed—Rosie getting it in her head Josh and Katie could live happily ever after at the lodge and have lots of babies for her to knit for. That would be a nightmare.

"Well, you tell your mom I said hi, even though I just talked to her. And tell Andy the same, since I hear he's been spending most of his spare time at the lodge."

Not the most subtle fishing expedition for Fran. She was usually better than that. "He works for Josh. Has since the summer."

"Even on Sundays?"

Katie just smiled and picked up her bag of groceries. "Guess so."

But as she walked to her Jeep, she wondered about what the older woman had said. Andy *was* spending a lot of time at the lodge, and not all of it working. He spent a lot of time with her mom, but her mom wasn't talking to her best friend about it.

Maybe there was something salacious going on at the Northern Star after all.

JOSH HEARD KATIE'S Jeep pull into the yard, but he didn't take a break from making the beds. His Slim Jim could wait until he was done with this last thing on the pre-guest checklist. Once the bedding was done, so was he.

He'd moved on to the second room when he heard Katie coming down the hall, and it wasn't long before she found him. "Hey, why didn't you wait for me to get home so I could help?"

Because, for some reason, he thought it would be weird crawling around on the beds with Katie, even if all they were doing was tucking sheet corners. "Don't need help. I've been making these beds since I was old enough to tell flat from fitted."

"I can help, Josh."

"You're here to take care of Rosie, not make beds."

"Don't be a dumbass. It'll take half as long if I

help." Then she climbed onto the mattress to tuck the far corner and he was presented with another delicious display of her ass.

He'd tried to tell himself last night that it was just the skimpy sleepwear that had caught his attention. Maybe little cotton boxers on a woman did it for him. But now he had to admit Katie's ass was no less great in her usual jeans. He just hadn't noticed before.

Now that he had, making the beds turned into a torturous chore that seemed to go on forever. Every time she bent over to straighten or tuck, he got a little bit harder. By the time they got to the last bed, he could barely walk.

"As slow as you're moving, it would have taken you until next week to do this alone," she said as she smoothed the last quilt. "Is your leg bothering you?"

"Yes." No, but blaming an aching leg was a lot easier on the ego than explaining the real problem.

"Okay, done." Katie put her hands on the small of her back and stretched, which effectively distracted him from thinking about her ass. How had he never noticed she had great boobs? "Mom wants fresh blueberry muffins for your guests, so I have to go make a test batch. That gives her time to tell me what I did wrong and make me bake more."

"So you're telling me we're having shitty blueberry muffins for supper."

"Yup."

He watched her walk out of the room and then he sagged against the wall. He would have flopped onto the bed, but he'd have to remake it, so he settled for just taking a couple minutes to get control of himself.

It wasn't working. Now that his body was having some kind of delayed reaction to Katie's, his dick didn't seem to understand why it wasn't getting what it wanted. When a woman was into him, Josh wasn't in the habit of denying himself.

The trouble was, he couldn't tell if Katie was into him. She seemed the same as she always did. It was him that had changed, and he was afraid if he made a move, he'd just embarrass them both.

Time to split some more wood. He went outside and set the first log on the stump before picking up the splitting maul. *Whack*. The log fell into two pieces. It was satisfying as hell.

After only five minutes or so, he shed his coat and tossed it on the pile. Maybe fifteen minutes after that, he heard a vehicle coming up the driveway. It sounded like Paige's car and, if he remembered correctly, Mitch was supposed to be home. He kept splitting, though, because he didn't want to lose his rhythm and cool off his muscles if it was only Paige stopping by to see the women.

"Holy shit." It was Mitch, and Josh followed his gaze to the mountain of split wood he'd created piling up around him, and then to the last batch he'd split and stacked. "You see a different long-range forecast than I did?"

"Just burning off some…excess energy."

"Sex is more fun than splitting wood for burning off energy."

Josh growled and swung the maul with so much force the log blew apart instead of splitting.

Mitch laughed. "Not a bad substitute if you can't get a woman to have sex with you, though."

"Screw you." He bent and set another log on end, then hefted and swung again.

"Maybe we should hire you a hooker before you clear-cut the entire property."

His oldest brother was a real freakin' comedian. He started to pick up another log, but then realized it was going to take him forever to stack what he'd already split. They were forecasting four to six overnight and he didn't want the split stuff freezing in, so he'd stack that next.

"So let me guess," Mitch said. "You finally realized your trusty sidekick is actually a woman."

Josh swore and wiped his sleeve across his forehead. "Did you know Katie has a really great ass?"

"Let's just say I'm aware she's attractive."

"How did I not see that?"

Mitch shrugged. "You're a late bloomer, I guess. You know hair growing on your balls is natural, right? You don't need to be embarrassed."

"Bite me."

"So you're splitting wood like a crazy man because Katie has a great ass?"

"I didn't see it before. She was just Katie, you know? Then she came into the kitchen in this white tank top and little boxer shorts and…I can't un-see it now."

"She's still the same old Katie."

"No, she's not, because I never had to shove my hands in my pockets to keep from bending the same old Katie over the kitchen table."

"Okay, that would probably piss Rose off on several levels."

Josh didn't want to talk about Katie anymore. He never should have brought up her ass in the first place. "Did you come over here just to bust my balls or did you have some higher purpose?"

"I'm not sure there *is* any higher purpose than busting your balls, but have you got anything going on here right after Christmas? Like the twenty-seventh, maybe?"

Josh tried to picture the calendar in his head. "That's Thursday. Since Christmas is on Tuesday, we left most of the week unbooked. I have people coming in for a long New Year's weekend, but none of them are arriving until Friday, so…no."

"Good. Ryan could use some help moving the last of Lauren and Nick's stuff down to Brookline."

"Oh, wait. Except for that group checking in Thursday. Damn. Forgot about them."

"Nice try."

"Yeah, I'm free. We're gonna do it in one trip, though, right?"

"Yes, and Ryan says it's the last trip," Mitch said, nodding. "They've been bringing stuff down each time she visits and when he goes back and forth, but he wants it done."

"We'll make it done, then."

"And Katie told Lauren she'd help her unpack, too, so she's going to ride down with you."

"You're an asshole."

"Enough with the girl talk. How are the trails?"

IF THE CONSTANT, heavy thump of the splitting maul was any indication, Rose's plan was starting to unfold. Nothing made a man split that much wood with that much enthusiasm but woman troubles.

That's why, even though she was feeling a lot better and itched to *do* something, she complied with their orders to do nothing. Which, sadly, included watching her daughter botch a batch of blueberry muffins.

"Should I help her?" Paige whispered.

Thrilled to have a surprise visitor, Rose had made a pot of tea and they were sitting at the kitchen table, watching Katie make a mess. "Nope. She can do it."

"She does know that baking soda and baking powder aren't the same thing, right?"

Rose might have shushed her, except Katie was being a pain and had insisted on putting her earbuds in so Rosie couldn't "interfere." She wanted to make them all on her own and, with music blasting straight to her eardrums, she couldn't hear any helpful suggestions.

"This is painful," Paige said. "Let's go in the living room and stop staring at her like she's a zoo exhibit."

They carried their tea into the other room and Rose settled in the couch corner she was getting all too tired of. But it was an easy reach to the coffee table and her teacup, so she smoothed the blanket over her lap and picked up her knitting. She could knit and visit at the same time.

"Christmas present?" Paige asked. She'd chosen the armchair with the side table for her tea.

"Nope. I finished my Christmas knitting in the hospital." She held up the little red sweater she was knitting, with a white band near the bottom separated from the red with thin blue stripes. "For Sean and Emma's baby."

"Guess those colors aren't girl or boy specific." After a beat, Paige's face lit up. "Oh, wait, I get it! New England Patriots colors, right? The football thing?"

It still blew Rosie's mind one of the boys had married a woman who knew absolutely nothing about sports, but the girl was trying. "Yes, the football thing."

Paige gave a self-deprecating laugh. "Since Mitch talked me into getting a TV and cable, I've tried watching the games with him when he's home, but I don't really get it."

"You must be a really good cook," she teased.

"Or pay two really good cooks who are willing to make things to go." After taking a sip of her tea and listening to see if anybody was coming, Paige leaned forward a little in her chair. "So? How are things going?"

"Something happened." When Paige's face lit up, Rose held up her hand. "Nothing big, I don't think. But Josh is definitely acting weird and there's tension in the air."

"It's almost inevitable. Everybody can see it but them."

"If I have my way, there will be a baby sleeping on a blanket in front of that tree next Christmas."

Paige looked at the tree, as if imagining it. "What about the fact Josh plans to leave Whitford as soon as they figure out how to make it happen? Mitch feels pretty bad about the way they all abandoned him. He's really dedicated to making it happen."

"Once Josh realizes he loves Katie, he'll lose that itch to wander."

"Or take her with him."

Rose's hands stilled, her fingers clutching the

needles. Not once had she ever considered Katie moving away with Josh. The possibility she could lose the lodge *and* her daughter made her hands tremble and she set her knitting in her lap so she wouldn't drop any stitches.

"Rosie, are you okay? You're pale all of a sudden. Should I get Katie?"

The panic in Paige's voice snapped her out of it and she forced herself to smile. "I'm fine. I just…I don't think Katie would leave her dad's barbershop. She worked too hard for it."

"I shouldn't have said that. Of course she won't leave Whitford. I can't imagine her leaving you and the barbershop at all. And all her friends are here."

"Of course she wouldn't." She said it mostly to make Paige feel better, though. Rose was old and wise enough to know women made sacrifices like that for men they loved all the time. "How are things at the diner?"

"Business is better than I ever expected. If the guys really do manage to connect the lodge to the ATV trails and get them access into town next summer, I might even have to hire more people. Ava's great, but if the supper rush gets any bigger than it is, she won't be able to do it alone. As it is, she's called Tori in two Friday nights in a row."

Rose didn't know Tori Burns very well, yet. She was Jilly Crenshaw's niece and she'd just recently moved from Portland to escape her parents' divorce. She was in her mid-twenties and worked from home, but liked picking up part-time hours at the diner, which gave Paige a little more freedom with her own hours.

"They'll have to make a concrete decision on the lodge before spring, I'd think," Rosie said. "If everybody goes through the red tape and elbow grease of getting the four-wheelers into town, it doesn't seem fair to cut it off again if somebody buys the lodge and doesn't want ATVs. If they decide they're for sure going to sell it, they should hold off and leave it to the new owners to deal with."

"Mitch is pretty torn up about it," Paige confided in a low voice. "He doesn't want to sell the lodge, but he's not willing to step in and run it day-to-day, so he doesn't think it's fair to make Josh do it. But it'll break his heart."

Rose's, too, though she didn't say so. This was a hard enough decision for the kids, and she tried not to make herself too big a factor in it. She knew they were worried about what she'd do, but she didn't want any of them sacrificing their own wants or needs because of her. No matter what happened, she'd have Katie.

Unless she moved away with Josh.

"When are you two going to make me a grand-baby?" she asked in a desperate attempt not to think about Katie leaving anymore.

Paige's eyes widened at the blunt question, but

then her face relaxed into a soft smile. "Soon. Mitch thinks it would be nice to have a baby close in age to Sean and Emma's."

"I agree. You should work on that."

Paige blushed and picked up her tea. "We'll probably wait until we get home."

CHAPTER SEVEN

DAVE CARMODY AND his son, Dan, rolled up to the lodge in the late afternoon on Friday. Josh met them in the drive and shook Dave's hand through his open window.

"You made it," Josh said, just as he did every year. Dave was always the first guest. He had a standing reservation for the weekend of the fifteenth and the only time he didn't make it was the rare occasion Josh had to call him and tell him there was no snow. Then his reservation was floated to the first weekend the trails opened.

"You've done some work around the place," Dave said. "Looks good."

Josh swept a critical eye over the lodge and the outbuildings. It did look good, and he felt a small swell of pride. Whether he'd wanted to or not, he'd been the one to keep the place going for a long time. And it had taken his brothers' help to make it look good again, but the heart and the bones of the place were all his.

"Let's get you parked and unloaded." He slapped Dave's door and stepped back.

Dave owned a trucking business down in Rhode Island, so he had no problem backing his truck and trailer into the patch of lawn off the driveway they kept plowed for just that purpose.

Dan jumped down from the truck the second his dad put it in Park, which released the door locks. Josh grinned at his enthusiasm. "How old are you now, Dan?"

"Almost thirteen. I've got a new sled. Wanna see?"

It made Josh feel a little old following the kid to the back of the trailer and watching him drop the door down so they could walk inside. If he remembered correctly, Dave had brought Dan along with him for the first time the winter before Josh's dad passed away. He'd been little enough to ride in front of Dave on one machine. Now he was on his third snowmobile and he didn't need any help unstrapping it and backing it down onto the snow-covered lawn.

He wanted to go for a ride, but Dave shook his head. "Grab your bag and we'll go say hi to Mrs. Davis. Then we'll go hunt up some supper."

"Is there enough snow so we can ride to town?" Dan asked.

Josh shook his head. "Not yet, bud. Sorry. You'll

have to take the truck into town, but at least they were able to groom the trails and get them open."

"I'll wear him out tomorrow."

That he would. It was a long ride from Rhode Island, so Dave spent every possible minute riding, not wanting to waste a moment of it. "Rose is getting over pneumonia, so her daughter's staying with us to help out. Her name's Katie."

Dave nodded. "Pretty sure we've met her. Pretty blonde about your age, right?"

"Yeah." A very pretty blonde.

The Carmodys headed for the door, but Josh held back for a minute. Since they had the first reservation every year, they had dibs on the room, too. Theirs was the only one with two double beds and its own bathroom, and they took it every time they came up, so they knew the way.

It twisted his gut a little, looking up at the lodge. Dave was right. It did look good. More like it did in his distant memory when the economy was strong, his father was still running things and they had so much business they had to turn people away almost every weekend there was snow.

It was times like these, sharing memories with a longtime guest, that he felt the connection to the Northern Star. It was home—*his* home—and he felt the emotional and nostalgic bonds that came with that. He loved the old place. But all he'd ever wanted was the right to make a choice for himself, and the lodge stood in his way.

Shaking off the melancholy, he went inside to make sure Dave and Dan settled in. Nothing much had changed since their last visit. When they woke up in the morning, they'd find the coffeemaker with a freshly brewed pot in the same spot on the counter, and a basket of home-baked blueberry muffins. Luckily for the Carmodys, Katie had mastered the recipe on the third try. Josh hadn't been so lucky, since he was the taste test dummy.

The Northern Star didn't offer meals to their guests, but they did offer the coffee and baked goods in the morning to hold them over until they rode by a place offering a real breakfast. And they did occasionally have a group who hadn't gotten dinner before every place closed for the night, and Josh would offer some reheated leftovers or access to the deli meats.

Katie was the only person in the kitchen, so he assumed the Carmodys were in their room. "Where's Rosie?"

"Apparently you guys replaced the television in that room since the last time they were here and she wanted to show them how to use it."

"Oh, I forgot about that."

"It's a little weird."

"What is?" He grabbed a soda out of the fridge and popped the tab.

"Having other people—strangers, I mean—in your house."

"I've never known it any other way, I guess." He shrugged. "And we get a lot of repeat business, so people don't stay strangers very long."

She leaned against the counter and crossed her arms in a way that would have drawn attention to her breasts if he wasn't *very* deliberately keeping his eyes on her face. "What does Rosie usually do while you have guests? I mean, what should I be doing right now?"

He laughed. "The guests being here is the easy part. It's the getting ready and the cleaning after that sucks. Juggling the calendar. Accounting. But they come here to ride the trails and we're pretty much just a place to sleep."

"That seems a little anticlimactic."

Katie not talking about climaxes at all would be good. "Every once in a while we'll get a phone call and have to take the truck and trailer out to rescue a guest whose machine broke down, if that keeps it exciting."

"I've been out with you on a rescue run, remember? Not that exciting. But I've never been staying here at the same time as paying guests. It's just a little hard to know what to do."

"*You* keep your focus on that stupid party. Let me worry about the guests."

"About the party—"

"Hold on, I think I hear a truck coming." As soon as it was quiet, they could definitely hear a truck coming up the driveway. "They're first-timers, so I need to get out there and tell them where to park and make sure they unload okay. Introduce them to Dave and his son and all that."

"I think you're using this as an excuse to avoid talking about appetizers."

"Would I do that?" He gave her his best angelic smile and then practically ran out the door.

EVEN THOUGH SHE didn't have to do anything, so to speak, living in a house that ended up with eight strangers in it for the weekend was a drain on Katie and she was so thankful when Sunday rolled around. They all hit the road back to their own homes and she and Josh made short work of stripping the beds and giving everything a quick once-over.

Of course, now she had a veritable mountain of bedding to wash and thorough cleanings to give when tomorrow morning rolled around, but right now it was Sunday night, Andy had offered to watch a movie with her mom, and she was parked on Max's couch to watch some *Sunday Night Football*.

It was made both more awkward and more amusing by Josh's inability to get comfortable. At least that looked like the problem to everybody else, she guessed, even though she knew all the shifting and rearranging was him trying to avoid his body coming into contact with her body. As a matter of fact, he seemed to be trying to pretend she wasn't there at all.

Funny, considering they'd ridden over together in his truck because it made no sense to take separate vehicles. He'd been fine on the ride over, talking about the trails and something about groomer parts and stuff, but once it came time to hit their usual sofa spots, he'd started getting weird again. He was also a little more enthusiastic than usual in his dislike of San Francisco's team and the referees. Katie had even spotted Butch turning down his hearing aid.

In the break between the first and second quarters, Katie decided to give Josh a short reprieve by going into the kitchen to replenish the chips and dip. A few seconds later, Max followed her in, carrying everybody's empties.

"Confession time," he said in a low voice. "What did you do to Josh?"

Katie shrugged, but the blush heating up her cheeks gave her away. "I ran into him in the kitchen on a midnight snack run a few nights ago. Tank top, skimpy shorts. No bra. He looked like somebody had just smacked him upside the head with a shovel."

"Ha! I knew you guys would hook up eventually."

"We haven't actually hooked up. He told me to put some clothes on and went storming up to his room. Alone."

Max stared at her for a few seconds, his head cocked to one side. "Okay, wait. It's midnight. You guys are alone in the kitchen and you're barely dressed and…he told you to put some clothes on?"

"Yeah. And ever since he realized I'm not actually one of the guys, he's been acting weird. Not all the time, but a lot."

"Probably only when he's thinking about having sex with you."

That gave her pause, because if Max was right, that would mean Josh thought about having sex with her a lot. "Wouldn't it make more sense to have, I don't know, kissed me or something, instead of criticizing my lack of clothing and leaving the room?"

"That's probably how most guys would have played it."

"So what's his problem?"

Max gave her a good impression of a deer in the headlights, before shrugging his shoulders. "I don't know. Maybe he's afraid of mucking up your friendship?"

That's what she figured, too. "It's pretty mucked up already."

"Maybe if you hook up, it'll kill the awkwardness and everything will be normal again."

"That's what Hailey said, too."

"Who's Hailey?"

She held up her hands in total disbelief. "Max, how can you have lived here five years and not know who Hailey Genest is? She's the librarian."

"Which librarian? I'm really bad with names."

"Whitford only has one. Blonde. Attractive. A little older than me?"

"Oh, her. She seems nice. And we seem to be in agreement on you and Josh having sex."

Katie laughed. "There you go. A consensus. You guys obviously have a lot in common. You should take her out on a date."

He recoiled. "With the librarian?"

"Why not? You can have some dinner and get to know each other better. Talk about her work. Talk about your work. Maybe have a drink or two."

The corner of his mouth twitched in an almost-smile and she guessed she hadn't been subtle enough. "This is my busy season, but maybe I'll at least say hello at some point."

A clue! "So you get busy before Christmas?"

"Yup. Hey, grab that bag of pretzels on your way out, would you? And maybe for that Christmas Eve thing I hear you're doing, you should wear a sexy dress and spike his eggnog." And just like that he was gone.

Katie refilled the chip bowl and grabbed a new tub of dip out of the fridge, but she stopped to scowl at the alarm panel on the basement door before grabbing the pretzels. She'd been close this time. She was sure of it.

A few plays had already been run by the time she got comfortable again and normally Josh would have given her a recap, but this time he didn't look away from the television.

This had to stop, dammit. If she was going to lose her best friend over sex, it certainly wasn't going to be because they *didn't* have it. That would be a waste all the way around.

Hailey's advice echoed through her head. *Seduce him, use the hell out of him, and then send the oversexed, possibly dehydrated husk of him out into the world.*

To hell with it. She had one week to find herself a drop-dead sexy dress.

"IF YOU COULD stop ogling your wife long enough to answer my question, that'd be great." Maybe meeting Mitch for a late breakfast-slash-early lunch at the Trailside Diner hadn't been Josh's greatest idea, but at least he'd been correct in guessing they'd have the place more or less to themselves at ten-thirty on a Wednesday morning.

"You asked a question?"

"I asked what you think I should get Katie for Christmas." He'd lost almost as much sleep worrying about that as he'd lost to picturing her naked.

"A vibrator, since you're too chickenshit to get the job done yourself."

Josh's jaw dropped, and then he closed his mouth with a snap. "I can't believe you just said that."

"I can't believe I left what I was doing to come and meet you so you could whine about shopping."

"I'm not whining. I just asked for a suggestion. And what were you doing that was so important, anyway?"

"Working on Paige's Christmas present."

"Really? What are you making for her?"

Mitch nodded his head toward Paige, who was refilling the salt shakers around the coffee counter. "Can't tell you. She has hearing like a bat."

Josh glanced over and saw Paige looking back. Her mouth turned up in an apologetic smile. "Just for the record, I think a vibrator would be a *really* awkward gift to receive at a family Christmas party. Sorry."

"Oh, for chrissake." Josh slid down in the booth, holding his head. "I should have known better."

"Fine." Mitch angled himself in the booth so that Paige wasn't in his line of sight. "What do you usually get her?"

"I dunno. Stuff. I got her a Patriots sweatshirt once. A Bruins cap. Last year I got her a poster signed by the Red Sox pitchers from the '04 team. But I'm stuck this year and I'm running out of time. Even though we're closed this weekend to guests,

Rose and Katie are driving me bat-shit crazy with this party. Sneaking out to the city and back's going to be a problem and there's no sense in even going if I don't know what to get."

"Sounds like you usually go the sports shop and play eenie-meenie-minie-mo. Why the stress this year?"

Damned if he knew. He'd never stressed about gifts for Katie before. Rosie, yes, until he'd figured out a gift certificate to the fancy yarn store a few towns over was her idea of the greatest gift ever. He thought gift certificates were boring, so he usually got her some little thing to go with them, but at least she was happy.

Mitch was right on the money about Katie. He always went into the sports shop and bought the first thing that caught his eye.

"Maybe she wants girly stuff," he said, frowning at his coffee cup.

"Josh, Katie didn't suddenly start being a girly-girl because you noticed her ass, okay? She's not the problem here. *You* are."

Maybe he was, but he couldn't seem to help himself. Now that his view of Katie had changed, he didn't know how to act anymore. It was exhausting, and he couldn't keep it up much longer. But how was he supposed to have that conversation with her? *Hey, Katie, I know you've been my best friend forever, but you either have to have sex with me or move back to your own place, okay?*

"What's holding you back?" Mitch asked, and Josh was both relieved and a little scared of his transition into serious big brother mode. Mitch was a damn fine big brother to have when the chips were down, but sometimes he threw stuff out there that Josh didn't want to see.

"She's Katie. I mean, what if I make a move and she's not into me? Or she is into me, but then it goes south. I don't want to never have Katie in my life again because I saw her half-naked in the kitchen and came unglued."

"That's a reasonable fear."

"And she's Rosie's daughter. That makes it weird, too. And harder because, not only could I lose Katie, but would my relationship with Rosie suffer?"

"Maybe."

Josh sighed and pinched the bridge of his nose. "So you agree that it's best I keep my hands to myself."

"No. Not really."

"But you just said—"

"I said they're reasonable fears. I didn't say you should let them stop you. I mean, you're driving yourself insane. You're probably annoying her, too, and she either hasn't said anything because she doesn't want to jeopardize the friendship, or she hasn't quite put her finger on what the problem is yet. How long do you think your friendship's going to survive your current state?"

"I don't know, but…" He didn't know how to articulate the deep, underlying thing that had a grip on him.

"But what?"

He shook his head. "I love Katie, you know? Like I love Rosie and you and…family. What if I take this step and really *fall* in love with her?"

"Maybe you're meant to."

"And what if I do and I never leave and eventually I feel the same way about her as I do about the lodge?"

Mitch was quiet for a few seconds, as if he wasn't sure what to say. Josh could understand that. His was a problem with no easy answer, so even his big brother wasn't going to be able to solve it that easily.

"Stop overthinking it," he said finally. "Stop worrying about years down the road. You know, coming back here was the last thing I ever expected to do, but when it came to Paige, I just went with it and eventually ended up where I was meant to be."

Josh drank some of his coffee to give himself an excuse not to answer right away. Buried in Mitch's response was the assumption that if Josh fell in love with Katie, he'd be happy staying in Whitford. The difference was Mitch had chosen to stay and he'd made that choice after he'd gone out into the world, gotten a degree and traveled all over the country building a successful business. Then, when he fell in love with Paige, he'd chosen to stay.

"Maybe I'll just let the chips fall where they will," Josh said when the silence had dragged on too long.

Mitch seemed satisfied with the totally bullshit answer, which was good because he didn't want to talk about Katie anymore.

"Now, because it's really important, I know Rosie's not supposed to be taking part in the party planning and prep," Mitch said in a welcome change of subject, even if it was about the damn party, "but she's going to make that chocolate truffle thing, right? With the cake and pudding and whipped cream and those toffee bits?"

CHAPTER EIGHT

KATIE COULD HEAR people arriving, but she was terrified to leave her room. Which was stupid, she knew, because it was Christmas Eve and everybody in the house was a friend or family. But every time she thought she might be ready, she'd catch a glimpse of herself in the mirror and panic all over again.

She either looked like a glamorous movie star or a cheap hooker. It depended on how deeply she was panicking when she looked at her reflection.

The black dress was soft and snug. It was V-necked and long-sleeved, so perfectly respectable. But Hailey had gotten her to wear one of her high-dollar bras and the boobs were not respectable at all. Even decently covered up, they demanded attention.

They never did that in her cotton bras and comfy sweatshirts.

Her hair was down and floated around her shoulders. And, thanks again to Hailey, she'd managed to do her makeup so her lips were subtle, but her eyes were all smoky and sexy.

The shoes had been a problem. Even after an hour of practice at Hailey's, Katie couldn't walk in high heels. When she'd fallen on the coffee table and snapped two of its legs off, they'd admitted defeat. There was little chance she'd make it down the stairs alive. Instead she was wearing low black wedges with thin ankle straps to make them cute. They weren't as sexy as the stilettos but, according to Hailey, walking like a linebacker in them had killed the sexy, anyway.

Her cell phone chimed and her hands shook as she read the text from Josh. Get your ass down here now. Clearly somebody was feeling overwhelmed.

Taking one last deep breath, Katie avoided the mirror and made her way down the hall. She could tell by the noise that everybody was in the living room, which meant she'd be making something of a grand entrance down the stairs. She pressed her hand to her stomach for a second and then stepped into the fray.

Josh saw her first—probably because he was annoyed and looking for her—and he froze. The butterflies in her stomach danced as his expression changed. She could see the hunger in his smoldering blue eyes and realized she'd just thrown down the gauntlet.

He was a man and she was a woman, dammit, and the chemistry sizzling between them wasn't going to be ignored much longer.

The moment was broken when the rest of them noticed her and a few seconds of what felt like stunned silence were followed by everybody talking at once. Hopefully more about how she looked like a glamorous movie star than a cheap hooker, but she couldn't really make out individual words.

As she greeted each of them, though, exchanging hugs and happy holidays, they all told her how beautiful she looked. And Paige and Lauren really made a fuss over her, which made her feel even more self-conscious. Still, none of them were as bad as her mother, who actually had tears in her eyes.

"You look so beautiful tonight," she whispered, looking Katie up and down.

"If you cry, I swear I'm going upstairs and putting on my Bruins jersey and my favorite black sweatpants. I mean it."

Rose sniffed and blinked a few times really fast, making the unshed tears disappear. "I'm so glad you listened when I said to dress up. You're going to look amazing in the pictures."

She was a little more dressed-up than everybody else, but eventually she relaxed, moving around the living room and kitchen, making sure she talked to everybody. But she was constantly aware of the way Josh watched her, and it kept those butterflies from settling down too much.

It wasn't until it was time to serve dinner that they ended up alone in the kitchen. Josh had carved the meats just before everybody had arrived, so all they had to do was carry the dishes out to the table. Seeing the steam rolling off the gravy made her extra glad she'd opted out of the heels.

"You clean up nice, Davis," Josh said, balancing a bowl of vegetables in each hand.

She smiled and gave him a little shrug. "You don't look too bad yourself, Kowalski."

Actually, in his jeans and a white button-down shirt with the sleeves folded back, he looked more than not too bad. Their eyes met and, for a few long seconds, she wondered if he might set down the vegetables and take a few steps closer to her.

Then Paige hurried in from the other room and the moment was over. "I'm sorry, but I can't just sit there and not help serve. It goes against my nature."

Because Josh and Katie were obviously the last to be seated, the family had left two chairs empty and, naturally, they were right next to each other. Somehow she guessed Lauren or Paige had a hand in the arrangements. And, even with both leaves in the table, the seating was tight, which meant she'd be extra cozy with her sexy neighbor.

Fortunately, there was enough conversation around the table to keep her distracted. She didn't notice *too* much when his arm brushed hers, or when his thigh pressed against hers for a few heartbeats before shifting away.

The meal seemed to go on forever, and she didn't

think she drew a full breath until everybody had risen and she was able to put some distance between her and Josh. They'd made an executive decision to use disposable "china," which hadn't gone over well with her mom, but made cleanup a little easier. Neither Katie nor Josh wanted to spend the next three days washing dishes.

"He can't take his eyes off you," Lauren whispered when they were at the sink, rinsing the serving dishes and stacking them for real washing later.

Katie blushed, hoping nobody else was close enough to overhear. While many people suspected, Lauren was one of the few people who knew Katie had been in love with Josh for a very long time. "This bra is very uncomfortable."

"You have to suffer to be beautiful, my mother always told me. And, trust me, your girls are beautiful tonight."

"He seems to think so."

"So...tonight?"

Katie didn't bother pretending she didn't know what Lauren was talking about. "I don't know. Depends on him, I guess."

"I think you should wait until Rosie goes to bed and then drag him over to the Christmas tree and unwrap him."

Now that made for one hell of a mental image. "Guess I'll be on the naughty list this year."

WAS THERE ANYTHING worse than spending an evening in a state of semiconstant erection in a room with the woman who was like a mother to you and two of your older brothers? Josh couldn't think of a single damn thing.

Except maybe if he'd almost had a heart attack when Katie had walked down the stairs in that dress and then had to get mouth-to-mouth from Andy Miller. That would have been worse, probably, but it was too close to call.

He couldn't look at Katie in that dress and not think about sex. He just couldn't do it. There wasn't a math equation or box score or any other damn thing he could concentrate on enough to draw his focus away from how she looked. And, as if that wasn't bad enough, he'd somehow ended up sitting next to her at dinner and she smelled as sexy as she looked. It was torture. Christmas Eve torture in front of his family, which was even worse.

At least everybody else seemed to be having a good time. The food was good, the music was playing softly and Rosie hadn't complained about a single thing. Unless something drastic happened with dessert or the gift opening, he and Katie had pulled it off.

He was talking to Ryan and Lauren when Mitch

bumped into him and then handed him a cookie. "Oh, hey, I need to find Paige. Can you bring this to Katie? She asked me to grab her one."

"She can't get her own cookie?"

"I don't know. She was doing something and they're almost gone, so she asked me to bring her one. Just give her the damn cookie."

Rather than argue, since Mitch wasn't really making any sense, Josh decided to deliver the damn cookie. It took him a few seconds to spot Katie, and then another minute to make his way to her side.

He held up the cookie. "Mitch asked me to bring you this cookie."

"He did?" She looked as confused as he felt.

"Hey, look, Josh and Katie are under the mistletoe!" Nick yelled. "Kiss!"

They both looked up at the same time and Josh saw that they were, in fact, standing under a sprig of mistletoe. The red ribbon tied around the end of it had been taped to the ceiling.

And he was standing under it with Katie. "Mistletoe? It's a family Christmas party. What kind of sick, twisted nut job hangs mistletoe at a family party?"

"Mistletoe's a traditional decoration," Rosie told him.

"I did the decorating and there was no mistletoe. And there's no way you hung that up there." He caught her quick glance at Mitch—who just happened to be grinning at him like an idiot—and silently called his brother a few choice words. The interfering, asshole traitor just kept grinning.

"Kiss! Kiss! Kiss!" Nick chanted, and everybody else joined in.

"I thought we were having dessert," he yelled, hoping to distract them with food.

"After you kiss her," the boy said. "I've been waiting all night for two people who aren't related to be under the mistletoe at the same time."

"I used to like you, kid."

"Hey, I didn't hang it. I'm just enforcing it. Kiss! Kiss! Kiss!"

Great. A mistletoe enforcer was just what he needed. The chant got louder and faster until he turned and kissed Katie just to shut them up.

Her mouth was soft and he felt the quick breath of surprise against his lips. She tasted like hot chocolate and peppermint and…Christmas, and only a raucous cheer going up around them kept him from sliding his tongue between her lips and pressing for more. He wanted so much more.

Everybody was clapping like idiots, and he didn't dare look at Katie when he broke off the kiss. Instead he looked at Lauren's son. "You happy now, kid?"

"Yup. Dessert time!"

Josh realized he still had the cookie in his hand and ate it himself. Even if she *had* asked for one, it was all clearly a setup by his brother, so he deserved the damn thing.

By the time they got the desserts laid out on the table—with some on the counter because they'd seriously overdone it—everybody seemed to have calmed down. Josh wished he felt the same. Now that he'd kissed Katie, he wasn't sure things would calm down in his mind anytime soon.

While everybody grabbed plates and gathered around the table for the good stuff, Josh stayed at the counter and grabbed a brownie. Drew, who also seemed to be avoiding the crowd, took a beer out of the fridge and joined him.

"Hell of a party," he said, popping the can open.

"It came together pretty well. Rosie hasn't found anything to complain about yet."

"Kinda surprised Sean and his wife aren't here."

"Emma's pregnant and Sean got all superstitious about making the drive during a holiday."

Drew nodded. "I can understand that. Nothing sucks more than responding to an accident scene during Christmas."

"I'm sure Aunt Mary's making sure he gets his fair share of figgy pudding."

Drew took a swig off his beer, then scowled. "What the hell *is* figgy pudding, anyway?"

"Damned if I know."

"Chocolate pudding I might stand on a doorstep

and sing for. Maybe even tapioca, if it's homemade. But figgy?"

"I'd ask Rose, but I'm afraid she'd make it and then we'd have to eat it."

"I'm all set with that." Drew set his beer down on the counter and picked up a sugar cookie. "Have you heard from Liz lately?"

"I talked to her for a few minutes earlier today, but she was in the middle of something. Rose talked to her a few days ago, though. She's doing good."

"She get back together with that artist guy?"

Josh shook his head. "No, that's over for good. Rose said she hasn't really figured out what she's doing next yet, but that she sounds happier."

"That's good. She deserves it."

Something about the way Drew said it sounded like more than polite conversation, but before he could dig any deeper, he heard Katie's laugher and he couldn't stop himself from turning to see her.

Her smile. Her hair. The eyes. That dress. It almost hurt to breathe when he looked at her, and he imagined he could still taste her on his lips. He wanted to kiss her again, preferably when the family wasn't gathered around, chanting like spectators at a blood sport.

She was standing at the table and he wanted to step up behind her. Run his hands over that shiny fabric, then under it. Bend her over the...

Damn it! He took a deep breath, forcing himself

to look back at Drew. "I've gotta check something. I'll be back in a few minutes."

He escaped out the back door without bothering to grab his coat. It was cold as hell on the porch. Not as effective as a cold shower, but at least the air chilled his skin a little.

He was so screwed.

How was he supposed to keep on going as though nothing had changed between them? Maybe she hadn't noticed, but he was having a serious problem staying in bounds as far as their relationship went. And the last thing he wanted to do was screw things up with her.

He had his brothers. And there were a lot of guys he counted as friends, with a few he'd call good ones. But Katie was his pal. His buddy. His best damn friend. He needed her to keep being that in his life.

There wasn't an official rule book that he knew of, but he was pretty sure a guy didn't bend his best damn friend over the kitchen table. And who would he ask about it? His best friend? *Hey, Katie, is it bad form for me to want to make you my own personal brunch buffet?*

Maybe it was just some weird phase brought on by watching his brothers fall in love. First Mitch and Paige, then Ryan and Lauren. Maybe it was catching, like the flu, and all he had to do was ride it out and the symptoms would pass.

He hoped it was a fast-moving bug, though, because he wasn't sure how much longer he could hold out without doing something really stupid he could never take back.

NOTHING MADE ROSE happier than the sound of family laughter ringing through the lodge. There had been too long a dry spell before Josh broke his leg and the other boys came home. The resentment he'd felt toward the lodge and his family had made him bitter, and he'd started going through more beer than she liked.

She'd just resigned herself to the fact she was going to have to interfere and call Mitch, which would have made Josh so angry he might never forgive her, when fate intervened in the form of a tree that needed limbing. To save money on a tree service, Josh had footed a ladder against the toolbox in the bed of his pickup and it had all come to a head with an ambulance ride and a cast.

Now their home was filled with love and laughter and, even if all the kids hadn't made it for Christmas Eve, this was the best night Rose had had in a very long time.

"Are those tears sparkling in your eyes, Rose?" Andy had slipped up beside her without her even noticing.

"Happy tears. Definitely happy."

"I thought maybe you were sad because you're standing under the mistletoe and nobody's kissed you yet."

She looked up and damn if she wasn't. Her skin suddenly felt tingly and she glanced around, but everybody was involved in their food and conversations and nobody was paying the slightest bit of attention to the fact that her face had to be as red as a Christmas stocking.

"I want you to know," Andy said, "that you forgiving me and making me welcome here has made me a very happy man. And I'd really like to kiss you."

Good lord, she hadn't been kissed by a man in fourteen years. And by nobody but Earle for decades before that. She wasn't sure she even remembered how it was done, but she found herself tipping her face up to his and leaning a little closer.

"Just a quick one," she whispered. "All the kids are in the room, you know."

He chuckled softly, and then his lips met hers and she clenched her hands to keep from touching him. Just as her body seemed to say, "oh, *yes,* we remember this," it was over. She sighed, wishing it could have gone on just a little longer.

"Maybe you should leave that mistletoe up there for a while." He winked and she giggled like a smitten schoolgirl. "Now, I'm going to go get me a slice of that banana cream pie before Lauren and Paige eat it all."

That was fine with Rose because she could use a minute alone to compose herself. Andy Miller, all of people. Who would ever have guessed that?

Once she was fairly confident she no longer looked like a girl who'd just been kissed by a boy she had a crush on under the mistletoe, Rose went in search of dessert. Something chocolate would be good. Chocolate and gooey and sinful.

She was spooning chocolate truffle into a paper bowl when Katie nudged up beside her. "I saw you kissing Andy Miller under the mistletoe."

Prickly heat crawled up Rose's neck as she mentally flailed for something to say. Was she upset? "I didn't kiss him. He kissed me."

"Wait until Fran hears about this."

"Katherine Rose Davis, don't you dare!"

Her daughter just grinned and walked away, sticking her tongue out at her over her shoulder.

"Whoa!" Mitch said, very loudly. "Katie just got middle named!"

"On Christmas Eve?" Ryan shook his head. "Hell of a time to end up on the naughty list."

"Speaking of naughty and nice lists, we need to open up the presents so Nick can get to his dad's before his little brother and sister go to bed," Rose said in a voice everybody could hear.

As she'd hoped—and expected—the excited rush

toward the tree distracted them from wanting details on Katie's transgression, which was a relief.

She wasn't sure how she felt yet about Andy wanting to kiss her, but she knew her feelings weren't going to be clarified any by getting everybody else's opinion on the matter. This was something she was going to have sort out for herself.

CHAPTER NINE

KATIE, ACTING AS official hostess in Rose's place, was in charge of passing out the gifts. Mostly, though, she was just trying not to pass out.

Josh had kissed her. Andy had kissed her mom. This whole mistletoe thing was out of hand and, if she could, she'd kick Mitch in the junk for hanging it. He had to have done it for his own twisted amusement, since Josh had made a good point about hanging mistletoe at a family party.

It had happened so fast, she barely had a memory of it to savor later. Just a fleeting impression. Everybody had been chanting and then his mouth touched hers, lingered for far too few seconds, and then was gone. She'd always imagined her and Josh's first kiss, if it ever really happened, would be some earth-shaking, soul-shattering event, not free party entertainment.

But she pasted on a grin, put on the Santa's helper elf hat Josh thought would be a cute gimmick, and handed out gifts. She, Josh and her mom would exchange theirs in the morning, but there were plenty under the tree to pass around.

Being the elf kept her so busy she only caught fleeting glimpses of the opened gifts. Her mom had knit a scarf and hat in Bruins colors for Nick, and Katie knew she'd knit Andy and Drew each a pair of fisherman's mittens. Mitch gave Josh a new splitting maul, which made both men laugh. They wouldn't let anybody else in on the joke, but Katie suspected her mother knew by her smile and made a mental note to ask her about it later.

She collected a small pile of her own, too. A really cute barber tree ornament from Mitch and Paige made her smile but, surprisingly, it was Andy's gift that made her teary-eyed. It was a really old photo of her father enlarged to fit a new five-by-seven frame, obviously taken by Andy on one of their pre-fallout sledding trips. Her dad was standing next to his snowmobile at the top of a steep, icy-looking hill, with his arms raised in victory and a huge grin on his face. She'd never seen the photo, so she assumed he didn't get a chance to give her dad a copy before her mom cut him out of their lives.

It was such a joyful picture the tears just blurred her vision for a couple of minutes without falling, and then she hugged him on impulse. "Thank you."

"Merry Christmas, Katie."

She set the photo on the mantel near the picture

of Josh's parents to keep it safe, swiped at her eyes and went back to being the elf.

When she handed Paige a big box, everybody stopped what they were doing to watch her open her gift. They all knew Mitch had made it himself, but nobody knew what it was. When she'd asked him earlier why he wasn't giving it to her on Christmas morning, he'd told Katie he wanted her to open it surrounded by family.

Of course, Paige took her time opening it. Slitting the tape with her fingernail. Slowly and ever so carefully folding back the wrapping paper. Lifting the lid on the box as if she was afraid whatever was inside might jump out at her. Although, that one Katie could understand. These were Kowalskis, after all.

Then, after all that, Paige burst into tears before she took whatever it was out of the box so they could all see it.

"What is it?" Lauren asked, straining to see.

Mitch, who'd looked startled at first by his wife's emotional outburst but moved in quickly to comfort her, lifted the gift out of the box. It was a sign—the kind that got mounted on a post outside a house or hung by the front door. Mitch had used a router to cut in letters, and then painted the recesses in colors that matched their new house.

In large letters, it read Welcome to Our Home.

And then, in smaller letters at the bottom, The Kow-alskis, Est. 2012.

Josh had to scramble for a box of tissues because there wasn't a dry female eye in the house. Even Katie got a little choked up. Paige had spent her entire life looking for a sense of home, family and community. She certainly had one now.

"Too much crying on Christmas Eve," Ryan grumbled. "I say next year we have a gag-gift rule."

It took almost half an hour to clean up the wrapping paper, but Katie didn't mind. Their Christmases had been a lot smaller in past years, and she was so thankful to have more of the people she considered family around her, she didn't mind the extra mess.

"I found out the other day," Josh said when he came to take the full trash bag of paper from her, "that Max's job involves shipping boxes more often than the average person does. And Miranda thinks I'm adorable."

Miranda had worked at the post office for as long as Katie could remember. Maybe even for as long as *anybody* in Whitford could remember. "Miranda is also like ninety years old. And no wiles."

"No, the condition was no *feminine* wiles. That's not an issue for me."

She laughed. "Go ahead, then. You seduce Miranda into letting you peek inside one of Max's packages. Just do me a favor and make sure it's caught on the security camera. I'll give Drew a heads-up and, as police chief, he can request the footage. I bet posting that on the lodge's Facebook page would really increase business with the elderly demographic."

"Maybe I can get you side work washing trucks for our guests after they see what a nice job you do on mine."

"Hey, you two," Rosie called. "Ryan, Lauren and Nick are getting ready to leave. Come say goodbye."

But Josh had one last parting remark. He looked at Katie, making no effort to disguise the heat in his eyes. "It's a good thing Max can't see you in that dress. There's not a man alive who could deny you anything tonight."

"Really?"

His smile was slow and sizzling. "Really."

JOSH WAS HAVING one hell of an argument with himself. Everybody had gone home, Rose had gone to bed, and he should politely help Katie clean up before following suit.

Or he could not so politely push her up against the wall, kiss her until their legs gave out and then take her right there on the floor with that killer dress shoved up around her hips.

He could almost imagine cartoon versions of himself, good and not so good, perched on each shoulder.

"She's your friend and you shouldn't mess with that," the polite him would say, while the not-polite him would counter with, "Look at those legs and think about what they'd feel like wrapped around you while she begs for more...."

The real Josh was feeling less polite with every passing second.

"I'm so glad that's over," Katie said, drawing his attention away from his internal debate and back to her body in that dress. It was a good thing her regular clothes didn't show it off like that, or he'd spend every football game in a drooling stupor. "But I think everybody had a good time."

"We did good," he agreed. "Hey, let me help you with that."

She was trying to move half a chocolate cake from its fancy serving plate into the plastic cake container and it was going to end up on the floor. When he moved closer to her so he could slide a spatula under one end of the cake while she did the same on the other, he could smell her shampoo and her soap. He knew it was French vanilla, because she'd left her shower stuff on the shelf in the bathroom, but they didn't smell as good in the bottle as they did on her.

He'd never really been a vanilla kind of guy, but right then he wanted nothing more than to lick every inch of her.

"You paying attention?"

He realized she was waiting to lift the cake, and he nodded. They managed to get it into the container without mangling the frosting too badly, but then he had to suffer through watching her laugh and suck chocolate frosting off her finger.

Josh could imagine the polite cartoon version of himself throwing up his hands in defeat and toppling off his shoulder into oblivion.

Katie looked at the food and dishes still left to deal with. "I should go change before I spill something on this dress."

"Don't."

He wasn't surprised when she looked at him as if he'd lost his mind. He had. That was the only explanation for why he'd known this woman his entire life, but now, all of a sudden, he was going to die if he didn't touch her. Insanity.

"Don't what? Change my dress?"

"I like that dress. A lot."

Her face flushed and his body heated in response. "Me, too. Which is why I'd rather not get cranberry stains on it."

He swallowed hard. "The dress makes me want to cross the line."

"What line?"

"The line between friends and taking you right here on the kitchen floor." He watched her face intently, waiting for shock. Maybe anger or laughter.

There was no predicting how she'd respond and that scared the hell out of him.

Because he was looking, he saw the flare of heat, and the smile, when it came, wasn't mocking but one of invitation. "Does this look like a sex-on-the-floor kind of dress to you?"

"That looks like the kind of dress that demands champagne and silk sheets, but I don't have either."

She took a step closer to him. "I'm not really a champagne and silk sheets kind of girl, so don't let it fool you. Under this dress, I'm still just me."

"I'd like to find out what's under the dress for myself."

When he reached out his hand and she took it, curling her fingers through his, some part of him was aware he was stepping across that line and he could never take it back.

Tugging gently on her hand, Josh pulled Katie close and used his free hand to cup the back of her neck. He felt her sigh against his lips as he pressed his mouth to hers. This time, he was thorough, sweeping his tongue over hers as he claimed the kiss he'd wanted under the mistletoe and couldn't have. He tasted the chocolate on her lips and felt her tremble under his touch.

"I've wanted to do that since that night in the kitchen," he confessed, releasing her hand so he could stroke her back.

"But instead of kissing me, you told me to put

some clothes on and went to bed. Interesting technique."

"I panicked."

She tipped her head back and closed the small gap left between them so her breasts brushed his chest. "Am I that scary?"

"Terrifying. I scared the hell out of myself, actually. I had no clue what to do."

"I can show you," she said, her lips curving into a smile. Not a regular old friendly smile, but a naughty smile that made his body tighten in response.

She took his hand and led him into the living room. For a second he thought she was taking him upstairs and almost balked, but she walked to the Christmas tree. It was still plugged in, the lights twinkling in the otherwise dim room.

"Lie down," she whispered.

He wasn't sure exactly what she was up to, but he hadn't been kidding when he'd told her earlier no man could deny her anything in that dress. Stretching out on the floor with his head almost under the tree, he waited.

KATIE KNELT NEXT to the Christmas present she was giving herself, her heart hammering in her chest. There was no turning back now, even if she wanted to. And she definitely didn't want to.

One by one, she slowly undid each of the buttons

on his shirt. His eyes never left her face and she felt the heat of his gaze. "You're killing me, Katie."

Oh, she could do better than that. She threw her leg over his, so when she sat back she was straddling his thighs, before she undid the next button. "I'm unwrapping you."

She had to pull the shirt out of his jeans to get the last two buttons, and then she parted the fabric. He sucked in a breath when she ran her hands over his chest and down the taut muscles of his stomach.

"When do I get to unwrap you?" he asked in a low, husky voice.

"We're taking turns. It's still my turn." Her voice was barely above a whisper because she couldn't seem to turn off the awareness they were in the living room. All she could do was keep it quiet and hope her mother didn't choose this night to get back out of bed and, for the first time, miss the squeaky floorboard at the top of the stairs.

When she'd gotten her fill of touching his chest, she popped the button on his jeans. His stomach muscles tightened and they twitched as she slowly, carefully, lowered his zipper.

"I must have been a very good girl this year," she said, leaning forward to kiss her way from his Adam's apple to his navel.

His hands fisted in her hair. "You're definitely on the naughty list now."

Katie pulled at his jeans, working them over the

hard length of his erection and his hips. She had to get off him in order to grab the hems and pull them all the way off, along with his socks, and then she ran her hands back up his legs.

But when she reached for the waistband of his boxer briefs, he caught her hands and, after pulling her flat on top of him, rolled so she was pinned under his body.

"It's my turn now."

She shuddered when he slid his hand up her thigh and under the hem of the dress, biting back a moan. She'd been waiting years for him to touch her like this and she intended to savor every second of it.

"I like this dress on you." He lifted himself off her so he could bunch the fabric in his hands. "But I think I'll like it even more balled up on the floor."

Katie lifted her hips and then sat up so he could peel the dress off and toss it away. He lowered her back to the floor, his gaze raking over every inch of her body.

"I thought I loved the dress, but I *really* love this bra," he said.

"I have to make a confession. It's Hailey's."

"Tell her you lost it. You're not giving it back."

Damn right she wasn't. Not when it got at least partial credit for getting an almost-naked Josh under the Christmas tree.

He bent his head and his mouth blazed the same trail hers had, from the base of her throat to the elastic waistband of her panties. Then he stretched out and lowered his body to hers. The delicious weight of him sent warmth curling through her, and she ran her hands over his back. The muscles twitched under her touch as she stroked the broad expanse of flesh.

This time when he kissed her, it was demanding and she buried her hands in his hair so he couldn't stop. Their breath mingled and his tongue danced over hers until her awareness centered around his mouth. She lifted her hips, rubbing against the length of his erection through cotton and his body jerked as his breath hissed against her lips.

Josh slid his hands under her back and she felt the bra's clasp give way. Seconds later, he pulled the black straps down her arms and closed his mouth over her nipple. She arched her back, biting her lip to keep from making any sound. He sucked harder and she dug her nails into his shoulders.

His hips pressed down on hers, holding her still against the floor while he turned his attention to her other breast. She whimpered, unable to stop the sound, and *finally,* he peeled her underwear off and tossed them onto the dress. He grabbed his jeans and pulled a condom out of the change pocket before stepping out of his boxer briefs.

Her breath caught in her throat as he knelt over her, his gaze hot in the twinkling lights as he rolled on the condom.

When he moved between her parted legs, Katie caught herself holding her breath and forced herself to breathe.

"I can't wait anymore," he said. "I've waited too long already."

He'd waited too long? She almost laughed. He'd waited all of a week and a half. But then he reached between their bodies and guided himself into her and everything left her mind but that delicious sensation. She lifted her hips as he pressed into her, withdrew slightly, then pushed a little more. It was excruciating and she put her hands on his hips, trying to pull him deeper.

But Josh refused to be rushed. With small, teasing strokes, he slowly filled her completely, and then he stopped. He looked down at her, his eyes full of heat and tenderness, and she lifted her head to kiss him. She wrapped her arms around his neck and moaned against his lips as he began to move again.

With stroke after stroke, he pushed her closer to the edge, and she tucked her hands behind her knees, lifting her legs. Deeper and faster he filled her, until her back arched and she bit down on the side of her hand to keep from crying out.

Josh groaned against her neck and his body jerked as he came, thrusting again and again through the orgasm.

Katie held on to him until the tremors passed,

stroking his hair as his breath came in hot, rapid puffs against her cheek.

"Merry Christmas," he whispered, and she had to stifle a laugh. "Beats the hell out of coal in my stocking."

"Merry Christmas." It was certainly one of the happier holidays *she'd* had.

They lay there for a few more minutes, naked in the colorful glow of lights, but she had just closed her eyes when Josh rolled away. It was probably a good thing. If they fell asleep, her mother would have had quite the shock in the morning.

She heard the rustle of the discarded condom wrapper, and a few seconds later his zipper. When she opened her eyes, Josh was gone. She grabbed the dress and pulled it over her head just to have something on, leaving the undergarments on the floor with Josh's shirt and socks.

When she went into the kitchen, he was just downing the last of a glass of water and he smiled when he saw her. "We didn't finish cleaning the kitchen."

"We saved the chocolate cake." She scanned the counter and shrugged. "There's nothing left to put in the fridge and the dirty dishes will keep until morning."

"I'm going to go around and lock up, then. It's time for bed."

She nodded, but hesitated because she wasn't

sure if she should just walk away or what. He solved the dilemma by crossing the kitchen to her. His kiss was sweet, especially since he took both her hands in his.

"That was amazing, Katie. I wish I could take you to bed and do it again."

But his bed was right across the hall from her mother's bed, which was awkward. "It *was* amazing. I'll see you in the morning."

Katie grabbed her underwear and went up the stairs, carefully avoiding all the squeaky spots. Being caught in the hallway with her bra and panties in her hand wouldn't be an easy one to explain.

When she closed her bedroom door behind her, Kate leaned her head back against the wood and heaved a happy sigh of utter contentment. That had been one hell of a Christmas Eve party.

CHAPTER TEN

DESPITE THE LACK of a full night's sleep, Josh woke up in a very holly, jolly mood. Waking up *alone* after the most incredible sex of his life wasn't ideal, but last night had been, in fact, the greatest Christmas Eve party ever thrown.

And, Jesus, when he thought about all the years he'd wasted having sex with women who weren't Katie, he could weep.

His eyes widened when he looked at the clock, and he threw back the covers. He couldn't remember the last time he'd slept until eight o'clock, but it felt pretty good. Or maybe it was the sex. Either way, he was whistling Christmas carols while he took a quick shower and threw on some clothes.

All he needed now was coffee. He went down the stairs and found Rosie and Katie sitting on the couch, both of them cradling coffee cups. There was an awkward moment when he felt like he should say something more than good-morning to Katie and couldn't with Rose sitting beside her, so he wished them a merry Christmas and kept on going to the coffeemaker.

"Have you guys been up long?" he asked once he was settled in the armchair with some coffee in him and a full cup on the side table.

"I was up at six, as usual," Rosie said. "But Katie got up just before you did. Sleepyheads on Christmas morning."

Josh looked at the twinkling tree instead of Katie, because he was afraid if he looked at her, he might laugh. It might appear as if they'd slept in to somebody who didn't know when they'd gone to bed.

Rose played elf this morning, since she wasn't still sucking down caffeine in a desperate attempt to wake up. She gave Josh her gift to him and then handed Katie hers, even though she grimaced a little when she had to put her coffee down.

She'd knit Josh a pair of his favorite gloves. They were cut off at the fingertips, but had a flap that folded over. His hands could be warm, but he could also flip back the flap if he was working on something that required some fine motor skills. He got up to kiss her cheek, pausing to admire the zip-up wool sweater she'd made for Katie, and then handed Rosie her gifts from them.

Katie had gotten her a slow cooker, which he wished he'd thought of. She'd been complaining for so long that hers didn't cook evenly anymore, that he might have started tuning her out. Missed gift opportunity. He, of course, gave her a gift certificate to the yarn store, this year hidden in the bottom of a box holding new slippers.

That left two presents under the tree, and Katie was smiling when she handed him the oddly shaped one from her. He wanted to pull her down onto his lap and give her a very thorough Christmas-morning kiss, but he had to make do with brushing his fingers along hers as he took his gift.

It was a five-gallon bucket, complete with a sponge, a bottle of car wash, a chamois cloth and a tub of wax.

"You're too much, Davis," he said when he'd stopped laughing.

"Look under the sponge."

He rummaged at the bottom of the bucket and found a small, wrapped box. After tearing off the paper, he opened the lid. It was a small snow globe with a picture inside of him and Katie.

It had been taken on the nineteenth of January in 2002. It was shortly before his dad passed away, and Josh and Katie had worked their asses off getting tickets to the last game the Patriots would ever play in Foxboro Stadium. It was the only game they'd ever seen in person. It had been cold and snowing, but it was a historic night and the Patriots beat the Raiders by three points. Katie had gotten a fellow fan a few rows up to take a picture of the two of them with the snow-covered field as the backdrop, and the excitement and happiness of the night lit them both up.

When he shook it, the snow fell in front of them, almost as if it was turning the photograph into a living memory.

"That was one of the best days of my life," he said softly, shaking it again.

"Mine, too."

"You have to open mine now," he told her. Then he smiled at Rosie. "Things are gonna get weird."

Katie gave him a questioning look, but he only shrugged and gestured for her to open it. Inside the box was a huge sponge, specially made in a jumbo size for washing trucks, according to the label. She laughed and threw it at him.

The second item in the box was wrapped, just as the snow globe had been. She tore the paper off and he wasn't surprised when her mouth fell open in surprise.

"You can't be serious," she said.

"What is it?" Rosie asked impatiently.

She took a plaque out of the box and held it up for her mom to see. It had been designed to commemorate the final game at Foxboro Stadium, with a photo of the snowy field and a smaller plaque with the games details. The bottom half had a photo of the field at the shiny new Gillette Stadium, as well as the pertinent details of that September 2002 game. Also a win for the Patriots, and over the Steelers, which was even better. The plaque was made complete with trading cards for Tom Brady and Tedy Bruschi mounted under plastic protectors.

"You're right," Rosie said. "This is a little weird."

"I was remembering that day and how amazing it was while I was shopping, and when I saw that plaque, it seemed like the perfect gift."

"It is," Katie whispered. "The absolutely perfect gift."

Their eyes met and he could see that she wanted to throw her arms around him and thank him, but she was holding herself back. He winked and gave her a smile, because they could thank each other later, when they had more privacy.

"What's with the car wash stuff?" Rosie wanted to know.

"Why was it so funny that Mitch gave Josh a splitting maul?" Katie countered, and the women were at a standoff.

Josh was tempted to explain the splitting maul, but Rosie might find it odd he'd so freely share the story of working off his sexual frustration by splitting wood with the woman at the root of that sexual frustration. He'd have to tell her later—once again, when they had some privacy.

"I'm going to bring the muffins in here so we can pick at them."

Rose went into the kitchen and, as soon as she

was out of sight, Josh and Katie met in the middle of the living room. He kissed her for as long as he thought he could get away with it, and then rested his forehead against hers.

"Thank you for the snow globe."

"Thank you for the plaque," she said in a soft voice. "I guess we both treasure the memory of that day."

"Always."

When Rosie came back into the living room, carrying a basket of warm muffins, they were both back in their seats. Josh smiled and took a sip of his coffee.

Best Christmas ever.

"AMAZING." KATIE LICKED powdered sugar off her fingers and reached back into the box.

"The sex or the doughnuts?" Hailey asked.

They were sitting on Hailey's couch with their feet on her brand-new coffee table and an open box of powered doughnuts between them. It was something of a Boxing Day tradition. They weren't sure how it was done in England, but they always had a box of something delicious the day after Christmas.

"The sex," Katie clarified. "But the doughnuts are pretty amazing, too."

"I can't believe you didn't call me immediately."

"I wanted to, but since it was about one o'clock

on Christmas morning, I thought I should wait. Plus I fell asleep."

Hailey sighed and gave the doughnut in her hand a mournful look. "I don't think these are amazing. They're not bad, but I think you have that really annoying happy afterglow that great sex gives you. *Everything's* amazing after an orgasm or two."

"That explains the coffee. Mine isn't usually as good as what mom makes, but it was really good this morning."

"I kind of hate you a little right now."

"Have another bite of your doughnut."

She did, and then washed it down with half her mudslide. "So what now?"

"No more doughnuts. I'm done."

"With Josh. Where did you sleep last night?"

"In my bed." Katie paused, and then grinned. "After we snuck out to the barn for a little while."

"The barn? Isn't it a little cold for barn sex?"

"It's heated. The guests like that, I guess. Heated storage for their snowmobiles."

"Beds are more comfortable, no matter how heated the barn is."

"Not when both beds are within earshot of my mother."

"There are tons of rooms in that house. Do the sex grand tour."

"We already made up the guest rooms for people coming in Friday. If we have sex in one of the beds, I have to change all the bedding again. Easier to sneak out to the barn."

"So tell me, besides being amazing, did the sex also stop the weirdness?"

Katie thought about that. "Mostly. We're fine with each other, I think, but it's a little weird being around my mom."

"Is it really a big deal if she finds out?"

"I don't think so. She might even be happy about it. But I think Josh needs some time to adjust to us before he has to deal with his relationship with my mom changing. It's a lot."

"You're probably right." Hailey covered her eyes and groaned. "Take the doughnuts away, Katie. They need to be out of my reach."

She picked up the box and set it on her end of the table, far out of Hailey's reach. "I don't know how you can even think about eating another doughnut."

"Because you've had amazing sex two nights in a row. I haven't. Not even one night of mediocre sex. And no, don't mention Max Crawford."

"I wasn't going to." Actually, she was, but Hailey didn't need to know that.

"I need salt after all that sweet. Potato chips. I need chips."

Katie leaned her head back against the couch and closed her eyes. She hadn't gotten enough sleep the past two nights, not that she was complaining. And she definitely wouldn't complain to Hailey.

It still blew her mind that she and Josh had not only managed to become an almost-couple, but had turned out to be so deliciously compatible in bed. Or on the floor and in the barn, as the case may be.

But, in her mind, they'd stay an almost-couple until everybody knew they were together. Yesterday morning, she'd waited with her mom on the couch and, when Josh got up, took her cues from him. It was pretty clear he didn't want Rose to know their relationship had taken a turn for the intimate.

"I bet having guests running around the lodge will really put a cramp on you guys hiding in closets," Hailey said, plopping down on the couch with an open bag of chips. She offered it to Katie, but she shook her head. She didn't know how her friend could eat another bite.

"I know. Tomorrow we have to drive to Brookline and back, to help Ryan and Lauren with the last trip from her house. Then the next day, guests are arriving. We might have to sneak away to my apartment, which wouldn't be fun since I have the heat turned down to fifty while I'm at the lodge. By the time that old boiler heats it back up, we'd be done. Or I could just let *him* warm me up, I guess."

"I think you're too salacious for me now," Hailey told her. "I'm not sure I can be your friend anymore."

Katie laughed and snatched the bag away from her. Maybe a few chips wouldn't hurt.

ROSE WAS CURLED up on the couch, feeling about as content as she'd felt in a very long time. The Christmas tree lights were twinkling, the fire was crackling and Andy's arm was warm and snug around her shoulder.

"I know you said Katie went to Hailey's, but where's Josh?"

That was another reason for her deep sense of contentment. "He's taking a nap."

Rose was fairly sure she knew why Josh wasn't getting enough sleep at night. It was obvious in the way he and Katie had been looking at each other since yesterday morning. The very air between them felt different. And, in her mind, the fact they'd both chosen gifts for each other that honored one of the happiest days they'd ever shared together was a sign they were meant to be together.

"You may have noticed I didn't bring you a gift Christmas Eve," Andy said.

She had, though she'd tried not to be disappointed by it. "I wasn't expecting a gift. Just your company."

"I had it in my pocket, but I wanted to give it to you like this. When it's just us." He pulled a small, flat box out from under a throw pillow, where he must have hidden it earlier. "Merry Christmas, Rose."

Her hands shook a little as she unwrapped the paper. That embarrassed her a little, but she was anxious about what she'd find—something he hadn't wanted lost in the chaos of the entire family.

She lifted the lid off the box and her breath caught in her throat. "It's… Oh, good lord, I'm going to cry."

Andy pulled his arm free so he could lift the charm bracelet out of the box and fasten it on her wrist. With tears running unchecked down her cheeks, she touched each silver charm, one by one. A pair of scissors for Katie. A tiny ball on a chain for Mitch. She supposed it was probably meant to jokingly represent the old "ball and chain," but it looked like a miniature wrecking ball. A hammer for Ryan. A combat boot for Sean, who'd served in the army. A coffee mug for Liz, and a tiny snow-mobile for Josh.

It was a perfect choice for him, she thought. She'd almost expected a little house, but the lodge didn't represent Josh. No matter where he went, though, he would always love sledding.

"Mitch almost did me in," Andy said. "They don't make explosives for charm bracelets that I could find."

"It's perfect," she whispered. "So very perfect."

When he slid his finger under her chin to tip

her face up, she didn't resist. The kiss was soft and sweet, and as perfect for her as the bracelet.

"Merry Christmas, Andy."

He put his arm up and she snuggled back against his chest again. It was a very nice way to spend the day after Christmas.

"So when are you going to let Josh and Katie know they don't have to sneak around the place like teenagers?"

She laughed. "When I stop enjoying watching them do it."

"Do you really think she'll be able to keep him here?"

"I hope so." It was a sobering question, taking a little of the shine off her mood. "Paige brought up the possibility Josh might leave and talk Katie into going with him. That worries me."

"I don't think she'd leave here. I don't think she'd leave *you*."

"People do unexpected things all the time. Look at me, for example. Go door-to-door and ask how many people in Whitford would believe you if you said Rosie Davis kissed Andy Miller in front of her Christmas tree."

His chuckle rumbled against her face where it rested against his chest. "Even I can hardly believe it."

"What I find hard to believe is that Josh would actually leave."

"I think he'll leave, but I think he'll come back on his own." He kissed the top of her head. "People have a tendency to find their way back to the ones they're meant to be with."

CHAPTER ELEVEN

WHEN JOSH HAD agreed to get up at the crack of dawn and drive down to Brookline, he hadn't known he'd be spending half the night before in the barn with Katie. He didn't want to get up and he certainly didn't want to drive four and a half to five hours—one way—to play moving guy.

On a more positive note, he had Katie to keep him company on the drive. She'd certainly kept him company last night, and he had the sore muscles to prove it. The good kind of sore, though, not the aches and pains he'd have after today. Four and a half hours in the truck, a few hours of heavy lifting, and then another four and a half hours in the truck was hard on the body.

They loaded up on coffee, grabbed some muffins out of the basket and hit the road. When they got to Lauren's house, Ryan was just pulling down and securing the back door of the rented box truck.

He shook Josh's hand and then hugged Katie. "I appreciate you guys giving us a hand. I'll be so glad to have this behind us. Lauren will, too, though she's a little emotional today."

"Where's Mitch?" Katie asked while they waited for Lauren to do a last sweep through cabinets and closets, making sure the house was really empty. Katie would have gone in and helped her, but she got the impression it was really a walk-through to say goodbye.

"He's coming down with something, I guess. He said he couldn't make the drive over here, never mind to Massachusetts."

"Sure he is," Josh scoffed. Funny how germs had a way of attacking when there was a moving truck to unload. It was the same principle as when they were kids and Sean always seemed to have an upset stomach when it was time to wash the dishes.

"He sounded like crap on the phone." Ryan shrugged. "Said it was a stomach thing, and I don't think he's playing hooky. To be honest, I don't think Paige would let him get away with it. She and Lauren are pretty close."

"If he's really sick, he needs to stay away from Rosie. And so does Paige. The last thing Rosie needs right now is a stomach bug."

Once Lauren had finished saying goodbye to her house and locked the door on her way out, Ryan climbed into the truck, but Josh saw Lauren hesitate. Her eyes were a little damp as she gave her home a last look. He knew this was the final transition from her old life to her new one in Brookline. When Nick's holiday visit with his dad was over, they'd be meeting her ex-husband halfway to pick him up—which they'd do every other weekend, too—and when they came to Whitford to visit, they'd be staying in Ryan's room at the lodge.

Once Lauren was ready to go, Josh and Katie buckled up and he pulled his truck out behind Ryan's. They hadn't gone twenty miles when he heard Katie's gentle snoring and shook his head. So much for company. He decided to leave her alone, though, because the more rested she was now, the better she'd be at keeping him awake on the drive home. He might even have her take a turn at the wheel. But for now, it looked as if it was just him, the radio and Ryan's taillights.

Amazingly for a weekday morning, they didn't hit too much traffic, so they pulled into Ryan's driveway before noon. Which was good because, even though they'd stopped a couple of times along the way, a *lot* of coffee had been consumed and it had been a while since the last pit stop.

Once the mad rush to the bathroom was over, Josh took a look around his brother's house. It looked a lot less like a model home and a lot more like a *home* home than the last time he'd been there. The living room was painted a dark, creamy-peach color and there were family photos on the walls instead of stock art. Lauren's knickknacks were here and there, along with obvious signs of teen-ager debris.

It must be nice, he thought, to get to choose your home. To be able to choose the style and how many bedrooms and whether or not you let strangers sleep in them. He'd always tried to be grateful he'd al-ways had a home and a job, but sometimes, when he saw others getting to make choices like that for themselves, he wished he could make them, too.

A couple of years before his dad died, Josh had started collecting pictures of houses. He found them in ads and magazines and the real estate pages. He'd been partial to log cabins that had a lot of glass, and he'd thought when he got to buy a house someday, it would look like those. Then his dad had passed away.

Mitch, Ryan, Sean and Liz had all been there for the funeral, of course. They'd even spent a few days together as a family, with Rose fussing over them. He could remember sitting on the couch with Liz because she wanted to look through the old photo albums with him. Katie had sat on his other side, holding his hand.

Then they'd all, essentially, told him to let them know if he needed anything and gone back to their lives. A week later he tossed his folder of house photos into the woodstove.

"If you guys start unloading the truck, we'll start unpacking stuff," Lauren said, pulling Josh out of the self-pity pool he'd been drowning in. "I know we can't waste any time, because it's a long drive back for you guys. Are you sure can't spend the night? We have plenty of room."

There was no doubt about that. It didn't have as many bedrooms as the Northern Star, but his brother was doing all right for himself. "I have people checking in tomorrow. I can't be away on Fridays, so we'll hustle and get back tonight."

He lost track of the number of trips they made from the truck to the garage. Every third or fourth trip, Lauren and Katie would appear and take a couple of boxes into the house. A few were so heavy that Ryan or Josh carried them and then they'd bring more from the truck.

Finally, just when he was considering crawling under the truck for a nap and hoping nobody noticed, Josh could see the back wall of the box truck. He grabbed one of the final boxes before they hit the few pieces of furniture Lauren hadn't donated to Goodwill and headed back down the ramp. Ryan was between him and the garage, but he didn't step out of the way. Instead, he decided it was a good time to make conversation.

"When did you start sleeping with Katie?"

Josh almost dropped the box, and since Lauren had written Fragile all over it in huge black letters, that probably wouldn't be good. "What the hell are you talking about?"

"I'm not blind. Not stupid, either. It's pretty obvious."

It was? "What do you mean?"

"You're treating her like a woman."

"She *is* a woman, dumbass."

"Yeah, but you've never treated her like one. You've always acted like she was one of the guys."

Josh wasn't sure what that meant. It's not as if he'd spent the day handing out roses or throwing his coat over puddles. And he'd been very careful not to touch her in front of his family. At least he thought he had.

"When you got here, you opened the screen door and then stepped back to let her go first," Ryan said.

"I have manners. You're right—I must be having sex with her."

"When we stopped to have a drink, you broke the seal on her bottle of water before you handed it to her instead of tossing it to her from across the room like usual."

"Lauren has nicer knickknacks than we do and Katie can't catch for shit."

"You're treating her differently than you have your entire life so, yeah, I think you're sleeping with her."

One of the things that had occurred to him *after* he lost his battle to keep his hands off Katie was how his brothers might react if they found out. Despite how he felt about Rosie, Josh had always seen

Katie as his friend rather than practically a sister. But Mitch and Ryan, being older than her, might have seen her differently growing up. Mitch, the mistletoe-hanging bastard, was obviously okay with it. Ryan? It was hard to tell with him, but lying wouldn't help his case any in the long run.

"Christmas Eve."

Ryan didn't look surprised. "That dress was…as an almost married man, there's nothing I can really say about the dress."

"Believe it or not, it was a tank top and boxer shorts that lit the fuse. The dress just blew the top off."

"I bet it did."

"I'm surprised Mitch didn't tell you." Josh shifted the box's weight in his arms. It wasn't light.

"Mitch knew?"

"I assume so. He knew I wanted to and he knew I was less cranky after Christmas than before it, so he probably figured it out."

Ryan nodded. "We all knew you were going to eventually. We just didn't know when, until I saw you with her today. I thought maybe it was Christmas Eve. Does this change anything? With the lodge, I mean?"

"Katie and the lodge are two separate things. What's going on with me and Katie doesn't change how I feel about the Northern Star."

"That's kind of messy, don't you think?"

And it wasn't going to get any less messy with the entire family in their business. "Yeah, it is. And this box is kind of heavy, so I think we're done here."

THERE WAS NO way they could unpack the boxes as fast as the men unloaded, so Katie and Lauren focused on digging the essentials out of the pile. It was kind of fun, actually, like a scavenger hunt, and they worked well together. Plus she had plenty of energy since she'd napped most of the ride down, though she felt kind of bad about that. She'd have to make it up to Josh.

Maybe in the barn tomorrow night. Between the driving and the boxes, she knew they wouldn't do anything but fall into bed—each in their *own* beds—when they finally got home. But by tomorrow night they'd be ready to scratch that itch again. And, surprisingly enough, the pile of older comforters Josh had snuck out of the lodge's backup supply was comfortable enough. Maybe not as good as a bed, but better than the living room floor.

They were unpacking a box marked Under Bathroom Sink when Lauren finally broached the subject she'd been hemming and hawing around since they'd started. "So, you and Josh, huh?"

Once Lauren decided to stop beating around the bush, she really went for it, Katie thought. "Yeah. Me and Josh. That obvious?"

"You're both relaxed, which means you probably stopped fighting the attraction. It also means that was one *hell* of a dress."

Katie laughed and split the tape on the Bathroom Drawers box. It was a small box because Lauren had had a small bathroom, but looking around Ryan's gorgeous master bathroom, she didn't think space was going to be a problem. "Now I get why women pay too much money for bras and don't wear jeans and sweatshirts on a date. I definitely got his attention."

"What does Rose think of you two being a couple now? She must be so excited."

Katie sat back on her heels, reminding herself this conversation was probably going to happen a few more times with the various family members and she couldn't let it slice at her like emotional razor blades. "We're more in a friends-with-benefits space right now. Not really a couple, and my mom doesn't know."

Lauren snorted. "Sure she doesn't."

"Okay, she's pretending she doesn't know and I'm pretending I believe that."

"You never know what'll happen in the future," Lauren said, giving her a look that clearly said she didn't believe the friends-with-benefits thing for a second. Not surprising, considering Lauren knew how Katie felt about Josh. But it seemed like everybody underestimated just how strongly Josh felt about leaving.

"How's Nick doing?" she asked, desperate to change the subject. "With the move and you getting married and all?"

"It's a lot of change all at once. Sometimes he's okay and sometimes he's not, but we'll get through it. I think once he starts school and gets back into a routine, it'll help. And he likes Ryan, so everything else just has to work itself out with time."

"Is he having a good visit with his dad?"

"Yeah. Dean's been really reasonable about us moving down here, which makes a huge difference. I hate to give the bastard credit, but if he'd chosen to be an ass about it, I can't imagine what that would have done to Nick."

"Brookline's a lot different from Whitford. That'll be an adjustment."

Lauren laughed. "You're not kidding. But we've been to the movies and gone to the mall and tried to show him the fun side of living in a town with more than one main intersection."

"Got a guest room?" Katie joked.

"As a matter of fact, we do. Anytime you want to come down and have a crazy shopping weekend, just say the word."

Katie wasn't into crazy shopping weekends, but she wouldn't mind a trip to the city now and then, just for something to do. And, now that she thought about it, they probably had a Victoria's Secret store in the neighborhood. She wouldn't mind blowing some money there.

"Lauren?" Ryan peeked in. "Hey, we're starving. You guys want pizza or Chinese?"

"Pizza," both women said at the same time.

"I'll call it in," Lauren said. "We'll probably finish up in here just in time to eat."

A half hour later, they were gathered in the kitchen, standing at the counter and devouring pepperoni pizza right out of the box. Katie was starving, so she concentrated on eating and watched Josh and Ryan talking between bites. They were discussing business, mainly Ryan's, so she tuned out their words and focused on their faces.

The Kowalski family resemblance was unmistakable. Nobody could doubt Josh and Ryan were brothers, and it was the same with the other three. They shared a lot of the same mannerisms, too, though she doubted they were aware of it.

"Good-looking guys, aren't they?" Lauren asked in a low voice. "We're very lucky women."

Katie nodded, but then she took a huge bite of her pizza so she could avoid having to respond out loud. Lauren was very lucky, she'd give her that. Ryan loved her, was going to marry her and didn't hide how happy he was to be starting a life with her and her son.

Whereas Josh didn't seem to want anybody to

suspect he'd made love to Katie last night. Apparently there were degrees of lucky.

"Ryan told me the lodge's projected numbers for the season look really good." Lauren wiped her mouth and then tossed the napkin in the trash.

"Yeah, business definitely picked up." Katie didn't want to talk about the Northern Star or Josh anymore. Hearing about projected numbers was a reminder they were watching them because they were waiting for the right time to put the property on the market or hire a manager so Josh could leave.

"This pizza's amazing," she said, changing the subject. "I'd give anything for a good takeout place in Whitford."

"Yeah, buying a frozen pizza from Fran and taking it home to microwave isn't the same at all. I have to say, being able to have almost any food delivered is one of my favorite things about living here, and Ryan's starting to wonder if I'll ever cook again."

A few minutes later, Ryan pulled the trash bag out of the can and gestured for Lauren to grab the pizza box they'd emptied. "Can you get that, Lauren? We'll be right back, guys."

After they disappeared through the side door into the garage, Katie laughed and shook her head. "That bag wasn't even full and he could have carried that box himself. They just want to make out for a few minutes."

Josh stepped up behind her and wrapped his

arms around her waist so he could nuzzle her neck. "Nothing wrong with making out."

She shivered and pressed her back against his chest. "They won't be long."

"Then we'd better make out fast." He spun her around and kissed her, his hands traveling up her waist to cup her breasts.

She pushed his hands away because there wasn't time for rounding that base, but wrapped her arms around his neck so he wouldn't stop kissing her.

"You taste like pepperoni pizza," he murmured against her mouth. "I like it."

He showed her how much, kissing her until she was tempted to lock Ryan and Lauren out of their own house and have her way with Josh in one of the guest rooms. At least they had beds.

When there was a scuffing sound outside the door, though, Josh broke away. And by the time Ryan and Lauren got through the door, both a little flushed, Josh had his back to Katie, taking another slice of pizza out of the box they hadn't finished off.

Because she knew her face was probably as red as Lauren's, both from the kisses and Josh's sudden pulling away, Katie turned to the sink and took her time running the water cold from the tap and filling a glass.

After guzzling the water, hoping it would cool her off, she filled the glass again. She wasn't holding out for proclamations of love and a diamond ring, but she wasn't going to be anybody's dirty little secret, either.

WHEN IT CAME time to get back in the truck for the ride back to Maine, Katie got a little teary-eyed leaving Lauren. Even though she'd been in Brookline for a while, somehow her house in Whitford being empty made the move more real. "We're going to miss you at movie night."

"I'll miss you, too. But I'll be dragging Ryan back to Whitford more often and we can watch movies at the lodge together."

Katie nodded, even though in the back of her mind, she was wondering if Lauren remembered she didn't actually *live* at the lodge. Not that she couldn't drop by and watch a movie if they planned it ahead of time, but somehow she didn't think that's what Lauren meant.

After going to the nearest drive-through for coffee, Josh hit the highway and Katie settled in for the long ride back. She was determined to stay awake this time if it killed her. Maybe she'd even offer to drive, although all of the Kowalski men had severe issues with riding shotgun. They weren't very good at turning over the steering wheel.

Josh reached over and turned down the radio. "Ryan asked me about us."

He didn't have to get more specific than that. She knew what he meant. "What did you say?"

"I'm not going to lie to him. There's no reason to do that, and it's not like we're doing anything wrong, right?"

"It sure seems like you think we are," Katie admitted. "Christmas morning, it was obvious you didn't want Mom to know, and you kept your distance from me today, too, except when nobody was looking."

He drummed his fingers on the steering wheel for a few seconds, then blew out a breath. "I know what's going to happen when Rose finds out, Katie. She's going to jump to the same conclusion Ryan did—that everybody else is going to."

"What conclusion is that?" she asked, though she suspected she already knew. Probably the same one Lauren had jumped to.

"Ryan asked me if this thing between us changes my plans for the lodge. You know Rosie will be even worse."

"I really wish we weren't having this conversation doing seventy-five miles an hour up the highway," she muttered.

"I didn't mean to. I think about things while I drive and it kind of came out of my mouth."

And it was easier for him to have meaningful conversations when he was behind the wheel, because it wasn't as intense as a face-to-face discussion. That wasn't a new thing for him.

"You know you and the lodge are separate for me, right?" he asked, glancing over at her for a second before turning his attention back to the road. "I mean, I like being with you, but it doesn't change how I feel about the lodge and Whitford."

In other words, *we're having a good time but at the first opportunity, I'm going to run like my ass is on fire and not look back.*

"I know that, Josh. This is me, remember? Katie? I know you." When she saw his hands relax on the steering wheel, she realized just how much tension the situation was causing him.

She'd be lying if she said it didn't hurt that he needed to clarify that having sex with her hadn't made him want to settle down with her and start filling the lodge with babies. Even though she'd known going in that this was how it was going to be, Josh had always been her dream. What she needed to remember, and what would be all too easy to forget, was that Josh had a very different dream.

"I hope you realize," she said, "that there's no way my mom doesn't know."

That made him laugh. "I'm pretty sure Rosie knows everything."

"So why the song and dance? I don't like feeling like a dirty secret, Josh."

His smile faded. "It's not that at all, Katie. Rose

just has a lot more emotionally invested, which means it's a lot harder to tell her that whatever she's imagining probably isn't going to happen."

Despite knowing it wasn't healthy emotionally, Katie latched onto that *probably* as if it was the last life preserver on a sinking boat. It was no doubt a throwaway word to him, but it left the door open just a crack. Maybe whatever her mother was imagining—and odds were it included grandchildren—*would* happen.

She forced herself to keep her tone light. "I think it would be easier for us to just enjoy what we have if we weren't sneaking around and hiding in barns."

"I kind of like the barn."

"It wasn't a complaint." She'd had a very good time in the barn, too. "We can still sneak out there if we want. But I don't like playing games. It is what it is, and people knowing that is better than speculation. And getting Mom's hopes up."

"You're probably right. You should tell her."

"Wait—*I* should tell her? While you do what? Pretend you have to change the oil in your snowmobile again?"

"Hey! I change the oil in my sled."

She gave him a stern look. "Not as often as you say you do."

"Not as often as you'll be washing my truck."

She snorted. "Yeah, we'll see about that."

He turned the radio back up and scanned through

the stations until he found guys talking sports. Within a few minutes, Josh was muttering at the guys under his breath. Katie smiled and turned to watch the miles fly past her window, their equilibrium restored.

CHAPTER TWELVE

Six in the morning came early on Saturday, and Katie padded down to the kitchen as quietly as she could in search of coffee. She could smell it, and she knew Josh would have a pot already in the carafe to stay warm while a second pot brewed.

The barbershop usually opened at six on Saturdays, so getting to sleep in should have been a treat. She'd known when she'd made the decision to stay at the lodge that their guests wouldn't be happy to hear her Jeep fire up at five-thirty on their vacation weekend mornings. Rather than risk upsetting the apple cart, she was opening at eight for the time being. To compensate for the later mornings, she was staying open until four instead of two on weekday afternoons, along with a full Saturday instead of half days. The hours were just different enough to mess with her internal clock.

Josh smiled when he saw her and gave her a good-morning kiss before pouring her a cup of coffee. "How'd you sleep?"

They'd been creative last night and had a very

quiet quickie in the shower, so she'd actually gone to bed at a reasonable hour. But somebody else might not have. "Did you hear what I heard this morning?"

He winced. "I was hoping you didn't. And that I was imagining things."

She hadn't imagined the sound of Andy Miller's snoring coming from her mother's bedroom. Even at her most congested, Rose didn't snore like a chainsaw in desperate need of some bar oil.

Katie wasn't awake enough yet to analyze how she felt about Andy being in her mother's bed, but that situation did lead to another that had been on her mind lately. "I guess Mom's feeling a lot better."

He nodded, sipping coffee and watching her over the rim of his cup. She'd put off bringing up the subject because her interlude at the Northern Star had been a lot more enjoyable than she'd anticipated. But writing out the checks to pay utility bills for an apartment she wasn't using and doing the end-of-the-month accounting for the barbershop had been a strong reminder her real life was on hold.

"I don't think she needs me here anymore," she continued. "It's been almost a month and she's hardly even coughing anymore. She seems as healthy as she was before the first bout."

"I agree. Though I do think you've gotten exceptionally good at doing laundry and, since you carry your own baskets, you should keep doing that for her."

"Funny. Anyway, I was thinking I'd stay through New Year's Eve because I may as well round out the holidays here, but I think I should move my stuff back to my place Tuesday night so I can open the barbershop on the second at its regular hours."

When he nodded again, she felt a quick pang of disappointment. Logically she knew he wasn't going to ask her to stay with him and, even if he did, she probably wouldn't. Yet. But a little show of reluctance to let her go would be nice.

"You're going to do the laundry after everybody checks out Tuesday morning before you leave, right?"

She gasped and tried to punch him in the arm, but he grabbed her wrist and pulled her close. The muffled sound of voices alerted them to impending guests, but he gave her a hard kiss before letting go of her. "Maybe I can come to your place and we can actually have sex in a bed."

"I might let you in, if you ask nicely."

"Although, as good as a bed sounds, remind me to tell you my fantasy about me, you and the groomer someday."

Nothing like greeting virtual strangers in the kitchen with a flaming-red face. The guests were all dressed and eager to get out on the trails, though, so their intrusion was more like a chaotic hit-and-run that left a trail of muffin crumbs and dirty coffee cups in its wake.

It swept Josh out the door, though, since one of the guys wanted his opinion on a suspension issue, and within fifteen minutes Katie found herself alone in the kitchen. She was tempted to leave the mess for her mom. If she was well enough to have a slumber party with Andy, she was well enough to wash coffee cups.

But she didn't feel right letting them sit for her mom to take care of, and the mess would look bad if any of the guests came back through the kitchen so, after glancing at the clock, she filled the sink with hot, soapy water. She could wash them and get out before having an awkward moment with her mother.

She wasn't quick enough, though, and her mom shuffled in before Katie made it out the back door. Rose kissed her cheek and then popped a mug of water into the microwave for her tea.

Her mom looked awake enough for a conversation so, after rinsing the last mug and pulling the plug, Katie dried her hands and leaned against the counter. "Josh and I talked this morning and we both agree you're pretty much back on your feet, so I'm going to move back home Tuesday night. I want to open the barbershop on its regular schedule post–New Year's Day. Get the year off on the right foot."

Rosie's lips tightened, and Katie could see the wheels turning in her mother's head. "And Josh thinks that's a good idea?"

She recognized the roundabout way of finding

out if Josh had asked her to stay. "Of course he does. He runs a business, so he recognizes that I have a business to run, too. You know he'd never expect me to let mine suffer just to help him out."

"The barbershop isn't that far from here. You've been driving back and forth since I came home from the hospital."

"On part-time hours," Katie reminded her. "Mom, I'm not staying here."

Rose sighed. "I'd been hoping that maybe plans had changed."

"Nobody's plans have changed, Mom. Especially his." It was best to be upfront about that. Well, as upfront as she could be without specifically referencing the fact that she and Josh were having sex. Luckily, she knew she didn't need to, just as her mother didn't. They both knew what was going on, so there didn't need to be a potentially embarrassing conversation. "Now, I have to run or I'll find a pissed-off, half-frozen old buck standing on the sidewalk waiting for a haircut."

"Have a good day, honey."

Katie fired up her Jeep with a sigh of relief. She'd made it out before her mother was forced into the awkward position of either explaining why she was heating two mugs of water or leaving poor Andy upstairs with no caffeine.

Josh stepped out of the barn to wave goodbye and she waved back before heading down the driveway. It was such a comfortable, domestic moment, she couldn't hold back the smile as she drove into town.

Maybe Katie's moving home wouldn't be as bad for her relationship as her mom feared. Josh could sneak over to her place while Andy "kept an eye" on Rosie. The town could be a problem, though. The Northern Star was far enough off the beaten track to offer a little privacy. If Josh's truck was in the overnight lot between the barbershop and the consignment store for children's stuff for an entire night, all of Whitford would be planning their wedding by dawn.

She didn't really care what people said. But, as she turned onto the paved road and hit the gas, she wondered if Josh would. Every subtle hint about marriage would strike him as a not-so-subtle reminder he was expected to spend the rest of his life doing what he was doing now instead of normal small-town gossip.

As Katie parked her Jeep in the lot beside the barbershop, she decided there was nothing she could do about other people's reactions. They couldn't camouflage Josh's truck, so she'd just hope the people of Whitford dug deep and discovered the concept of discretion.

Laughing out loud, she unlocked the barbershop and prepared to start her day.

JOSH USUALLY LOVED guests who were up and checked out at the butt crack of dawn on Sunday. For them, it was a matter of getting a head start on a long ride home. For him, it meant stripping the beds, spraying down the bathrooms, emptying the trash cans and still making it to Max's for a football game. The more thorough cleaning wouldn't get done until Monday.

This Sunday was a little different, though, because Monday was New Year's Eve. All their guests would be taking advantage of the long weekend and not leaving until Tuesday morning. The Patriots would play at one o'clock, which meant the guests would all be out on the trails, racking up the miles, but he wouldn't be able to stay at Max's for the late game. Once evening came, he liked to know who had or hadn't gotten back safely yet.

It sucked that Katie wasn't going to be here today. When he mentioned the one-o'clock game, she had sworn she'd thought the Patriots' game was the later one and had made plans with Hailey. On the flipside, he still had a bet to win and her not being around might be an advantage for him.

Max was in the kitchen alone when Josh walked through his door, and it struck him as the perfect opportunity to get a leg up in the quest for Katie's car-washing services. "Hey, Max. How's it going?"

"Good. Just looking for some mustard. Mike

brought pretzels and I like mustard on them, but I can't find the bottle I *know* I just bought."

"You know, you and I should get together for lunch sometime. Grab a burger at the diner or something." Max stopped rummaging through the cupboard to look at him. "I enjoy hanging out with you, but we're always here and there's a game on. It'd be cool to talk about something other than sports, know what I mean?"

"Not really. I'm not very good at small talk."

Okay, so Crawford was a tough nut to crack. "Just a thought. I'm usually busy on the weekends, and I guess you probably have to work on the weekdays, anyway, huh?"

"Yeah. How come Katie's not here yet?"

And, right on schedule, the subject change. The guy was definitely doing it on purpose. "She's not coming today. Something else going on, I guess."

"I hear you two are a thing now."

"A thing?" Josh shrugged. It was as good a word as any. "I guess we're a thing, yeah."

"It's about time. I thought I was going to have to talk her into kissing me in front of the television or something just to get you riled up."

Maybe he didn't want to have lunch with Max Crawford after all, even to win a bet. The idea of Katie kissing some other guy made Josh's stomach churn and it was all he could do to keep his hands from curling into fists.

The surge of jealousy took him off guard. He'd seen Katie kiss a guy before. They'd even gone out as a group when he and Katie were both seeing other people. But now the thought of Katie kissing Max, even if they were just trying to make him jealous, raised his blood pressure.

"I'm glad I didn't have to resort to that," Max continued. "Katie's a sweet girl, but she's all yours. Has been as long as I've known her."

Josh nodded and grabbed a beer out of the fridge, but he kept replaying those words in his mind as he walked back to the couch. He'd thought maybe living under the same roof had sparked the fire between him and Katie, but even well before Rosie got sick, he'd been an idiot not to catch the hints here and there that Katie's feelings for him weren't platonic.

The day he'd had lunch with Mitch, Josh had been worried about falling in love with Katie. He'd never stopped to realize she might already be in love with him.

But he was certain he would have known if that were true. They'd spent so much time together, and there was no way she was that good an actress. If Katie had been thinking steamy thoughts about him before Christmas Eve, she couldn't have hidden it from him. It looked like Whitford suffered from the same overactive imagination, with a dash of wishful thinking, that Rose did.

Josh had just gotten comfortable when he looked up and saw Katie. She had a bottle of water in one hand and she grabbed a handful of chips before she settled herself in the corner.

"What are you doing here?" he asked.

"I came to watch the game, like I always do." He scowled and she rolled her eyes at him. "Oh, what? Now that we sleep together, I'm supposed to stay home and make you a sandwich?"

"That's not what I meant and you know it. You told me you were doing something with Hailey today, so I was surprised to see you. No big deal."

"Change of plans."

It was their first time at Max's since Christmas Eve, and he wasn't really sure how he should act. Or how *she* expected him to act. She didn't want to feel like a dirty secret, but that didn't mean she necessarily wanted a public display of affection here at Max's house, either.

To test the waters, he twisted around to face her and rested his hand on her knee. "What happened with Hailey?"

"She wanted me to help her do some winterizing, which she obviously put off too long, but she stayed up half the night watching some dumb movie marathon and she canceled on me. So now I get to be here with you, instead."

When she leaned forward and planted a kiss on

his mouth, he squeezed her knee. That answered that question.

Butch stirred in the recliner and muttered, "It's about goddamn time."

KATIE SAW THE opportunity to make her move during the third quarter. Max went into the kitchen for more drinks and, since Josh had nodded off, she eased herself off the couch and followed. Whether or not Josh was her boyfriend—and she wasn't holding her breath for that kind of definitive label from him—a bet was a bet and she intended to win.

"How was your holiday, Max?" she asked when they were alone in the kitchen. "Did you go somewhere for Christmas?"

"I went home to Connecticut to see my parents."

"Connecticut, huh? How'd you end up in Maine? Was it for work?" When he gave her a look that clearly said *really?* she knew she'd overplayed her hand. Again. She wasn't very good at subtle interrogation.

"What's with you two today? You're both acting more openly nosy than usual."

Katie laughed, knowing they were busted. "Josh and I have a bet going about who can find out what you do for work first. Loser washes the other's vehicle once a month for a year."

Max chuckled. "I thought it was a well-established fact in Whitford that I'm a serial killer."

"You know about that?"

"Of course I do."

"So why don't you say something?" It was weird to let a town think you were killing people in your basement rather than name your job.

"Because it amuses me. And I'm waiting to see how long it takes for somebody to point out that serial murder isn't really a sustainable career choice. How would that make me money?"

"Maybe you steal from your victims."

"Enough to buy that television and pay taxes and otherwise support myself? What kind of people do you guys think I'm killing down there? I think somebody, especially Fran Benoit, would notice if people carrying wads of cash in their wallets kept wandering into Whitford only to never be seen again."

"You're the only person in the entire town who has a separate security system just for his basement."

"Why a serial killer, though? Why not the CIA or a mad scientist?"

Katie felt herself blush. "That's probably my mom's fault. She's Fran's primary gossip buddy and she spends most of her spare time watching *Criminal Minds* repeats."

"I'll show you what I do if you don't ruin the fun by telling everybody."

"Really? Just like that?"

Max shrugged. "Josh is always talking shit about your Jeep. I think the idea of him having to wash it once a month is funny, don't you?"

"I think it's hilarious."

She looked away while Max punched numbers in the security box, but she was right on his heels as he went down the steps. Even though, once he hit the switch, the lighting was excellent and the climate control system was obviously top-notch, she had to admit it was a little thrilling going into the basement with the town's alleged serial killer.

When they reached the bottom of the stairs and he stepped aside, holding his arm out in a *ta-da* motion, she stopped short. "Toy trains?"

He clutched a hand over his heart as if mortally wounded. "These are not toy trains. They're highly collectible, precision-engineered brass HO-scale models."

She was confused. "So you, what…play with them?"

"I paint them. See that one?" He pointed to a brass train engine in a glass case on a shelf, then pointed to his workbench. "I take the brass ones and paint them, making them look authentic with weathering and whatnot."

Katie walked closer to the bench to look at his work in progress. There were jars of paint, the tiniest brushes she'd ever seen and an airbrush gun around a train lying supported on its side. It looked

as if he was in the process of lettering Central
Maine Railroad down the side.

Off to the right were more glass cases, and she
eyed one engine that looked really old. It was a
Union Pacific and the detail was incredible. He
didn't paint them to look nice. He painted them in
such a way that the engines looked as though they
had actually been worked for decades. "It looks
so real."

"It's not as exciting as serial killing or the CIA,
but I'm very good at it."

"You're an artist."

"And a historian. I have to know the locomo-
tive, the railroad, the numbering system. When
people want passenger cars painted, I want them
to be one hundred percent authentic. And doing
freight means knowing what the different rail lines
shipped. I work off of real photographs from the
time whenever possible."

They both turned when footsteps thumped down
the stairs and Josh came into view, looking concerned. "Oh, there you are. I couldn't figure out
where Katie went and then I saw the basement door
was ajar and…"

"You thought I was torturing and murdering her
during halftime."

Josh gave Max a chagrined look. "Not really,
but you have to wonder how many serial killers'

neighbors laughed off the idea they might be living next door to one."

"True."

"Are those toy trains?"

Max went through the spiel again and, when he was done, Katie poked a finger at Josh's chest. "Just to be clear, though, I knew before you did."

"Shit." He shook his head, obviously peeved at losing the bet. "Why the extra security?"

"Some of these locomotives are really rare, and even the ones that aren't cost more than you might think. At any given time I've got twenty- to thirty-grand worth of other people's property down here and sometimes more. I prefer not to advertise that."

"If anybody asks what we saw down here," Josh said, "we'll tell them nothing but an industrial sink, a meat hook and a dozen chest-style freezers."

Max grinned. "Excellent."

Katie followed Josh back up the stairs and, after locking up, Max grabbed the drinks off the counter and headed for the living room.

She hooked her finger through Josh's belt loop and pulled him close. "I think it's really sweet how you came running down to the rescue when you thought he might be killing me."

"I didn't want to have to tell Rosie I let Max Crawford stuff your body in his freezer."

She laughed and pushed up on her toes so she

could plant a kiss on him. "Chicken. I can't believe you'd face down a serial killer, but not my mother."

"At least with a serial killer, I've got a fighting chance."

CHAPTER THIRTEEN

JOSH HAD NEVER considered putting a couch in the lodge's office, a lack of foresight for which he was now kicking himself in the ass. He had, however, put a lock on the door to keep guests out, so he didn't have to worry about anybody walking in unannounced.

A long leather couch would have been nice, though, beating the hell out of being bare-assed on the hundred-year-old braided rug on the office floor.

There were families in the living room, watching the New Year's Eve countdown show together, and the closer it got to midnight, the louder they got. Rose and Andy had retreated to her room to do the same privately. Some of the men from the families in the living room were hiding in the barn from the merriment, drinking beers and talking sledding. Privacy was at a premium at the Northern Star.

It had been tempting to head to Katie's apartment for the night, even if she did have the heat turned down, but he didn't like leaving Rose with a party going on in the house. It wasn't a big party—

or even technically a party, really—but there were enough people and enough alcohol that a problem could pop up. Even with Andy in the house, Josh wasn't taking the chance of things going to shit while he was away.

The office had been their last resort, and it served the purpose even if it wasn't the most comfortable place in the house. Naked on his back, with Katie straddling him, the braided rug didn't bother him as much as he'd thought it would. Hell, with her breasts filling his hands, he could have been lying in a bed of puckerbrush and he wouldn't care.

With a hand braced on either side of his head, Katie could look at him while she rocked her hips in slow circles that damn near drove him out of his mind. "You know, I've heard that however you ring in the New Year is how you'll spend the entire year."

"I think chafing would kick in sometime around February at the latest."

She laughed and lightly slapped his chest. "Not literally."

"Then what? Is this some kind of riddle?" Why were they even talking right now? He was buried inside her and she was talking about some stupid holiday tradition.

"Quit being a dumbass. It means if you're happy and having fun and everything when it turns midnight, you'll have a happy, fun year."

Together, he thought. If they were together when

the ball dropped, did she think they'd spend the year that way? While being in bed—or on the floor, actually—with her wasn't exactly a hardship, he had his bags mentally packed. If the door to his leaving Whitford opened even a crack, he'd be through it so fast it wouldn't have a chance to hit him on the ass on the way out.

That's what he kept telling himself, anyway. Right at this moment, the need to get away wasn't quite so urgent.

"And you," she said, "are apparently at risk for spending the next twelve months scowling at ceiling fans."

"I'm lying on my back, facing up. I can't *not* see the ceiling fan."

"You can not scowl at it. What were you thinking about?"

He put his hands on her hips and rocked her forward, then he lifted his hips in a hard thrust to remind her what they'd been doing before she felt a need to have a conversation. "Less talking. More moving."

"Oh, I don't think so. I'm not ringing in the New Year with you telling me what to do."

Before she could resist, he pushed one of her knees back and rolled until he was on top of her. "What was that?"

She wrapped those amazing legs around his hips,

holding him close to her. "Maybe this was my master plan all along."

He started moving his hips, slowly thrusting until she dug her nails in his back and made that impatient sound low in her throat that made him incredibly hot. Quickening the pace, he watched her face, loving the way she caught her bottom lip between her teeth.

When she moaned, her breath coming faster, he ran his tongue across her lip and pressed a kiss to the spot her tooth had been catching. "Shhhh."

Her frustrated growl would have made him laugh if he wasn't aware of just how close she was, and the fact he wasn't far behind. She felt so damn good, and he thrust harder as she buried her face in his neck to muffle herself. Her body clenched around him and he couldn't hold back anymore.

When his breath returned and his heart stopped hammering in his ears, he rolled to the side so he wasn't crushing Katie into the rug. With his arm thrown over her, he rested his head against hers and enjoyed the afterglow.

"We're stuck here until they all go to bed, aren't we?" she asked after a few minutes.

He chuckled and kissed the top of her head. "Of course not. For all they know, we have a TV in here and wanted to watch a different channel than they did. We should probably get dressed before we go out there, though."

"I'm getting dressed, anyway. Wooden floors in old New England houses in the winter don't make for cozy beds, rug or no rug."

As much as he liked feeling her naked body up against his, he didn't mind watching her get dressed again. But once she'd covered up the best parts, he decided she was right about the cold floor so he dropped the condom in the trash can next to the desk and pulled his clothes back on. Once they were both dressed, the office became boring in a hurry, though.

"I wonder if they ate all the snacks," Katie said.

Because they knew their guests would be staying up later than usual, they'd made the kitchen more accessible. Cheese and crackers, popcorn, a nice assortment of goodies from Rose. They couldn't supply alcohol, so it was strictly BYOB, but they wanted to give a little extra to people who'd chosen to a spend a holiday at the Northern Star.

"Doing this as long as I have, you learn a few things," he told her. "Like squirreling away some of the goodies before you lay them out for the guests. There might be some cookies, cheese and a pepperoni stick hiding behind the baking powder in the pantry."

"You keep your stash behind the baking powder, huh? I'll have to remember that."

Josh grinned. "I've caught guests digging around for some weird things, but I've never had one try to sneak off with the baking powder. What do you think? Want to go eat cookies in the pantry?"

"Let's do it. Should I let you go first and then wait a few minutes?"

He laughed so hard he knew there'd be no doubt he wasn't alone in the office, anyway. "Jesus, Katie, we're not sixteen. Just walk to the kitchen and say hi or happy New Year or whatever to anybody who talks to you. Don't forget, this is *my house*."

Sure, it would be nice if he didn't have to lead the woman he'd just made love to through a gauntlet of guests who didn't seem to realize that once the ball in Times Square dropped, it was time to go to bed. But he was polite and kept moving, so they made it to the pantry without Katie passing out from embarrassment.

He closed the door behind him, the only light coming through the slats in the louvered doors, and rummaged behind the baking powder for the cookies. He handed her one, then took one for himself. Sure, hiding in the closet was stupid, but he was having too much fun with Katie and her adjustment to sharing living space with strangers not to.

"Gee, Josh. Sex in a barn. Cookies in a closet. You sure know how to show a girl a good time."

"I'm a hell of a catch, huh? Wait 'til I show you what I can do in the basement." He grinned and popped the cookie in his mouth.

Rose was always thrown off by holidays. People checking out on Tuesday and then more people checking in on Friday would make for a short week. Adding in the fact she'd stayed awake long enough to ring in the New Year with a kiss from Andy, and she was out of sorts. Even though she'd only been up a few hours, she could have gone for a nap.

Katie was moving back to her apartment today, and Rose had no good excuse to offer why she shouldn't. She'd thought—or maybe just hoped—that Josh and Katie would just go along as they were for a while. The longer they played house, the more *right* it would feel to them. But Rose could understand Katie's desire to get the barbershop back on schedule, even if she didn't understand why she couldn't drive to work from the lodge and back. It wasn't very far.

And Josh didn't seem upset at all by seeing Katie's bag next to the back door. If anything, he seemed happy about the fact she was leaving, and Rose couldn't understand that at all.

Andy walked into the kitchen, probably looking for coffee. "Uh-oh. You look like you want to slap somebody upside the head with a shovel."

"I'm trying to think of a good excuse for Katie to stay."

He slid an arm around her shoulders and kissed her before reaching past her for the coffeepot.

"You're back on your feet now, and that's the only reason she was here. It makes sense she'd go home."

"Maybe if I cough a few times, she'll stay." When Andy gave her a stern look, she laughed. "I was kidding. But why does Josh seem so okay with her going? I thought he was falling for her, but if he was he'd want to keep her here."

"Privacy." He blew across the top of his coffee and then took a sip, closing his eyes as he savored the brew. "Josh can, uh…visit her there instead of in a houseful of people."

Rose hadn't thought of that, but Andy had a point. Maybe spending time at Katie's apartment, where he could totally relax and enjoy her company, would strengthen their relationship more than continuing on in the routine they had now.

Before she could say anything else, the door to the basement opened and Katie emerged. When she saw them standing there, she smiled and then blew out an exhausted breath. "All the bedding's downstairs. First load's in the washer."

"I could have done that, honey. I really do feel better."

"I know, Mom. But I figured I'd get it all downstairs for you before I leave."

Rose couldn't help herself. "Why don't you stay for dinner and then go home after?"

Katie gave her a sweet smile, as if she knew her silly old mom was just trying to keep her there a little longer. "Because it'll take a few hours for my apartment to come back up to temperature and I don't want to crawl into a freezing bed. Where's Josh?"

"He went for a quick ride," Andy said. "One of the guests said there was a tree down across the trail. They had a few guys, so they were able to hold it up enough to pass all the machines under, but it needs a chain saw. Would've given him a hand, but he was ready to go and I wasn't. Said it wouldn't take him more than a half hour."

As if they'd summoned him just by talking about him, they all heard the whine of his snowmobile cutting across the yard, heading toward the barn.

Katie picked up her bag and shoved her feet into her boots. "I'm going to head out, then. You call me if you need anything, Mom. And you're still on semilight duty, no matter how good you feel."

"I won't let her overdo it," Andy said.

Rose shushed him and hurried forward to kiss her daughter's cheek before she went out the door. Then she watched through the window as Katie walked to the barn and waited while Josh took off his helmet and put the chain saw away.

They were easy together, smiling and happy, and Rose forced herself to relax. They were still okay, she thought. Her pneumonia had thrown them together and now all she could do was see if it stuck.

"I think you're right," she told Andy as the kids

disappeared in the direction of Katie's Jeep. "Being under the same roof was the kick in the pants Josh needed, but now they'll have a chance to build a real relationship."

She smiled as he slid his arm around her waist and kissed the back of her neck. "You're good at this matchmaking thing."

"I am, aren't I?" she agreed, and then she turned her head toward him so his next kiss was a proper one.

MOVIE NIGHT, HELD on the first Saturday of each month, was a longstanding tradition for some of the women of Whitford. The hosting duties rotated and this time it was Jilly Crenshaw's turn.

Katie was partial to movie night at Jilly's because Gavin usually put out some of his incredible food for them before he and his dad left for Max's to watch whatever sport they could find on the television.

Tonight the movie was the new romantic comedy on the block, which didn't do much for her. Gavin's buffalo-chicken dip, however, would have been worth sitting through *The English Patient* again. She was hesitant to try it, but once she did she wanted to bury her face in the pan and devour it like she was in a no-hands pie-eating contest. She needed that recipe.

Luckily, there was plenty of dip to go around,

because attendance was light. The forecast had hinted at the possibility of sleet, which kept some of the less adventurous drivers—including Rose—at home. Paige wasn't giving up a Saturday night with Mitch, especially since he'd be traveling again in less than a month. Hailey had gone to her sister's house in Massachusetts to have a belated Christmas with her family.

But Fran was there, and Jilly. Tori, the part-time waitress who was Jilly's niece, was sitting at one end of the couch, looking a little lost. There were a few others there, too, and she waved to them as she sat on the other end of the couch, balancing a plate with crackers and dip on it. Jilly sat between her and Tori, picking up the remote.

Holding the plate in one hand, Katie fumbled with her phone, switching it to vibrate before the movie started. She tucked it under her thigh and used a throw pillow to help balance her plate.

"I heard you and Josh are a thing now," Jilly said, leaning close to her as if every other woman in the room wasn't listening.

"Yeah, I guess we are."

"That's awesome. Everybody knew you guys belonged together, so we're all happy for you. Plus, the Kowalskis throw great weddings, you know."

Katie felt her eyes widen and shook her head. "We're not there yet. Not even close, actually."

Jilly patted her leg. "You'll get there. Don't worry."

"Okay, Jilly, I'm ready," Fran said as she lowered herself into Jilly's rocker and set her knitting basket on the floor next to it.

Jilly hit the play button and Katie sat back with a sigh of relief. At least the attention was off her and onto the television where it belonged. They were already talking about a wedding?

Ten minutes into the movie, Katie found her attention wandering. The romantic leads had no chemistry and the plot was ridiculous. She consoled herself with the knowledge it was her turn to pick the movie next, and trying to narrow down the choices was a nice distraction. Something with action, she thought. And explosions. Less witty banter and more shooting.

She wasn't even sure why she still showed up for these things, other than having an opportunity to hang out with Hailey. At least she and Josh had the same taste in movies, and she'd always enjoyed watching with him more than all the women, even before there was sex involved.

Katie dredged another chip through the dip to keep her focus from shifting to sex with Josh. All that would do was make the movie seem that much more endless. She should have texted him before she'd arrived to see if he was going to be busy later in the night, but she hadn't thought of it then and now it was too late.

When her phone buzzed under her thigh, Katie looked around to see if anybody had noticed. They were all focused on the television and nobody even glanced in her direction. Reaching down, she pulled the phone out enough to read the text message from Josh.

Blow off the movie & meet me at your place.

Blowing off the movie was one thing. Blowing off Gavin's buffalo-chicken dip was another. Keeping the phone down beside the pillow, she was stuck using only her right thumb to text back. Can't. It's movie night.

Only a few seconds passed before she got a response. I've made you come on the office floor and in the barn. Imagine what I could do in a bed.

Stop. There's a no texting during the movie rule, she sent back. Fran had instituted the rule months ago when women texting with their men had ruined her something-hundredth viewing of *Breakfast at Tiffany's*.

Tell them your stomach hurts.

He was going to get her kicked out of movie night. Stop. I can't.

She tried to ignore the vibration when he responded, but she couldn't. *Too bad. I wanted to see how many licks it takes to get to the center of your Tootsie Pop.*

Katie tried to disguise a quick snort of laughter as a cough, hoping like hell there wasn't a tearjerker scene on the television at that moment. *Later.*

Limited time offer. Sure it was.

"Katie's texting," Jilly said, and her voice was loud during a quiet moment in the movie. "And look at her face. She's texting Josh."

"Gimme the phone," Fran said, pushing herself out of the rocking chair and advancing on Katie with her hand held out.

"I don't think so."

"You know the rules. You'll get it back when the movie's over." When Katie crossed her arms, effectively hiding the cell phone in her armpit, Fran narrowed her eyes. "Katherine Rose Davis, you give me that phone right now."

That had been the drawback to running with the Kowalski kids growing up. She'd gotten in trouble often enough that every woman of her mom's generation knew her middle name. "Middle-naming me isn't going to work, Fran. I'm an adult and I'm not giving you my phone."

She yelped when Jilly reached under her elbow and snatched the phone out of her hand. Before she could get it back, Jilly tossed it to Fran. "Sorry,

Katie. It's a rule and, since it's my house, I have to help enforce it."

Unfortunately, when Fran caught it, she hit the button to wake up the screen—which was still showing the text messages—and she watched the older woman's eyes get big. Katie was surprised she didn't melt into a puddle and disappear between the couch cushions when Fran looked at her.

"Oh, honey, you have to go. I didn't know your stomach's upset." Katie froze, wondering if it was a trap. But Fran's eyes danced with mischief as she held the phone out to her. "You should definitely go."

Katie stood up and grabbed her coat out of the pile by the end of the couch. Then she approached Fran, who was still holding Katie's phone. She tried to take it, but the older woman resisted for a few seconds so she could lean in close.

"Katie, honey, there are some things a woman should never refuse."

Her face burning, Katie took the phone and nodded, her cheeks burning. Then, with a small wave in the general direction of the women behind her, she fled while the fleeing was good.

CHAPTER FOURTEEN

THE PHONE CALL from Mitch came out of the blue, while Josh was about to change the oil in his sled, and almost knocked him on his ass.

"We've had an offer to buy the lodge."

It took a few seconds for Josh to wrap his mind around what his brother had said. "An offer? To buy it?"

"I was surprised, too. I figured if we ended up selling it instead of hiring a manager, it wouldn't be for a while yet."

Josh put the gallon of oil back on the shelf and sat sideways on his sled. "I don't get it. It's not even on the market yet."

"You had a married couple there two weekends ago. Older, plenty of money?"

"Yeah, I remember them. Asked a million questions about the house and they kept going for walks around the property. I didn't think anything of it because a lot of people love the house."

"They fell in love with the place and called a Realtor in the city to arrange making an offer. The real estate agent called the town office for contact info and they called me. And now I'm calling you."

"I must have made it look too easy if the inmates think they can run the asylum," Josh joked while he tried to wrap his mind around this development.

Mitch was silent for a few seconds, then he cleared his throat. "It wouldn't be a lodging establishment anymore. Just a private home."

But it's been in the family for four generations and the Northern Star Lodge for three. The thought screamed through his head, though he managed not to say it out loud. He couldn't very well tell his family he wanted to get rid of the place and then come undone when a chance arrived.

"We've worked so hard to connect to the ATV trails," Josh said. "The access was going to help out other Whitford businesses, not just the lodge."

"Like my wife's diner, yes."

Josh closed his eyes, trying to fend off the guilt. The Trailside Diner was doing really well. It wouldn't live or die based on this decision. "I guess it must be a decent offer if you're bringing it to the table."

"It's a generous offer," Mitch agreed. "Although I have an obligation to bring it to the table even if it was only a hundred bucks. It's a family business."

"So…what now?" Besides figuring out why the possibility of having what he'd wanted made his gut twist into knots.

"We need to get together and have a discussion as soon as possible. And we'll have to call Liz and put her on speakerphone or something, since we can't make the decision without her. I'm going to send a group email so we can nail down a time to discuss it. Hopefully this weekend."

He had a full house for the weekend, but the family had their own rooms, so it shouldn't be a problem. "I'll be here, so whenever."

"You should probably tell Rose."

That wasn't something he wanted to do. "Okay."

When the call was done, Josh got up and walked toward the house. He wasn't into changing the oil now and there was no sense in putting off the conversation. Rose sometimes checked the lodge's email account and if Mitch used that address instead of Josh's personal one, it could be an unpleasant surprise for her.

He found her in the living room, dusting. When he sat on the couch, she gave him a questioning look and he patted the cushion next to him.

"You look unhappy," she said, taking a seat. "What happened?"

"I'm not unhappy. I just… Mitch called. We've had an offer from somebody who wants to buy the lodge. They want to make it a private home."

It broke his heart to watch her expression change. Confusion. The realization that, if they accepted the offer, she would need a new home. And the reso-

lution—she'd deal with it when the time came because that's the kind of woman she was. "So you
haven't talked to Ryan, Sean or Liz yet?"

"No. He wants us all to get together, with Liz on
speakerphone. Sean, too, if he can't make it here
in person."

"When?"

"Hopefully this weekend."

"I'll make a big lasagna, then, and put it in the
freezer so it'll be ready whenever they come." Before he could say anything else, she stood and went
toward the kitchen. "Speaking of which, I need to
start the ham for tonight. And put some laundry in
the dryer."

He let her go because he didn't trust himself not
to be too choked up to speak. What kind of selfish
bastard was he? The woman had pretty much devoted her life to taking care of the lodge and five
kids who weren't even her own and now she didn't
even get a say in what happened to her?

There was no doubt in his mind she was hiding
her true feelings about the lodge being sold so he
wouldn't feel guilty. Not only would she not want to
influence the family's decision, but she knew him
better than anybody. Even better than Katie. So she
knew how he'd felt trapped by obligation for years,
and she wouldn't hold him back.

Josh leaned his head against the cushion and
closed his eyes, hoping to ease the throbbing al-

ready starting at his temples. He wanted to go—
no, he *needed* to go—but he loved Rose. He didn't
want to hurt her.

And what about Katie?

It had been easy enough to tell her, the day they'd
gone to Brookline, that she and the lodge were two
separate things, but they weren't. Selling the lodge
meant leaving Whitford. And that meant leaving
her.

They'd always been friends. Granted, they'd
fallen into a friends-with-benefits deal, but it wasn't
like they'd talked about marriage. She hadn't even
hesitated when it had come to moving back to her
own place, and most women, if they were hoping for
a ring, would have clung to living under the same
roof. Even if he left, they'd still be friends.

But he didn't know how he could look her in the
face and tell her he was leaving town.

KATIE WAS HAVING one of *those* days. She'd somehow run low on small bills in the register, which
was a problem since most people in Whitford still
operated on a cash-only basis. After writing a note
that she'd be back in fifteen minutes and the time
she'd left, she'd locked up the shop and driven to
the bank. Normally she would walk, but she usually did her banking when the shop was closed and
she could take her time.

Of course there was a line at the bank and the

minutes seemed to tick by on fast-forward, so she ended up rushing back. She was halfway there when the blue lights flashed in her rearview mirror.

"Please don't be Bob Durgin," she said as she put on her blinker and pulled as close to the sidewalk as she could get without being on it. Officer Durgin hated the Kowalski kids and she was close enough to be lumped in with them, as far as he was concerned.

Luckily it was Drew Miller who got out of the cruiser, and she rolled down her window as he approached her door. "Hi, Drew."

He sighed and shook his head. "You guys are never going to catch on. You're supposed to call me Chief Miller when you're in trouble."

"Even if it's just a little bit of trouble?"

"You think seven miles over on the main street is a little bit of trouble?"

She gave him her best smile. "Sorry?"

"What's really sorry is that I just busted your boyfriend on the other end of town doing the same damn thing." It tickled her a little to hear Josh called her boyfriend. She could get used to that. "But he gave me a shitload of attitude, so I wrote him a ticket."

Hearing that killed the tickle. She wasn't sure what was going on with Josh, but his mood had definitely taken a turn for the worse and she didn't know why. She'd called him a couple of days before and he'd sounded tired. When she'd brought up getting together, either at his place or hers, he'd put her off, claiming he had a lot to do. That was two days ago and she hadn't heard from him since. Maybe she should give him a call later in the afternoon and drag him out for a burger or something.

"I needed change," she told Drew, "so I thought I'd run to the bank real quick, but it was busy, so…I was speeding. Sorry."

He pointed at her and gave her his stern police chief face. "Slow down. Next time, you won't get off with a warning."

Once he'd walked back to his cruiser, she pulled back into traffic and did the speed limit back to the shop. Of course she had a customer waiting on the sidewalk, looking unhappy.

The afternoon passed quickly as customers came and went, but she was thinking about calling Josh during a lull when the door opened and her mom walked in. "Hi, Mom. I didn't know you'd be out and about today."

"I needed a few things from the market and it's been ages since I've sat and visited with Fran, so I decided to drive in myself instead of sending Josh."

"I guess he's in town, anyway. Drew said he gave him a speeding ticket earlier today."

Rose frowned. "He must have been speeding a lot to get a ticket from Drew."

"Actually it was the attitude he gave him, I guess.

Drew didn't like it. And when I talked to him the other day, he was cranky, too. I don't know what's up with him. His mind's definitely somewhere else."

"Getting an offer on the lodge is a pretty big deal."

"An offer?" Katie thought maybe she'd misunderstood. "To buy it? But it's not even listed yet."

"He didn't tell you?" Rose pressed her lips together and shook her head. "I guess a couple that stayed there recently wants to buy it and make it a private home."

Katie did her best not to show it, but her mom's words made her stomach clench. So Josh's mind *was* somewhere else. It was wherever he was planning to go when he was free of the lodge.

"No, he didn't. Guess it's none of my business." The fact he hadn't told her hurt so much she didn't know what else to day. She was supposed to be his friend and he hadn't even bothered to tell her about what had to be one of the most important things to happen in his life in years. So much for the word *boyfriend* meaning anything.

"Katie, don't be like that. Maybe he can't figure out how to tell you."

"That's a tough one. 'Hey, got an offer on the lodge.' I can see how that would be hard for him."

"Maybe before, but now it's different. By telling you he might sell the lodge, he's also saying he might be leaving town."

And therefore leaving Katie. She wasn't stupid. She knew what it meant. "Has he made a decision yet?"

"They have to make the decision together. Ryan and Sean are both driving up tomorrow night, and Saturday morning they're going to call Liz and put her on speakerphone."

"So it'll be two days before we know if he's leaving us or not?"

When her mom walked over and pulled her into her arms, it was a struggle not to cry. "You knew this might happen, honey. So did I."

"I can't get over the fact he hasn't told me."

"It's weighing heavy on him, Katie. You know Josh. He'll talk about the weather and sports and snow and almost anything else you can think of, but not what's going on in his head."

Katie stepped back from the hug and shrugged. "Whatever. He knows where to find me if he wants to talk."

Despite that, it wasn't five minutes after her mom had left that Katie pulled out her cell phone. She got Josh's voice mail after the second ring, which meant he'd seen her name on his caller ID and silenced her.

She wasn't sure what the rules were now. A few months ago she might have jumped in her Jeep and driven to the lodge to ask him what had crawled up his ass. But now she wasn't sure if that was too girlfriendlike and, despite being tickled when Drew had called Josh her boyfriend, she wasn't sure *what* they were.

In the end, she settled for going to the diner and asking Ava to make her a massive hot fudge sundae. With chocolate and whipped cream came a little bit of clarity.

Being hurt that Josh hadn't reached out to her wasn't going to get her anything but misery. Josh had never reached out to her. He didn't reach out to anybody. Even when he'd been miserable and on the edge of snapping, he'd kept it to himself until he broke his leg and finally told his brothers he wanted out.

The best thing she could do was wait and, when he was ready to talk, he'd talk to her. No amount of pushing or nagging would make that happen any sooner, so there was no sense in potentially driving him away.

And now that her mom had told her what exactly was weighing on his mind, she wasn't really in a hurry to have that conversation with him, anyway. She knew feeling hurt that he hadn't confided in her wasn't going to hurt anywhere near as bad as hearing him say he was leaving.

ROSE PULLED A BATCH of oatmeal cookies out of the oven and closed the door with a snap. She wished she hadn't told Andy to make himself scarce for the weekend. The tension in the lodge was almost unbearable and she could have used his comfort.

Instead she was baking cookies after her bedtime, waiting for Ryan and Sean to show up. Lauren had opted to stay home because they'd done so much running back and forth that Nick wasn't even unpacked yet, and Sean was coming without Emma because she had a prior commitment. It would be just the kids, which was probably for the best. It wasn't going to be an easy decision to make.

When Josh walked into the kitchen, she was thankful he grabbed a soda instead of a beer, at least. "Do you want a cookie? They need to sit a few minutes, but they're fresh and hot."

He glanced at the cookie sheet, disappointment all over his face. "No chocolate chip?"

"Not tonight. Sean's partial to my oatmeal cookies."

"Lucky Sean."

She smiled, but didn't bother to point out that Josh got to eat her baked goods all the time and Sean didn't. Mary was a good cook, but the boys' aunt wasn't quite as good with oatmeal cookies as she was. And, from what she'd heard, cooking wasn't very high on Emma's priority list. After driving from New Hampshire, the boy deserved some of his favorite cookies.

"Have you told Katie about the offer?" she asked, even though she knew he hadn't. It was the only way she could think of to open the conversation without sounding accusatory right off the bat.

"Not much sense in telling her until it's final one way or the other."

Nothing in his tone invited further comment, but these were the two people she loved more than anybody and they obviously needed help. "I assumed you'd talk to her. I know this is a big deal for you and she's a good shoulder to lean on."

"You think she'll be happy for me?"

That was an almost impossible question to answer, but she could see on his face he wanted her to try. "I think she'll be happy for *you,* knowing you're getting what you've always wanted."

He didn't like the answer, but it was all she could give him. Truth was, if they decided tomorrow to sell the lodge, Josh was going to get what he wanted while Katie was going to lose what she'd always wanted. And it would be especially hard because now her daughter knew what she'd be missing. It would have been better for everybody if Katie had never worn that damn dress to the Christmas Eve party.

And Rose's dreams would crash to the ground, too. Losing the Northern Star would make her sad, of course. It had been more than her responsibility for decades—it had been her home. But she'd been so sure Josh and Katie were finally going to be together, and now it probably wasn't going to happen.

Before either of them could say anything else, not that there was much to say, headlights swung into the driveway. She wouldn't have thought it possible for Josh to get any more tense, but his jaw tightened and his thumb left an indent in his soda can.

When the truck pulled up close to the lodge, she saw that it was Sean and her spirits lifted a little. Even if the occasion wasn't a joyous one for her, she wasn't going to let it ruin a visit with one of the kids.

After parking in line with the guests, who were hanging out in their rooms, Sean went in the back door to the kitchen, bringing a blast of frigid air with him. He shut the door, dropped his bag and enveloped Rose in a bear hug that lifted her right off her feet.

"Are those oatmeal cookies?" he asked, setting her back down so he could burn his fingers on the pan.

"Of course. They're your favorite. But you should probably let them cool a few more minutes."

She started moving them to the cooling rack while he greeted his brother. It started as a handshake, but Sean pulled Josh in for a hug and slapped him on the back. "How's it going?"

"Not bad. Better if those cookies were chocolate chip."

Sean laughed. "Not my fault she loves me best, little brother."

Rose rolled her eyes, letting the familiar sibling banter roll over her. She wished they'd all come home more often, like they had for Mitch and Paige's wedding. But that thought, happy as it was, reminded her there probably wouldn't be a home to come back to very much longer.

She shrugged off that depressing thought and put a few cookies on a couple of napkins and set them on the table, gesturing for them to sit. Oatmeal cookies weren't Josh's favorite, but favorite was relative when it came to cookies. As long as they didn't have coconut, he'd eat his fair share of them.

"How's Emma doing?"

Sean grinned, pulling out a chair to sit. "She's great. She's at twenty-one weeks now and Sprout, who won't uncross his or her legs for the ultrasound, is kicking her now."

"Sprout Kowalski?" Josh laughed. "I like it."

"I'm not allowed to share any of the names we're thinking about, so Sprout it is for now. Emma's into plants, being a landscaper, and once she called the baby a sprout, it kind of stuck."

Rose chuckled. "I hope you realize that poor child's cousins will never let that go."

"I know," Sean said. "Unfortunately, we didn't think of that until *after* we said it in front of them and they all thought it was the funniest thing they'd ever heard."

WHILE SHE FUSSED around the kitchen, cleaning up after herself, Rose watched the two brothers catching up over their late snack. Sean's mood seemed good, but she didn't miss the way his eyes moved around the room, taking in the details as if it were the last time. Under the jovial smile that came so easily to the Kowalskis, she could see the underlying sadness and knew he was, in his heart, saying goodbye.

There was no more possibly or probably about it. No matter how much it hurt, she knew the kids were all going to agree to sell the Northern Star because they loved Josh. They'd gone off and made lives for themselves and they'd sacrifice the home that bound them together so he could have that same chance.

She loved them even more for it—she was as proud of them as if they were her own—but when she followed Sean's gaze to the Bless This Kitchen sampler his mother had cross-stitched when he was just a baby, she saw her own heartbreak reflected in his eyes.

CHAPTER FIFTEEN

JOSH WAS UP before the sun, brewing coffee and laying out the muffins and banana bread Rosie had baked for the guests. Since he'd spent most of the night tossing and turning, he was glad to be up and about.

He should have talked to Katie. Even more than the upcoming family meeting, that thought had kept him awake.

Rosie was right about Katie being a good shoulder to lean on. God knew he'd leaned on her many times in the past. But what Rose didn't understand was his fear—no, his certainty—that Katie would be hurt. He knew how hard the idea of selling the Northern Star was for his brothers and Liz to swallow, and there was a limit to how many people he could let down at one time. Today he would see loss in the eyes of every one of his brothers and hear it in his sister's voice. He couldn't take Katie's hurt, too.

Sometime during the wee hours, he'd forced himself to face the fact that leaving her would be harder than he thought. That had led to wondering if she'd consider leaving Whitford with him. It was only the slim possibility that he could have his cake and eat it, too, so to speak, that had allowed the gears in his mind to stop grinding long enough to fall asleep.

But in the light of day, he knew that wasn't going to happen. Katie wouldn't leave her mom—especially while Rose's life was being turned upside down—or the barbershop to go wander around the country with Josh.

Two hours later, he watched the last group of guests disappear into the woods on their sleds, and took a deep breath. Ryan and Sean would probably appear any minute, because it wasn't easy to sleep through a pack of snowmobiles firing up in the morning. Rosie had been in and out of the kitchen, fussing over things, but she was in a quiet mood, so they hadn't said much beyond exchanging good mornings.

Josh had just finished washing the guests' breakfast dishes when Mitch walked through the door. Because it looked like he'd slept about as well as Josh had, Josh filled the carafe to start a fresh pot of coffee.

"I see Ryan and Sean's trucks out there," Mitch said, wiping the traces of a fresh snow dusting off his boots. "They still in bed?"

"Haven't seen them yet. There's some banana bread left, but the guests demolished the muffins."

"Where's Rosie?"

"I think she's doing a quick check of the guest rooms. Making sure nobody used all their shampoo or clogged the toilets."

"I'll go say hello while the coffee brews."

Left alone, Josh picked at a slice of banana bread, not really tasting it, but knowing he needed something in his stomach besides caffeine.

As if they were waiting for the last spurt of coffee into the pot, Sean and Ryan appeared just as it finished brewing. Josh said good-morning, but didn't bother to get up. They both knew where the milk and sugar were.

"Thought I heard Mitch," Ryan said as he picked through the mugs in the drying rack until he found the biggest.

"He's here. He went to say hi to Rosie." Once his brothers fixed theirs, Josh got up to pour another cup of coffee.

"I'm going to hit the trails when this is over," Ryan said. "I haven't been out in…I don't even know how long."

"That's what happens when you live in the big city." Sean broke off a chunk of banana bread and popped it into his mouth. "I've gotten out a couple of times, but Uncle Leo's starting to give me a hard time about borrowing his sled."

"Throw yours in the back of your truck and take

it home," Ryan said. "I'll give you a hand after we put some miles on."

Sean snorted. "That thing's older than dirt. If I keep borrowing Uncle Leo's and Emma has to listen to me bitch about him giving me shit, maybe she'll tell me to buy a new one just to shut everybody up."

"You've really got the hang of this married thing."

Josh drank his coffee, trying to focus on the conversation, but it was hard to pay attention when they'd essentially be deciding his future any time now. It was pretty early in New Mexico, but Liz had always been a morning person and she'd said she wanted the call over with before leaving to work a double shift.

"You guys better not have eaten all the banana bread," Mitch said as he walked back into the kitchen.

"Left you two slices." Josh handed them to him on a napkin.

"Gee, thanks."

"Hey, your wife owns a restaurant. You should have brought *us* food."

Mitch laughed. "She brings me food all the time. In Styrofoam to-go boxes."

"Rose didn't find any problems with the rooms, did she?" Josh asked, surprised she hadn't joined them in the kitchen.

"No. She said she was going to go upstairs and

read for a while," Mitch told him, and Josh nodded. She'd gone to her room to wait for the verdict.

He tried not to imagine her up there alone, staring at the pages of a book she was only pretending to read while waiting to learn her fate. For three decades, her life had been as wrapped up in the lodge as his was.

When Mitch's cell phone finally rang, Josh almost dropped his coffee mug. He wasn't ready for this. How could he not be ready for something he'd been waiting for most of his life?

"Hey, Liz," Mitch said, setting the phone in the middle of the table, and they all echoed him.

"Hi, guys. I wish I was there with you."

Josh set his cup on the counter because his stomach was too jumpy now for any more caffeine, then took a seat at the table while Mitch recapped. A retired couple wanted to buy the Northern Star and the offer was *very* generous. They wanted to take up residence in the spring and it would be a private home. Evidently they had a bunch of kids and grandkids and it would be perfect for them.

They talked it out for a few minutes—what the property was worth. How long it would take them to vacate. The attic alone, which was the repository of several generations of family memories and debris, would probably take weeks. They talked about the impact on the town, with regard to the ATV trails, but in the end they all agreed it was a good offer.

"Honestly," Liz said, "my biggest concern is for Rosie. She sold her house when she moved into the lodge to pay off the last of the mortgage on the barbershop building, and Katie's apartment isn't big enough for both of them."

Ryan cleared his throat. "Lauren and I talked about it and if we accept this offer, she'll take her house off the market and I'll pay it off so Rosie can live there rent-free."

"That's very generous," Mitch said. "But I think we should subtract the payoff on Lauren's house from the profit on the lodge before we split up the money."

"I agree," Liz said, and Sean added his agreement.

They had it all figured out, Josh thought. They'd all spent days dwelling on the situation and they'd found a way to make it work. For him.

He suddenly realized he was cold. Not like a chill from a draft, but a cold that seemed to come straight from his bones. They were all willing to sacrifice the Northern Star to make him happy, but none of them wanted to. He could see it in their eyes and hear it in Liz's voice.

His family would be hurt. Whitford would lose the ATV access to town before they'd even gotten to reap some benefits from the work they'd put in so far. People like Dave Carmody and his boy would have to find a new place and start new traditions.

And then there was Rose. Even though the offer of Lauren's house was there, it wouldn't be her *home*. He tried not to think about Katie, but she was in his head, too.

"So what's it going to be?" Ryan said, his tone letting everybody know he wanted this conversation to be over.

One by one, starting with Mitch and going down by age as if it had been planned that way, they all agreed to the sale until it came down to what should have been Josh's vote.

"I guess it's unanimous, then," Mitch said, probably assuming he was a yes vote, and the silence that followed was a boulder crushing the air from Josh's lungs.

It was right there—everything he wanted. He'd have freedom from the lodge and enough money from his share of the sale to figure out what he wanted to do and where he wanted to do it.

"Wait." Everybody turned to him, but he couldn't seem to squeeze any more words out.

"Don't do this to yourself, kid," Sean said after a long silence. "It's a big deal, so it hits home a little, but we told you we're one hundred percent behind you. We mean that."

"It's okay, Josh." Liz's voice sounded small over the speakers, but he could hear the tremor.

"I can't." Even as he got the words out, he knew

they were the truth. He couldn't sell the Northern Star.

"This is an excellent offer and not one we're likely to see again anytime soon," Mitch said in a tone that was all business. "This season's going well, but we're not in a place yet to offer an outside manager financial security, so hiring a manager's not an option yet. You want out and this is the best opportunity."

"I wanted a choice." Josh dropped his head into his hands and rubbed his temples. "I just wanted a goddamn choice."

"Nothing's changed for the rest of us," Ryan said. "We can't run the lodge, so either you're in or we're all out."

"I can't do it." He stood abruptly, barely noticing that his chair fell over. "We're not selling. Sorry you all had to drive up here for nothing."

He walked out the back door, his chest so tight he felt as if he couldn't breathe, even though evidence to the contrary hovered in front of his face in frosty clouds. For the first time in his life he'd been given a choice. And he'd made it.

Picking up a chunk of wood, he hurled it as hard as he could at the barn.

KATIE HEARD THE footsteps coming up the stairs to her apartment and knew it had to be Josh. The door at the street locked automatically, requiring most people to be buzzed in. There was a spare key to all the barbershop building's doors, hanging at the lodge, but the footsteps sounded too heavy to be her mom's.

Suddenly, she didn't want to answer the door—didn't want the answer to the question that had been hanging over her head since yesterday—but she figured if he used his key on the street door, he wouldn't hesitate to use his key to the apartment if she didn't let him in. He had to be coming to tell her in person he was leaving town. Anything less and he probably would have called.

Since there was no avoiding the conversation, she opened the door just as he lifted his hand to knock, and she stepped back to let him in. He looked beat, both physically and emotionally. And he didn't kiss her as he walked past.

"Sorry I didn't call first," he said.

"No problem. You want a beer?"

"No, I'm good." He sat on her couch and flopped back against the cushion. He looked like a man who needed a hug, but he'd gone out of his way to put distance between them and she was having a hard time crossing it. "Did Rosie tell you we had an offer on the lodge?"

"Yeah, she mentioned it, assuming you had told me."

"Why didn't you say anything about it?"

"Why didn't *you?*" The exhaustion on his face

made her regret the sharp tone and she tried again. "I was hoping you'd tell me yourself. I don't know why you couldn't talk to me about it."

"I should have." He blew out a breath, staring at her ceiling. "I met with my brothers today. And Liz, by phone."

She waited a few seconds but, when he didn't say anything else, she went and sat next to him. "How did it go?"

"They all agreed to the sale."

Even though she'd been expecting it, the words cut a lot deeper than she'd prepared herself for. There was a part of her—the part that had been Josh's friend for their entire lives—that was happy for him, but most of her wanted to curl up and cry.

"I said no," he added in a low voice.

Oh, God, she thought, what did that mean? Even though she desperately wished he'd decide to stay in Whitford to be with her, she didn't actually want to be the reason he said no. Eventually he'd resent her as much as he resented the Northern Star. "Why? I thought it's what you wanted."

He lifted a hand, then let it drop back to his lap as if he didn't know what to say. Then he turned his head to look at her. "Selling the lodge to that couple was a forever thing. It would never be home again and not just for me. For Rosie and the others. Did you know I sleep in the room that was Uncle Leo's when he was a kid?"

She smiled and put her hand on his so he'd stop tapping it on his leg. He curled his fingers through hers. "I didn't know that."

"He carved my aunt Mary's initials in the windowsill."

She squeezed his hand. Generations of family might bring a sense of obligation, but they also came with a shared history and bond that couldn't be easy to break away from. "What are you going to do now?"

"What I've always done."

Something about the way he said it pulled at her heartstrings. He might not have been able to part with the place, but it hadn't been a total change of heart. In a way, he still hadn't really had a choice.

She let go of his hand so she could put her arm around his shoulders. Shifting a little into her embrace, Josh rested his head on her chest and tears blurred her vision as she stroked his arm

"Maybe plan B won't take as long as you think," she said. "The way business is going, it won't be long before you can hire a manager to run it for the family."

"Yeah." She could tell by the flat way he said it that he didn't really believe it.

"Do you want to go somewhere? We can go for a drive and find some food along the way."

"I should get back to the lodge. I've been driving around half the damn day and Rosie just read

me the riot act on the phone. Sean and Ryan want
to say goodbye before they head out."

"They're not staying over another night?"

"I guess not. The storm track shifted, so it might
be sloppy tomorrow. They all went out on the sleds
after I left this morning and now they want to get
home before the weather goes south. We've got a
guy and his kids checking out early, too."

"I'm glad you stopped by. And I'm glad you finally talked to me."

He grabbed the hand she'd been rubbing his arm
with and kissed her knuckles before holding it to his
cheek. "I'm sorry I didn't tell you sooner. I don't...
talk about things well."

"I know. Someday you'll realize talking things
out with somebody who cares about you can make
things easier. Maybe."

"I don't want to go home. I want to stay here with
you and relax." He kissed her palm before pushing
himself to his feet. "But I don't want my brothers hitting bad weather because they were waiting for me."

She stood and pulled him into a hug. "Call me
if you want to talk later, okay? After you see your
brothers again, I mean."

He kissed her, and it was a long, slow, sweet
kiss that made her tremble. "Thanks, Katie. I guess
you'll be stuck with me now, huh?"

She smiled, but after he'd let himself out, she

sank onto a chair and let out a breath. She'd been so sure he'd come to tell her he was leaving Whitford she was still having trouble believing he wasn't.

And even though she knew he was conflicted about the decision and probably angry to find himself still stuck in Whitford, she couldn't help but be a little bit glad.

SEAN WAS ALONE in the living room when Josh got home. The basement door had been ajar when he'd gone through the kitchen and he'd heard faint voices down there, so he'd assumed Andy and Rose had gone down there for something. And since he'd already noted that Ryan's and Mitch's vehicles were missing, he wasn't surprised that Sean was the only one there.

"Just me, I guess," Sean said when he saw Josh in the doorway. "Somebody just came out to ask for a lightbulb, so Andy and Rose went down to get it, but they knocked something over so they had to go back down. Said they'd be up in a few minutes."

Josh nodded. Sounded like a normal Saturday night at the old home-sweet-home.

"You okay, kid?"

"Sure." Josh shoved a hand through his hair and blew out a breath. "No, not really. What a total mind-fuck."

"Mitch said to tell you he's not responding to

the offer until Monday. You can still change your mind."

"I won't."

"Don't make yourself into some kind of martyr for our sakes, Josh."

"Screw you. I'm not playing the martyr here." He sat in one of the chairs and rested his elbows on his knees. "It wasn't all about you guys. Some of it, yeah, and Rosie. But it's me, too. There's a difference between wanting to get away from home and wanting home to go away forever."

"Okay. As long as you're not throwing yourself on the sword because of us." Sean relaxed against the couch. "Ryan couldn't wait. With the storm coming up from the south, he didn't want to chance it. I'm going to hit the road myself pretty soon."

"I feel like an asshole, making you drive here for nothing."

"It wasn't for nothing." He was quiet for a moment, then cleared his throat. "I owe you an apology, Josh."

"For what?"

"You know I had a really hard time growing up here. I wanted a regular house that didn't have strangers in it all the time."

"Katie had a hard time with it, too," Josh said, smiling at the memory of New Year's Eve.

"When I got out of the army, I told you I wanted

to visit Uncle Leo and Aunt Mary in New Hampshire before I came home."

"Nothing wrong with that. You hadn't seen them in a long time."

"I did want to see them, but I also didn't want to come back to Whitford. I was afraid I'd end up stuck here helping you and I didn't want to do that. I should have come anyway, and I'm sorry I didn't."

Josh winced, though he hoped it didn't show too much. Having one of his brothers around to shoulder some of the responsibility might have made a big difference in his attitude. Then again, two of them having shitty attitudes because neither of them wanted to be there wouldn't have done anything but drive away the rest of their customers.

"You had to do what was right for you," Josh told his brother. "And if you hadn't, you wouldn't have met Emma and we wouldn't be waiting for little Sprout. I'm going to be that kid's favorite uncle, just so you know."

The stress lines smoothed from Sean's face as he smiled. "I can't imagine not having Emma."

"I'm happy for you. One hundred percent."

"Thanks. So tell me about you and Katie. Is it serious?"

It wasn't *not* serious, but he still wasn't sure how to answer that. "We've been having fun, mostly. That probably sounds messed up, but we haven't exactly had a State of the Relationship talk."

"Hey, you're talking to a guy who pretended to be a total stranger's fiancé and ended up marrying her. I know 'messed up,' and two friends hooking up doesn't qualify."

"Even though it's Katie?"

Sean shrugged. "Maybe if it was a different one of us, but you and Katie have always been a pair. All you guys did was take it up a level."

What level that was, exactly, remained to be seen. He hadn't spent too much time analyzing what was going on between him and Katie, but if he was going to be stuck in Whitford for the rest of his life, he'd have to think about it pretty soon.

Stuck in Whitford for the rest of his life. He felt the familiar tightness in his chest and rubbed at the spot. At least this time he'd had some kind of choice, even it had been a crappy case of all or nothing.

"I hope you know Mitch will be crunching numbers as the year goes on, especially if you get the four-wheeler trail through here in the summer. As soon as we can, we'll see about hiring a manager."

Josh nodded, just as he had when Katie had brought up the possibility, but he didn't put too much faith in that plan. A manager whose last name wasn't Kowalski would expect a salary and benefits and all that good stuff. Business was increasing, but it would be a long time before the lodge could bear that kind of expense.

"I should probably get going," Sean said after he glanced at the clock. "It's a long drive."

They both got up and Sean went to the basement door. "Hey, Rosie, I'm leaving!"

Josh stood off to the side while Sean hugged Rose and shook Andy's hand. Now that the day was almost behind him, he just wanted to stretch out on the couch and close his eyes.

"I'm going to head out, too," Andy said. "I told Drew I'd stop by tonight and hang out for a while."

After the flurry of goodbyes, Josh closed the door and rested his forehead against the cold windowpane.

"Are you okay?"

Obviously that was the question of the hour. He turned to face Rosie, not bothering to force a smile. She'd see right through it, anyway. "I will be. It's not like everything took a turn for the worse. It's just more of the same now."

"I'm still sorry it didn't work out for you. I know it had to be a hard decision."

"I know it was the right one," he said, and the smile he gave her when she arched a doubtful eyebrow was genuine. "It really was and, yes, for *me*. I can't let her go to strangers. Besides, you and I make a good team, right?"

She touched his face, nodding, and he really hoped she wouldn't cry. "Yes, we do."

"I'm going to sit down for a few minutes and relax. Is everybody in now?"

"Bob Watkins and his cousin are still out, but he told me they wouldn't be back until nine or ten based on the trails they wanted to take. But everybody else is in."

So he'd be up until at least nine or ten, but probably later. "Okay, thanks."

He went into the living room, grabbing the TV remote on his way to the couch. But when he sat down, he didn't hit the power button. He could hear Rosie moving around in the kitchen and the low murmurs of a television coming from a guest room.

Closing his eyes, he let the familiar sounds of the Northern Star wash over him. It was a good thing he was used to it, because he wasn't going anywhere anytime soon.

"Excuse me?"

He opened his eyes and smiled at the woman who was staying in room three with her husband and two kids. Mrs. Grant—that was her name. "What can I do for you, Mrs. Grant?"

"I'm so sorry, but my youngest dumped his juice on the rug. It's more than we can blot up with tissues and toilet paper."

"It's not a problem." He stood up, still smiling. "I'll soak up what I can tonight and I'll steam it tomorrow."

Back to work, he told himself. He might not have chosen this life for himself, but at least he was good at it.

CHAPTER SIXTEEN

ONE OF THE nice things about living in what passed for "downtown" Whitford was that everything was within walking distance. So, when the snow kept everybody from wanting haircuts or library books, Katie and Hailey were free to lock up and play hooky.

Katie was ready when Hailey called. She'd already swept and mopped and sanitized everything, since it was obvious this nor'easter was keeping everybody inside. Now she just needed an excuse to hang the Closed sign and she'd be done for the day.

Her cell phone finally rang. "I thought you'd never call."

Hailey snorted. "If I wasn't responsible for salting the walkways, I'd have been gone already. I called Paige and there's no sense in going to the diner. Because Gavin rented her trailer, he offered to open the place, but it's mostly just coffee and he'll make sandwiches for the road crews or any random customers. But she won't be there."

"Well, I have food and drink and the library doesn't."

"I'll be there in fifteen minutes."

She'd just hit End when the phone rang again. Without looking, she answered and said, "What did you forget?"

"Is this one of those boyfriend tests?" Josh asked.

She laughed, though she was secretly thrilled to hear the word *boyfriend* come out of his mouth. It was the first time he'd used it. "I thought you were Hailey."

"Sorry, just me. How's business?"

"Funny. Business is so good I'm closing up shop. Hailey's coming over and we're going to eat junk food and watch TV for the rest of the day."

"She's walking, right? It keeps swapping between snow and sleet, so the roads might be slick."

"Yeah, she's walking. How are things with you?"

"I'm tired of moving snow, I can tell you that. But at least it's not the weekend, so I don't have to deal with people canceling at the last minute. I usually reschedule them instead of refunding their deposit—which we don't have to do, but I do when it's Mother Nature's fault—but we're pretty booked. Not easy to move people around."

She'd been wondering more about his state of mind than his reservation book, but it sounded like he was in a good mood, so she didn't push it. He'd called her yesterday morning and told her everything was okay with his brothers, but hadn't said much about how *he* felt. If not for the damn storm, she could have driven over and seen for herself, but the storm had been a little more severe than they'd forecast.

"It's supposed to wrap up by midday tomorrow," Josh said. "It's my turn to do the groomer run and I was thinking I'd go out tomorrow night so I can catch up on sleep Wednesday and Thursday nights. You want to go?"

"Sure." She'd gone out with him many times in the past, but it had been a while and she hadn't done it at all this year. Spending six or seven hours overnight doing eight miles per hour down the trail was best done with company.

"How about if I swing by about five? We can go to the diner, grab some dinner and get Ava to fill the thermos, and then we'll head to the clubhouse."

"I'll be ready."

"I was hoping to get over to see you tonight, but it's a mess out there. And Andy went out in the tow truck with Butch to pull morons out of ditches, so it's just your mom."

"I'd rather you stay home where you're safe," she said, and almost laughed at herself. It was a very *girlfriend* thing to say. "I'll see you tomorrow, anyway."

"Five o'clock. Good night, Katie."

"Good night."

She was still smiling when Hailey knocked on the window. After turning the sign around, Katie locked up and they went up to her apartment together. After shaking the snow out of their hair, they hung up their coats and put their boots on the mat she kept by the door.

"Just as I was leaving," Hailey said, "the phone rang."

"And you were dumb enough to answer it."

"Yeah. Can you believe this woman threw a fit when I told her I was closing? She said she was going to call the town and file a complaint."

Katie shook her head. "What did you do?"

"I gave her their number." She laughed and started rummaging through the cabinets. "Doesn't your mom send you home care packages?"

"I'm not away at college. I don't think grown-ups get care packages."

"Well, that sucks." She pulled out a package of store-bought cookies. "These will do. So tell me what's going on?"

"With what?"

"Paige told me about the offer on the lodge. And that Josh decided not to sell. How's he doing?"

Katie shrugged, snagging a cookie out of the package. "He seems okay with it, actually. He called me right after you did and he was in a good mood, except for having to clean up all this snow."

"So do you think he'll be ready to commit to you now?"

"Whoa." Katie frowned, holding up one hand. "What do you mean by *commit*?"

"If he's going to stay in Whitford, he should just marry you and get it over with."

"You're so romantic, Hailey. One, I don't want to be a consolation prize. And, two, there's no talk of marriage. He just called himself my boyfriend for the first time about ten minutes ago."

"You know, you're not as salacious as you used to be."

Katie laughed. "He wants me to go out in the groomer with him tomorrow night. Is that salacious enough?"

"Riding in the groomer?" She grimaced. "That's so boring. I did that once with a guy I was trying to impress about ten years ago. The fact he thought it was the greatest date ever was the end of that relationship before it even really started."

"Josh did mention once he had a little fantasy about me and him in the groomer."

Hailey made a *hmm* sound. "That could be salacious. If it is, you'll tell me, right?"

"Maybe."

"Do you love Josh?"

Katie frowned, snagging another cookie. "Of course I do."

"No, I mean do you *love* him, love him?"

"I've loved him like that for years, Hailey. You know that. And now that we're together, yeah. It's been harder in some ways, because now I'm not just doing it from afar. It's messy and there's the lodge thing and everything, but it's worth it."

"Even if he breaks your heart? Because I hate to say it, but refusing that offer wasn't like some kind of fairy dust that cured his need to roam."

"I should have sent you to voice mail. This is *not* fun snow-day talk." When Hailey only waited, still giving her the look that said she was only looking out for Katie's emotional welfare, she sighed. "Yes, it's worth it even if he breaks my heart. Which is why I'm not overthinking it to death like you apparently are. I'm taking it day by day and if the bridge crashes and burns in front of me, I'll cross that river when I come to it."

Hailey tilted her head, her eyebrows almost meeting over her nose. "I think you totally screwed that up."

"It's the sugar rush. Now shut up and turn the TV on. See if you can find something salacious for us to watch."

BY MID-TUESDAY morning, the snow had stopped falling and Josh got to work removing it all from the driveway and parking areas for the third—and hopefully last—time this storm. With Andy using the snowblower to clear the walkways, they were done by a little after noon, which was even earlier than he'd predicted.

Luckily he was better at predictions than the weatherman, who'd said four to six, so he was going to have plenty of time to jump in the shower before he picked up Katie. Spending seven hours in a groomer with a guy who smelled like sweat and two-stroke fumes probably didn't put a woman in a loving kind of mood. He might even grab a quick power nap, since he wouldn't be sleeping tonight.

He was whistling when he walked into the kitchen and he stopped to sniff the warm air. "Are those my special apple pies?"

"Of course." Rose pointed to where they were cooling on the rack. She made little individual pies, pinched off at both ends, like they did at fast-food restaurants. She'd wrap them in foil he could peel back as he ate while driving. "When's the last time you groomed the trails without my apple pies?"

"You're too good to me, Rosie." He kissed her cheek, but when he reached for a pie, she slapped his hand.

"Still too hot. Go take a shower."

"Yes, ma'am."

"Do you want me to heat up some beef stew before you go?"

He shook his head. "I'm picking Katie up and we're going to grab something at the diner before we head to the clubhouse."

"You make sure you share those pies with her."

He grinned at her over his shoulder as he left the kitchen. "Maybe, if she's nice to me."

It was already quarter after five when he pulled up outside the barbershop and beeped his horn. He wouldn't have been late, but halfway there when he'd realized he was so intent on seeing Katie after several days without her, he'd forgotten the pies. He had to turn around and go back for them.

He smiled when she stepped out onto the sidewalk, juggling stuff while making sure the door locked behind her. She'd remembered to dress in layers. It could be hard to regulate the heat in the groomer, because keeping the windshield clear sometimes meant overheating the cab. But other times it could get chilly and if, heaven forbid, there was a problem, she also had to be prepared to stand out in the cold for hours at a time. The groomer had died on him a few years back out in the middle of freaking nowhere in a cell dead zone and he'd worked on that sucker for five hours before a passing sledder finally stopped, then rode for help.

She shoved her snowmobiling gear and her heavy sweatshirt in the backseat of the truck, along with her hat and gloves, then climbed into the passenger seat. Before she even got the door closed, he leaned over to kiss her.

"I missed you," he said, and her face got that

soft, gooey feminine look that probably should have scared him, but didn't.

"Missed you, too. I didn't think it was ever going to stop snowing."

The diner parking lot was more full than he'd expected. Probably a bunch of people suffering from cabin fever after the storm had felt the need to get out. In Whitford, after business hours, there weren't that many places to get out *to*.

"They're busy for a Tuesday night," Katie said as he backed the truck into an open spot. "Either people were sick of being inside or Gavin's cooked up one hell of a special."

It wasn't the special. They overheard grumbling before they even got to an open table, and Ava looked cranky as hell when she slammed two coffee cups on their table. "The special's some weird, tropical chicken thing. It has coconut, Josh, so don't order it. Katie, you might like it, but fair warning—it comes served over rice, not with mashed potatoes. I swear to God, if a man in these parts doesn't get mashed potatoes with his flippin' supper, you'd think he was being starved half to death! Now... Josh, what do you want to eat?"

He gave her the charming Kowalski smile that usually worked pretty well on highly annoyed women. "I'll have whatever you think I should have, Ava. And I'll like it."

She laughed and rested her hand on his shoulder. "I've always liked you boys."

"And, if it's not too much trouble, if you could brew a pot of coffee for the thermos, I'd appreciate it."

"Grooming tonight, huh?" When he nodded, she tapped her pen on the order pad. "I guess you'll be wanting a double dose of the meat loaf, then?"

"That sounds perfect. Mashed and extra gravy, and you can keep whatever the veggie is."

"Katie, what'll you have?"

"I'll have a single serving of the same, please."

Ava nodded and started to walk away, but then she leaned down to squeeze Josh's shoulders. "I'm awful glad you're not leaving us, Josh."

"I hope people find somebody else to talk about soon," he said when Ava was out of earshot. "I hate being the center of attention."

"I'm glad you're staying, too, you know," Katie said quietly. "I mean, if you'd sold the lodge, I would have been happy for *you,* but not so much for me."

"It's a moot point now, anyway. I'm not going anywhere."

"Sometimes it seems like you're okay with that and sometimes it doesn't."

He didn't see much sense in lying to Katie. "Because sometimes I am and sometimes I'm not. But mostly I am. Hey, I get to hang out with you, right?"

"Is that enough for you?"

The question hung between them, the conversation suddenly a lot more serious than he liked to have. Especially in the middle of the Trailside Diner. "For now."

He saw a quick flash of uncertainty cross her expression, but then she smiled and seemed to shrug it off. "You wouldn't know what to do without me, Kowalski."

"I know I'd get bored as hell in the groomer tonight."

She laughed and, just like that, the tension was broken. "Maybe, if you're nice to me, I'll sing for you."

"Oh, please no," he groaned. Singing was not one of Katie's strengths. "Rosie made her special apple pies. You want me to share, don't you?"

The normal balance of their relationship restored, they talked about the usual stuff while they ate meat loaf and drank coffee. After she filled the thermos for him, Ava brought the check and Josh pulled enough cash out of his wallet to cover it.

"What are you doing?" Katie asked, holding a twenty in one hand.

"I got it."

"We've always gone Dutch."

"That was before." He shrugged and put out his hand to help her up. "I guess you must officially be my girlfriend now."

ONCE THEY ARRIVED at the snowmobile club's club-house and Josh opened the massive overhead door, Katie made trips back and forth between his truck and the groomer, transferring their stuff to the cab.

Josh grabbed a clipboard that hung on a nail by the door and started his inspection, which covered everything from the windshield wipers to the huge tracks that moved the thing. After she locked his truck, she put his keys in the inside pocket of her coat and zipped it up. Her dad had gone riding one year and lost his truck keys out on the trail. As far as she knew, they'd never been found, and not for a lack of looking.

Once Josh had pulled the groomer out and she'd helped him hook it to the two-ton drag, she climbed into the cab, which had as many controls and buttons as a plane cockpit, while he locked up the club-house. Finally they started churning their way down the trail. While she knew Josh had been through a lot of training to drive the thing, the concept was pretty simple. The blades on the groomer swept snow onto the trail and the drag packed it down. And it all happened at a crawl.

Because it was a little tricky navigating the machinery down the trail leading away from the club-house, Katie was quiet, which gave her mind plenty of time to wander.

I guess you must officially be my girlfriend now. Even though it was a dumb thing to say, since his picking up the entire check did not a relationship make, there had been something in his eyes that made her wonder if he was talking about more than not going Dutch. As if not selling the lodge meant he was resigned to staying, so he might as well make his relationship with her official.

She wasn't sure how she felt about that. On the one hand, she knew Josh wasn't the best when it came to talking about feelings. His feelings about the Red Sox taking the pennant next year? He'd talk about that all day long and half the night. But his feelings about anything personal or intimate were generally not up for discussion.

On the other hand, as she'd told Hailey, she didn't want to be a consolation prize. It felt like she'd come in second in a contest, then had been pronounced champion by default when the real winner was disqualified. It was silly, but part of her would probably always wish he'd had to actually step up and deliberately choose her.

"You're awfully quiet over there."

She shrugged. "I'm resting my voice so I can sing for you later."

"I'll be the first guy in the history of the club to run himself over with the groomer."

"I'm not that bad. Give me something to talk about."

"Andy and your mom."

She groaned. "I'd rather not."

"What's the matter? I thought you were okay with Andy?"

"I am." And she sincerely was. "It's just weird, talking about my mom being in a romantic relationship with somebody. I don't think she ever dated after my dad died. Not until Andy started visiting."

"I don't think she did, either. But I like him. He's a good guy."

"If she's happy, I'm happy."

Josh laughed. "If Rosie's happy, we're *all* happy."

After Josh got quiet for a few minutes while steering the groomer through a particularly winding stretch of trail, they talked about the Celtics for a while and griped about the price of gas. By the time three hours had passed, they'd gone through most of their standard conversation topics and half of Rosie's pies.

Katie was getting bored. And she was also thinking more and more about what she and Josh could be doing in the groomer besides flattening snow. Those thoughts were making her antsy and she was having trouble keeping up her end of the conversation.

"Okay, so no interest in the new NASCAR rules going into effect this year," he said, and she realized he'd been talking to her. "What do *you* want to talk about?"

"Maybe you should tell me a little more about that fantasy of yours. The one with you and me and the groomer." She could tell by the way he jerked his head to look at her and then shifted in his seat that it was probably a good one. "Isn't there a wide spot in the trail just a little further up?"

"Yeah." His voice sounded hoarse and he cleared his throat. "The trail's narrower than usual through here, so if there's night traffic, sleds can bottleneck behind the groomer. They cut in the pull-off so the groomer operator has room to let them go around."

"I haven't seen any night riders, but maybe we should take a little break. You can tell me all about it."

By the time they reached the pull-off and Josh maneuvered the equipment off the trail, Katie was already flush with anticipation. Not only did she know she was really going to enjoy this portion of her ride-along, but there was something almost naughty about it. While it wasn't exactly outside in the woods, it was pretty damn close.

"You're going to need to take those jeans off before you climb over here," Josh said the second the groomer had come to a complete stop.

"Jeez, doesn't a woman get a little foreplay?"

"Thinking about it all night doesn't count?" He snorted. "You are such a girl. I'll kiss you first. How's that?"

"You are such a guy."

She did end up kicking off her boots and wiggling out of her jeans without foreplay, but only for logistical reasons. The cab was small and, instead of a bench seat, there were basically two captain's chairs smooshed side by side. Trying to turn herself so she could get over to his lap without hitting her head or pressing any of the control buttons with her ass required a level of flexibility she didn't have.

And the bastard was laughing at her.

"This is *your* fantasy," she snapped. "How the hell did you picture this working?"

"I think you're more flexible in my imagination."

She would have hit him, but her arm being braced against the dash was all that was keeping her face from bouncing off the steering wheel. "Maybe you should imagine how you're going to get that condom on *after* I'm in your lap."

"This was a lot sexier when the real you wasn't actually involved, just so you know."

"I already took my jeans off, so we're doing it."

"If you leave an ass print on the inside of the windshield, I'm putting that in my report."

She really wanted to flip him off. "If I wasn't stuck right now, I'd get out and walk home."

He finally took pity on her and gently rearranged her, supporting her when necessary, until she was straddling his lap. It was a tight squeeze, getting her knees on either side of his thighs, but they managed.

"Better?" he asked, amusement still making his eyes sparkle.

She was hot, flustered and was probably going

to ache in a dozen places tomorrow, but she could feel the hard ridge of his erection through her panties and that made it worth the less-than-graceful effort. "Much."

Especially when he kissed her, his hand sliding up into her hair to hold her close. He nipped at her bottom lip and she sighed against his mouth. When his other hand slid between her legs, she moaned and kissed him harder, sweeping her tongue across his.

She rocked against his hand, but it wasn't enough. "How the hell are we supposed to get *your* pants off now?"

He smiled and reached between them to undo his fly and his zipper. "Raise up a little."

When she did, he lifted his hips and slid his jeans down enough so he could roll on the condom he'd stuck in his sweatshirt pocket.

"Must be nice," she muttered, wondering how she was supposed to get *her* jeans back on without getting out of the groomer.

"No, this is nice." He slid his hand under the elastic of her panties and stroked her until she was panting and growled his name in frustration.

Only then did he pull the fabric to one side and slide into her. She braced her hands against his shoulders as she moved her hips, taking him in inch by inch. Finally she'd taken him all and Josh threw his head back with a groan as she started to rock.

"Is this how your fantasy went?" she asked, nipping at his jaw.

"This is better," he said, his voice husky as he slid his hands under her shirt.

She quickened her pace as he ran his thumbs over her nipples, and his ragged breaths told her he was close to the edge. She rode him harder and he moved his hands to her hips, his fingertips pressing into her skin as he guided her.

The orgasm hit her fast and hard, and she gasped as he thrust hard upward, finding his own release. She moved against him, grinding, until the tremors faded.

"That was…a very nice fantasy," she said when they'd finally caught their breath.

"One of my favorites. And I think, by the time the windows are defogged, we might have figured out how to get your jeans back on."

In the end, it was easiest to get out of the groomer. She stood in the freezing cold and managed to pull her foot out of her boot, then shove it through the leg of the jeans and back into the boot without falling over. Then she had to repeat it for the other leg. By the time she ran around the groomer and climbed back into her seat, she was half-frozen.

Josh handed her one of her mom's little apple pies with the foil already partially peeled back. "I think we're going to have to act out this particular fantasy more often."

"Yeah, we need the practice."

He paused in the act of folding back the foil on his own pie to grin at her. "You know what would make it easier? If you wore that black dress."

"I think you need a new fantasy."

"You're the fantasy, Katie. The rest is just the setting."

Warmth curled through her insides, and she was smiling when she bit into the apple pie. Maybe they *should* go out in the groomer more often.

Rose snuggled closer to Andy and he squeezed her. "Cold?"

"Nope." The down-alternative comforter Josh had bought her for Christmas several years back, and given to her wrapped around her yarn store gift certificate, was far too warm for her to get chilled in bed. That and the body heat.

An old black-and-white Western was playing on the television, but she wasn't really watching it. The movie had been his choice, not hers, but she didn't really care what they watched when he cuddled with her like this. She'd missed cuddling a lot.

"I hope the kids are doing okay," she said during a commercial, because her mind had turned to them instead of focusing on the cowboys. "I always get nervous when they're out in the groomer all night in the middle of the woods in the freezing cold. So many things could go wrong."

"The club spares no expense when it comes to maintaining that equipment and I know Josh gives it a thorough inspection before he takes it out on the trail, because I've seen him do it. And they're together."

"It's a good opportunity for them to talk."

He laughed. "Not much else to do when you're putting through the woods at eight miles an hour."

"I hope they have enough food. And they're going to drink too much coffee. It's not good for their stomachs, especially since Katie's only going to sleep for a couple of hours before she opens the barbershop."

"You worry too much, Rose."

"Do not. Besides, what else am I going to do?"

"You could talk to me instead."

Rose knew he didn't mean for her to talk to him about the kids. He wanted to talk about *them*. She'd known it was coming, but she was still trying to sort through just how she felt about Andy Miller.

"I don't think what we have here is just casual anymore," he continued.

"It may have started as casual, but this part—you being here with me right now—was never casual. I'm not a casual kind of woman."

"I didn't think you were. But you're also not a woman who wears her emotions on her sleeve, either. It's hard for me to know where I stand with you."

She rolled onto her side so her head rested on his shoulder. "I've only ever told one man I loved him and I was married to him for a good part of my life. I'm not quite ready to say it again."

"I'm a patient guy." He kissed the top of her head. "All I need is a little encouragement that we're headed in that direction."

"Consider yourself encouraged, then. I like your company, Andy, and I'd like to have more of it. I know you rent your place, and it doesn't really make sense for you to keep running back and forth between here and there. Unless you prefer it that way."

"Are you asking me to move in with you, Rose Davis?"

She laughed, feeling a little bit scandalous. "I guess I am."

"I'd like that."

"I have to talk to Josh first," she said. "When push comes to shove, the kids own this house and I work for them."

"Your relationship with them could never be described as just that." He took his arm from around Rose so he could prop himself up on it and see her face. "Before you talk to him, though, I have a thought I'd like to run by you."

She listened to what he had to say, then took a deep breath. "I need to think about that, Andy. I need to see how things are. Promise me you won't say anything to him right away."

"Not until you tell me it's okay. Nobody knows those kids like you do."

CHAPTER SEVENTEEN

ON SATURDAY MORNING, after making sure all his guests got out on the trails okay, Josh drove over to Mitch and Paige's house. Mitch had business travel looming on his horizon and he wanted to finish the home office before he left so his time at home could be spent with his wife and not remodeling.

The rest of the house had been finished in a hurry so Paige could host Thanksgiving, but they'd been putting off the home office. Now, with the clock ticking, Mitch had asked Josh and Drew for help.

By the time he got there, Drew had already arrived. They were still in the kitchen when Josh walked in, and he held up his hands. "I thought there was work to be done."

"Just waiting on you, as usual." Mitch led the way down the hall and into a large room that had great windows looking out over the yard.

It also had fresh paint over new Sheetrock and trim, and new switches, outlets and plates. Even the light fixtures were in place. "I thought you needed help finishing this room."

"Wait until you see the garage."

"This can't be good," Drew muttered, but they both followed Mitch back through the house and out the side door into the garage.

There was an army of massive cardboard boxes in front of them, all with photos of a different piece of office furniture pasted on the sides.

"Oh, hell no," Josh said. "This is above and beyond, Mitch. And you know it, too. That's why you didn't tell us up front."

"You can't put together furniture?" Mitch gestured at the boxes. "They all come with directions. And there are pictures even."

"You couldn't just go buy shit at the furniture store so they'd deliver it all put together?" Drew asked.

"Paige saw this stuff online and fell in love with it. It was less expensive than some of the stuff I looked at, so I told her to order it."

Josh snorted. "It's less expensive because it'll take you three days and a bottle of Valium to put it all together."

"Or three guys only one day."

"Jesus, Mitch." Josh hated this stuff. It was like doing a big, heavy 3-D jigsaw puzzle that required tools.

"I'll beg if I have to," Mitch told him. "When they started rolling these cartons off the delivery truck, I lost all my pride."

"How do you start and build a successful business blowing up buildings and not know better than to order assemble-yourself office furniture. A small bookcase is okay in a pinch, but that big-ass box over there has a picture of a desk on it."

"There are two," Mitch admitted. "His and hers desks."

Josh and Drew both stayed silent, staring at the line of boxes.

"It's for my wife," Mitch said. "If I don't get these done, she might try to finish building them while I'm away and hurt herself."

Josh laughed. "Really? That's low, even for you."

"I told you I'm not above begging."

"Fine." Josh threw up his hands in surrender. "Which one are we doing first?"

"The bookcases. They take up the most floor space to build, but the least amount of room space while building other stuff," Drew said. They both looked at him and he shrugged. "Mallory loved this shit."

Josh and Mitch each grabbed an end of a bookshelf box while Drew held the door. When Josh passed by him, he paused for a second. "How's that going, anyway?"

"The divorce is final. I'm now officially a middle-aged guy with no wife, no kids and a killer loan so I could buy Mal's half of the house."

"Sorry to hear that."

Their marriage had ended right around the time Mitch and Paige had gotten together and, looking back, it was hard to say which had created the bigger buzz around town.

Shortly after their tenth wedding anniversary, when Drew had pushed, Mallory had confessed she not only didn't want children, but she never had. It had gone downhill from there.

Once they got started building Paige's furniture, it wasn't as bad as Josh had feared it would be. They got a good rhythm going, almost like an assembly line, and managed not to jab any fake wooden corners through her new walls.

They were about halfway done when Drew brought up the subject Josh had managed to go almost an entire half day without hearing about.

"I was glad to hear you decided against selling the lodge, Josh."

Josh focused on setting the screw in his hand in the right place before he responded, so he had time to moderate his tone. He kept telling himself people were bound to get it out of their systems at some point. "Yeah. It was the right thing to do."

"I've got a lot of memories of the Northern Star myself, since I was always running around with Mitch."

Josh remembered. Sometimes it seemed like everybody had memories of the lodge, or at least a good reason for him not to sell it. Of course, none of them wanted to *run* it, but everybody was glad he'd be sticking around to take care of what was important to them.

"I saw one of the rooms down the hall is empty," he said, because changing the subject was something he was becoming very good at. "If you buy assemble-at-home furniture for whatever that room's going to be, it'll be assemble-alone furniture."

"That's going to be the baby's room." Josh and Drew both stopped what they were doing to stare at him. "When she gets pregnant, which she's not. Yet."

"But soon, huh?" Drew asked.

"That's up to Mother Nature." Mitch grinned. "We're certainly doing our part to make it happen."

"I don't want to hear anything about sex," Drew muttered. "From either of you."

Josh went back to what he was doing, which was trying to tell if he was holding the board he needed and the instructions in the same direction. He had to admit, sex was the one thing he had going for him.

Maybe it would snow again soon and they could make another groomer run. He'd take any perk of the job he could get.

KATIE MADE A whooping sound and laid down her cards. "Gin!"

Muttering a curse, Josh threw his cards on the

table and pushed more of his M&M'S across the table. She had almost all the chocolate now.

"You're not really paying attention," she said, since she'd been thinking it most of the evening.

"This isn't the game I want to be playing with you right now."

"If you'd come to my place instead of me coming here, we wouldn't be playing gin rummy for M&M'S."

"I might have, but the couple staying in room two are not only new to the trail system, but new to snowmobiles. I want to be here, where I can be reached and have easy access to my truck and trailer, just in case." He gathered the cards and started shuffling them. "That's how it is. Weekends I'm tied to the lodge and weekdays, when I have a little more freedom, everybody has to go to bed so they can work in the morning."

This was one of those pissed-at-the-world days he'd told her about, she thought. And there wasn't much she could do about it. "I heard you spent the day putting together Paige's office furniture."

He dealt the cards, scowling at the deck the whole time. "This town will talk about anything."

"Always has."

She was only a couple of cards away from taking the last of his M&M'S when the lodge phone rang. Frowning, Josh pushed back from the table to answer it just as Rose walked into the kitchen.

"I got it," he told her.

Katie took advantage of the short reprieve from the game—and the fact her mom was there to guard her cards and chocolate—to head to the bathroom.

When she came back out, Josh was putting on his coat and boots. "I told you."

"Room two? Are they okay?"

"Yeah. Just a little undereducated about important details like gas mileage. They're not too far out, so I'm just going to meet them with the gas can."

"Do you want me to go with you?"

"No, I won't be very long, so there's no sense in getting all bundled up." He grabbed his keys off the hook and opened the door. "Don't touch my M&M'S."

Once he was gone, she might have cast a sideways glance at his tiny pile of chocolate, but her mother gave her a look and she didn't touch them.

"I hardly get to spend any time alone with you anymore," Rose said, taking silverware out of the drying rack to put in the drawer.

"Where's Andy?"

"Helping Butch Benoit work on the transmission in Fran's car. He said he'd probably be late, so he was just going to go straight home from there. But I want to talk about you. How have you been doing?"

Katie laughed. "I'm here half the time, Mom. You can see how I am."

"Are you happy?"

The question hit her like a sucker punch and she sat down hard in her chair. Was she *happy?* "Why wouldn't I be?"

"I don't know. Just checking. I'm your mother, remember, so I'm supposed to keep track of these things."

She was happy enough, but she had a feeling that answer wouldn't satisfy her mom. The barbershop was doing well and she had Josh. Granted, things had been a little touchier since he'd turned down the offer on the lodge, but emotional upheaval did that to people.

Until he put it behind him, though, their relationship was treading water. They weren't sinking, but they weren't making any progress toward distant shores, either.

"It was rough on him, you know," she said, because maybe she *did* want to talk to her mom. Not only was Rose her mother, but she knew Josh better than anybody else, too. "It's going to take him some time to reconcile how much he *wanted* to leave with how much he *needed* to keep the lodge."

Rose put her hand over Katie's and leaned down to look at her face. "Do you think he can be happy here with you, honey?"

Katie saw the love and concern in her mother's eyes and couldn't lie. "I hope so, more than you can even imagine, but I really don't know."

EVEN THOUGH HE woke in a much better mood than he'd gone to bed in, Josh didn't shed any tears when the last guests—who were naturally the couple from room two, running an hour past checkout time—drove away.

After he stripped their room, which was the last one he had to do, he went into the kitchen to see what he could scrounge up for lunch. Then, as long as nothing went wrong between now and then, he was going to call Katie and try to drag her out for a ride on his sled with him. It wasn't really built for two, but she'd just have to snuggle close.

He'd just finished demolishing his second bologna sandwich when Rose walked through carrying a basket of dirty towels. "Did they finally leave?"

"Yeah. I made a note next to their name in the book so if they come back, we can give them a little extra coaching."

"Maybe we'll be so busy next winter they won't be able to get a room."

Josh didn't want to think about next winter. That was nothing but a reminder he'd still be here next winter. And the winter after that and the winter after that. And now, thanks to the ATV trail access coming together, it would be year round. It was a good thing. He knew that in a practical, logical way. But emotionally it made him tired.

"What's the matter, hon?"

"Nothing." He tried to shake it off while he dumped his plate in the trash.

"I know you're still upset about the offer on—"

"Maybe I'm still upset about it because people won't stop *talking* about it. *Hey, Josh, you almost escaped, but you didn't and you just need to resign yourself to that.* Maybe if everybody just let it drop, it would be a lot easier to forget."

She shook her head, tears sparkling in her eyes, and he had to fight a sudden urge to bolt out the back door. "Escaped? Resigned? You're more unhappy than you're letting on."

"I know you worry about me like a mom, Rosie, but you have to let me be."

"I do worry about you like a mom. I also worry about my daughter."

He reminded himself this was Rosie and managed not to raise his voice. "I'm doing the best I can to be what everybody needs me to be."

"What about what *you* want to be?" she demanded, and she didn't seem to have any trouble raising *her* voice.

"I don't *know* what I want to be, dammit." He stopped, inhaling what he hoped was a calming breath. "No, that's not right. I do know what I want to be. I want to be happy. I want Katie to be happy. And that scares the hell out of me because I don't think I can do both."

"You can't make Katie happy until you're happy, Josh. That's how it works."

"Please, Rose, just…" He grabbed his coat off the hook by the door. "I'm going for a ride. If Katie stops by, tell her I'll call her later, okay?"

"You shouldn't go out on the sled alone when you're upset."

"I'm not going to be stupid. I just need some space. Some quiet so I can try to get my head on straight and stop being an asshole to people who love me."

When she smiled and kissed his cheek, he wrapped his arms around her and held her close. "I'm trying, Rosie."

"I know, Josh. Just remember everybody needs some help sometimes and you have people who love you, even when you're being an asshole."

CHAPTER EIGHTEEN

JOSH WAS SURPRISED when he emerged from the office a little before noon on Tuesday, his head aching from hours of catching up on transferring stuff from paper to the computer, to find Mitch sitting at the table with Rosie and Andy. It struck him as ironic, seeing as how he'd just been thinking foul thoughts about his computer-happy oldest brother. Ledger books had been fine for generations, so Josh didn't see why they weren't fine now.

"Hey, Mitch. Come to mooch food?"

He gave a closemouthed smile and nodded, since his mouth was full of pastry.

"I called him and asked him to come over," Rose told him. "Andy and I have something we'd like to discuss with you boys."

Josh paused halfway to the coffeepot. What the hell was that supposed to mean? He knew Andy had been spending a lot of time with Rose lately, but that sounded as though it could be the opening of a getting-married announcement.

He loved Rosie, but he'd be pissed if he'd passed

up the opportunity to sell the lodge and she up and left *him*.

Deciding he might need the coffee after all, he poured himself a mug before taking a seat at the table. He glanced at Mitch, who only shrugged.

"You know Andy and I have been spending a lot of time together," Rose began. "And it's pretty obvious he's been spending the night lately."

Josh and Mitch both shifted uncomfortably in their chairs. She was way too close to being the mom of the house for them to want to be a part of any conversation even hinting at sex.

"We were thinking it would make more sense if he just moved in. With me."

Josh's mind seemed to be having a little trouble keeping up with the conversation. So it wasn't an engagement announcement, then. They just wanted permission for Andy to move in, from Mitch, as the oldest he guessed, and him, as the guy who ran the place.

Andy cleared his throat. "And if you guys don't have a problem with that, it also brings up the fact I'd be here all the time and, between Rosie and I, we can run this place for the family. I can take care of stuff in exchange for my room and board so you, Josh, would be free to do…whatever you want to do."

Josh sat back in his chair as the implications of that sank in. He'd be free to leave. He could leave

Whitford, the family could keep the Northern Star and Rosie could keep her home. It was pretty much everything he wanted, tied up with a neat bow.

He looked over at Mitch, who just held up his hands in an *I don't know what to say* gesture. He knew the feeling.

"Wow." Thoughts were careening around his head and he couldn't seem to grasp on to any of them long enough to form a sentence.

"That's a big commitment," Mitch said. "The lodge, I mean. Not Rosie. Although, that's a big commitment, too. I just meant that—hell, I'm happy for you guys."

Rose laughed and reached over to cover Mitch's hand with her own. "Thank you, honey."

All of the careening thoughts in Josh's head slammed to a stop as one word filled his mind. *Katie.*

At some point along the way, he'd stopped pretending they were doing the friends-with-benefits thing. Or if they were, at some point he could see them signing on for the full, long-term benefits package. They were best friends, unquestionably compatible in bed, and he knew he'd never want to spend all his time with any other woman.

But he also knew that the second Andy Miller opened his mouth and offered to run the lodge with Rose, his relationship with Katie was doomed.

The rush when he realized what those words

meant for him was too intense to be ignored, and if he tried he'd always wonder, *What if?* And someday he'd blame Katie for it.

"When are you thinking of moving in?" Mitch asked, and Josh was glad he was there to be the guy who could think straight.

"Anytime," Andy said. "Hell, Josh could take off tomorrow if he wanted to."

Tomorrow. He could get in his truck, put it in Drive and not have to be home to tell strangers where to park in his yard or get up before six in the morning to make them coffee. He could just drive until he found a place he wanted to be.

"Not quite," Mitch said, chuckling. "We'd have to get you added to the bank account and the account at the market and some legal stuff. It'd be a few days."

"I…" Josh forced himself to stop and take a breath. He needed to slow it down. "Maybe I should stay through the season."

"Why?" Rosie asked. "It's all under control and you know if you stay until spring, you'll get all wrapped up in the ATV trails and you'll never leave."

You'll never leave. How many times over the years had he tried to resign himself to that possibility and failed? He couldn't even begin to count.

"As far as you moving in," Mitch said to Andy, probably because Josh had stopped making words again, "that's between you, Rose and Josh. The rest of us own the lodge, too, but we don't live here. But nobody's going to make managing the Northern Star a condition of you being with Rose."

"That's true," Josh agreed. He sat up straight and gave himself a mental slap upside the head. He needed to get his shit together and figure out what the hell was going on. "I don't have any problem with you moving in, but you don't have to earn your keep. Just make Rosie happy and it's all good."

"Look, son. I've known your family my entire life. I knew your parents well and I've watched you kids grow up. Mitch and my son were almost inseparable as kids. And while I might not have been here, thanks to Rosie's stubborn streak—" he paused to smile at her "—I know you've sacrificed for this lodge and for your family."

"And they've sacrificed for me. They were willing to give up the Northern Star and everything it means to make me happy."

"I bet walking away from that was the hardest thing you've ever done."

Josh nodded. "Yeah, but it was the right thing and, even if I'm still doing this when I'm eighty, I'll never regret not selling."

"You're a good kid," Andy said quietly. "I'm here and I'm not going anywhere, so take this chance."

Maybe if the rush had died down and his mind wasn't reeling from all the possibilities in front of him, it would be easier to think. But the excitement was still burning and he was afraid it wasn't going to die down.

He looked at Rose, because nobody could understand better than Katie's mother what his leaving would mean. He saw the knowledge in her eyes, but she just gave him a gentle smile. "You'll never be truly content until you feel like you're free to make your own choices, Josh. I believe that in my heart."

She was right. He knew it with the same conviction he heard in her voice. But to leave, he'd have to say goodbye to Katie, and all he could do was hope like hell she understood.

Or maybe, he thought as he glanced at Rose with guilt growing in his gut, he could talk Katie into going with him.

KATIE DROVE UP to the Northern Star and killed the engine. She'd been out doing errands and decided to stop into the lodge to visit her mom. She wasn't sure what Josh was up to, but his truck was there, so he had to be around. Unless he was out on his sled, of course.

When she walked through the door, she was a little surprised to see Andy holding her mom in the middle of the kitchen. Rose was more of a quick hugger, unless somebody was upset.

"Mom?" Rose turned as Andy dropped his arms,

and Katie was relieved she wasn't crying, at least. "What's up?"

It seemed like she hesitated for a long moment before she took hold of Andy's hand. "Andy's going to move in with me."

"Oh." Katie wasn't sure what to say. She really was happy for her mom, but it was still a little weird to see her mother going through the process of dating and eventually falling in love. "Congratulations."

"Thank you, honey." There was more her mom wanted to say—Katie was sure of it—but when Rose didn't add anything else, Katie chalked it up to a weird vibe.

"Is Josh around?"

Her mom nodded, her lips pressed in a tight line, but it was Andy who said, "He's in the office, I think."

"Thanks." She went through the house, trying to solve the puzzle of her mom's strange silence. Rose rarely held back if she had something she wanted to say.

The office door was open, but she rapped on the doorjamb as she stuck her head in. "Hey, what are you doing?"

He was writing something, and she saw what looked like guilt flash across his face when he saw her. "I was going to stop by your place in a little while. I thought you'd still be in the shop."

"I closed early. Business was slow and I had errands to run." She moved closer to the desk and saw he was making a schedule for the Northern Star—what needed to be done and when he usually did it. "Afraid you're going to start forgetting things in your old age?"

"Did you see Rosie?"

"Yeah, downstairs. She told me Andy's moving in with her, which is kind of…" Whatever she was going to say drifted into oblivion as the pieces of the puzzle fell into place. Andy was moving in—a man to help Rose around the lodge—and he'd need to know what chores Josh did. "You're leaving."

"I was coming to see you," he said again. "I planned to be there when you closed the shop, but I didn't know you were closing early."

He was leaving. Andy was moving in with her mother and he was going to take over for Josh so he could leave Whitford like he'd always dreamed of doing. The pain was so real—so physical—she almost doubled over.

"You're supposed to wash my Jeep for a year." She said it jokingly, knowing it was a dumb thing to say, but wanting to buy herself a few seconds to process what was going on here.

After the roller coaster the offer on the lodge had been, she'd thought they'd have a smooth ride for a while, but this was one doozy of a pothole.

"Come with me."

And the pothole caved, growing into a sinkhole. "Josh, that's crazy."

"Why? I still want to go see things I've never seen and do things I've never done, but I want to see them and do them with you."

The excitement in his eyes and the lure of seeing new things was enticing, but she refused to let herself get swept away by emotion. "I can't just leave everything behind, Josh. I own a business. You own a business. What are we supposed to do? Drive around the country, washing dishes for food and gas money?"

"I have a little money. And, even if I didn't, why not?"

"Seriously? You've waited your entire life for the opportunity to be a drifter?"

"I need to see what's out there to know what I want, Katie. Let's go together."

"I can't leave my mom."

"She won't be alone. Andy's moving in with her and they'll be doing their own thing, anyway."

"Okay, fine. I don't *want* to leave my mom. I don't want to leave my barbershop. I've never once, in all the time you've known me, ever talked about leaving Whitford, have I?"

The excitement faded and she knew he'd realized she wasn't going to go.

"I guess I thought maybe you'd want to go with me."

"Like how I thought maybe you'd want to stay with me?"

"You, more than anybody, know how I feel. I've spent my whole damn life waiting for it to be my turn to go."

"And now's your chance, so go."

He rubbed his hand over his mouth, like he wasn't sure what he wanted to say.

"You never made me any promises, Josh. You're right. I know you've spent your whole life waiting for this and I'm not going to hold you back."

"You're making me choose between you and the life I always wanted."

"The fact you still think of me and the life you always wanted as two separate things means there isn't really a choice."

"What the hell is that supposed to mean?" The desperate tone in his voice was almost her undoing, but she told herself she could cry later. That she *would* cry later, because the only thing that had ever hurt as much as this was the day her dad had died.

"I've loved you for as long as I can remember, Josh," she said. "But I don't want to spend the rest of my life watching you turn bitter and hateful because you never got out of Whitford, so I'm taking away the choice and saying goodbye."

There wasn't anything else left to say, so she turned to leave, but his voice stopped her. "Katie, please. I need you."

"You and I will always be friends. I'm here. Call me, email me, whatever. But you need to go find the thing that's going to make you happy. I'm just sorry it wasn't me."

This time she didn't look back. She went out the front door so her mother couldn't catch her and got into her Jeep. Without a single glance in the rearview mirror, she drove down the driveway and away from Josh, and she made it almost halfway to town before the tears started falling.

TWO DUFFEL BAGS, Josh thought, looking around his bedroom for the last time. Not the last time ever, of course, because Rosie wasn't going to put up with him not visiting. But it would be a while before he saw it again.

Everything he needed to go out and find himself fit in two duffel bags, which didn't seem like it should be enough. But he'd tossed his boots on the floor in the backseat of his truck, along with his small toolbox, and his clothes and toiletries fit in the two bags. And the snow globe Katie had given him for Christmas. It had hurt like hell to look at their happy, smiling faces in the picture, but he couldn't leave it behind.

He hadn't seen her in the week since he told her he was leaving. He'd talked to her on the phone a couple of times, but he could hear the strain in her voice. Seeing her face-to-face would be too hard on both of them.

So he'd concentrated on the process of handing over the lodge to Andy and figuring out what he needed to take with him. The rest would all be here waiting for his visits, like the others' bedrooms did. He did a sweep of the bathroom to make sure he hadn't missed anything vital, then cursed himself for a moron when he saw his cell phone charger still plugged in next to his bed. He coiled that up and stuck it in the side zipper of one of the duffels and then he was done.

After carrying them downstairs, he set the bags by the front door and went in search of Rose and Andy. She was nowhere to be seen, but he found Andy in the kitchen, sneaking a cookie from the jar.

"Ready to go?" Andy asked, offering him a chocolate chip cookie.

Josh took it, even though there was a box on the passenger seat of his truck stuffed with enough baked goods to last him to the Mississippi or farther. "I guess so. Where's Rosie?"

"When I left her, she was sitting on the bed, looking at your baby pictures."

"Oh, Jesus." Josh shoved the entire cookie in his mouth and chewed. This sucked.

"I'm sure she heard you come down the stairs, so I expect she'll be down when she gets herself together."

Josh swallowed hard to get the mass of cookie down. "How about you? You got any questions for me before you go?"

"I think we've covered everything. And I'm pretty sure there's nothing about this place Rose doesn't know."

"Got that right. She even knows the stuff you don't want her to. But, anyway, the division of labor's always come pretty easy to us. If it makes you sweat, it's my job. If it makes the guests feel at home, it's her job."

Andy laughed. "Sounds about right. You know where you're headed?"

"I'm going to have a steak in Kansas City." He shrugged when Andy's eyebrow shot up. "Years ago, when Mitch first started traveling for work, he told me about the steaks there. Said there weren't steaks like that anywhere else in the world and, dumb as it sounds, of all the things they've seen and done, I was most jealous of that steak."

Andy grinned. "Then, by God, you should go get you a steak."

"And on my way to Kansas City, I'm going to think about what I'd like to do for work and where I want to do it. Maybe someplace that won't give me frostbite."

"You make sure you call Rose on a regular basis. I'm the one that gets to hear about it if you don't. Maybe text her some pictures along the way."

"I will. And, trust me, I'm going to miss her as much as she's going to miss me. We've been a team for a long time."

"Stop it or you'll make me cry," Rose said as she walked into the kitchen. "I'm *not* going to cry, dammit."

Oh, she was definitely going to cry. The only question was whether she'd be able to hold off until he was gone. And, since he knew that was what she wanted, he needed to do this clean and fast, like ripping off a bandage. "You going to walk me out to my truck?"

"Of course."

She managed to keep a smile on her face, but the closer he got to the front door, the more his emotions weighed on him, until he felt as if he was wading through semidry cement. He picked up his bags and went out the front door, then stopped on the porch and took a deep breath.

The porch had always been his favorite part of the lodge. It was too cold to sit out this time of year, but nothing beat a cold beer on a muggy summer night on the Northern Star's front porch.

"You look like you're going to a funeral, not setting off on a grand adventure."

He snorted. "Grand isn't in the budget."

"You'll be fine. You have some savings and we'll deposit your share in your account so you can draw from it every month."

"I wish you two would take more. It doesn't seem fair."

"Honey, we don't need more than what we have."

Because they had each other, he thought. That was what mattered. "I lost my best friend, Rosie."

"Oh, hush. My girl has loved you for so long I probably made a note of it in her baby book. You'll never lose her."

"I need you to understand I have to do this. It rips me up to hurt her, but—"

She captured his cheeks between her hands, leaving him no choice but to shut up and look her in the face. "I do understand. And when the hurt wears off a bit, so will Katie."

"I hope so. No matter where I am, I'm going to need a friend and—to me—that'll always be her."

"I want you to promise me two things."

"I'll try."

"To hell with trying, young man. I've given you and your brothers and your sister as much of the best years of my life as I've given my own daughter and—"

"Okay!" He held up his hand to stop her. "I'll promise. What are the two things?"

"You're all as stubborn as a June day is long, but when it comes to pride you got a concentrated dose. Promise me if you don't find what you're looking for out there or you get lonely, you'll come home."

He gave a short laugh. "Wouldn't that be great,

if after all this time whining about leaving, I turn around and come home?"

"That's exactly what I'm talking about. I don't want to hear that. You promise me if you want to come home, that'll you'll damn well come home."

Home to a lodge he couldn't wait to leave behind and a woman whose heart he'd broken. But he couldn't deny Rosie anything when she looked at him like this. "I promise. What's the second thing?"

She gripped his hands in hers so hard it was almost painful. "Promise me you'll stop beating yourself up and embrace this opportunity. Enjoy your freedom and find what it is you're looking for in life, or all of this was for nothing."

All of this meaning the pain he'd caused Katie and, by extension, her mother. And himself. "I promise."

She gave him a skeptical look and he laughed. "I swear, Rosie. I promise both things."

"Good." Her bottom lip began trembling and he saw the tears glimmering in her eyes before she grabbed his face and kissed his cheek. "Now, go so I can cry in peace. I love you, Josh."

He hugged her hard and pressed his face to her hair. "I love you, too, Rosie."

"Go."

He went because he was afraid if he was still there when her control crumbled and she cried for him, he might not be able to go anymore. In his rearview mirror he saw Andy step forward to put his arm around her and they both waved.

He beeped the horn as he neared the end of the driveway and didn't look back again.

CHAPTER NINETEEN

"HEY, DO YOU have plans for Valentine's Day?"

Katie actually pulled the phone away from her ear to make a *what the hell* face that Hailey couldn't see on the other end of the line. Sure, she had plans for Valentine's Day, because in the two weeks since the love of her entire life had driven out of town—to get a steak in Kansas fucking City, according to his email—she'd found herself a hot new guy who was going to romance the hell out of her on the most romantic day of the year.

"No, I don't have plans" was all she said out loud.

"Neither do I. Which isn't a surprise since there's an extreme lack of romance-worthy men in Whit-ford. Let's do something together."

Katie smiled, which she hadn't been doing enough of lately. "Are you asking me to go on a date with you for Valentine's Day?"

"Yes. Yes, I am. You should know up front, though, that I'm not going to let you kiss me good-night." There was a short pause. "Well...probably not. Depends on how much I drink."

The laughter felt good and Katie decided that, no matter what Hailey wanted to do for Valentine's Day, she was going along for the ride. She was tired of moping. Tired of not having any appetite and crying herself to sleep.

Josh had left. He'd never made any secret of the fact he would if he got the chance, so she would try to treasure the time she'd had with him the same way she did all the other gifts he'd given her and try to put aside the heartache.

"Where are we going?" she asked.

Hailey sighed. "That's where I'm having an issue. I want to dress up and have a few drinks and dance."

"We'd be the talk of the diner for months."

"So you see the problem. The nearest bar with a dance floor is like forty minutes away."

"Screw it. Rent a motel room and we'll split the cost. We can put up signs that the library and the barbershop won't be opening until ten on Friday. I need to get out and so do you."

She hadn't really done anything but work and hide in her apartment since the Super Bowl, which had been the least fun she'd ever had watching football. Without Josh, it wasn't the same, and the other men at Max's had acted weird, as if they were looking at her differently now. Instead of just being one of the guys, she'd been a *girlfriend*. Apparently, it changed things.

She knew that would pass, as the pain eventually would, but for right now everything was awkward, all of the women in town were fussing over her and she was in real danger of becoming a hermit.

When the night came, Katie wore the black dress. It was too nice to be kept as some kind of shrine to sleeping with Josh for the first time, so she put it on and made up her mind to attach fun new memories to the dress.

"Damn, you look hot," Hailey told her when Katie slid into her passenger seat.

"So do you." Hailey was wearing a red jersey dress with a gold necklace and hoop earrings. She closed her door and buckled her seat belt. "Let's dance."

Four hours later, Katie was hot, tired and her stomach hurt from laughing. She hadn't danced like that in years and she was going to be sorry tomorrow when she had to be on her feet all day. Tonight, she didn't care.

Sliding onto her barstool, Katie pushed the half-empty glasses, which they'd abandoned when ABBA blasted out of the speakers, toward the bartender. "Two fresh drinks, please."

"This is the most fun I've had in years," Hailey said, still slightly out of breath. "We should do this more often."

Katie was pretty sure she wouldn't survive doing this more often, but she nodded anyway. At least the blaring music, the alcohol and the crush of dancing bodies kept her from thinking too much.

After their next trip to the dance floor, Katie switched to straight-up soda while Hailey ordered *her* cola with rum again. It was probably a good thing she worked in a library, Katie thought, because she was going to want things quiet the next day.

They gently brushed off the men who approached them hoping to get lucky with single women on Valentine's Day. Katie flat-out wasn't interested, and she'd stopped trusting Hailey's ability to judge genuine interest about an hour after they'd walked in the door. They laughed and danced and sang along with the songs until the DJ called it a night and the bartender turned off the disco ball.

Katie hooked her arm through Hailey's as they walked the hundred yards or so to the motel room they'd checked into earlier. Hailey was definitely going to wake up with a headache, she thought. But it had been worth it.

Hailey flopped onto the queen bed and almost immediately started snoring, so Katie took her time taking off the black dress and changing into the pajamas she'd tossed in her overnight bag. There was no waking up her friend, so she took off Hailey's necklace and the big hoop earrings and left her alone. The jersey dress would look like hell in the morning, but it wouldn't be too uncomfortable to sleep in. Or be passed out in, as it happened.

Katie had to nudge and push to get enough space in the bed for herself, but then she sighed and felt her overworked muscles relax as the exhaustion and low alcohol buzz zapped the rest of her energy.

She was just drifting off to sleep when her phone rang, and she knew before she looked at the caller ID screen it would be Josh. The whole time zone thing was something he struggled with.

"Hey you," she said, smiling so he'd hear it in her voice.

"How's it going?"

The low timbre of his voice across the line made her chest ache with need. "Not bad. Did you call to wish me a happy Valentine's Day?"

"Oh, shit, it's Valentine's Day? I forgot. I'm sorry. Did you do anything to celebrate it?"

Just nursed a broken heart on the day dedicated to love. And hearing his voice wasn't helping any. "I went dancing and had a few drinks. It was fun."

The silence on the other end of the line went on so long, she checked the phone's screen to make sure it hadn't dropped the call. "Did you go dancing *with* anybody?"

The tension in his voice made her want to laugh and cry at the same time. He was jealous, which meant he cared a lot more than he wanted her to know. But the fact she *knew* he cared about her, but not enough to stay in Whitford, made it harder to keep her voice on an even keel when they talked. She didn't want Josh to know how much it hurt or he might stop calling her out of some misguided idea it was for her own good.

"A friend asked me to go, actually," she told him, being deliberately vague. Let him chew on *that* for a minute or two. "It was nice to get out of town, and I wore my black dress."

Crickets again. Maybe it was a little mean to bring up the dress, but she didn't feel even a second of guilt. Tonight she wouldn't be the only one who closed her eyes and remembered Josh peeling the dress off of her under the Christmas tree.

"I should have stolen the dress and taken it with me. I can't stand the thought of some other man putting his hands on it. On you."

Katie closed her eyes, letting the hot, rough tone of Josh's voice wash over her. Maybe only somebody who'd been his friend for all of their lives would hear it, but he was hurting, too, and she lost the desire to poke at him.

"So are you...am I interrupting anything?"

She could only guess what a hit to his pride it was to ask. "I'm in a motel, actually, in bed with Hailey."

"Oh. Sorry I missed that."

She laughed, then covered her mouth, not that

Hailey so much as stirred. "She's passed out, so you're not missing much."

"As much as I hate to change the subject away from that dress, how's everything in Whitford? Everybody doing okay?"

"The same as always," she told him. "You know how it is."

"I talked to Rosie yesterday and that's exactly what she said."

"How are the riding lessons going?" That one had surprised her. She'd had no idea he'd always wanted to learn to ride until he sent her an email telling her he'd stumbled across a place in Kansas that would give him lessons in exchange for some manual labor.

"Not so well. Turns out horses are a lot harder to ride than four-wheelers. They have minds of their own."

She tried to picture Josh riding a horse, but couldn't. "So you're not the next rodeo star?"

He laughed. "Not even the clown in the barrel. I'm thinking about working my way toward New Mexico."

"I bet Liz would love to see you."

It sounded lame to her own ear, when what she really wanted to do was ask if he was finding what he was looking for. Was what he was doing worth breaking her heart? But she wouldn't ask, because if she didn't keep it light—if she wasn't just his old hometown buddy—she was afraid he'd stop calling.

"I should let you go," he said. "You sound tired."

"I'm going to send you a picture of a time zone map. You should make it the wallpaper on your phone."

"Oh shit, I didn't think of that." He chuckled in her ear and her fingers tightened on her phone. "Again."

"It's okay. I like hearing about your adventures." And she craved hearing his voice. She didn't care what time he called as long as he called. "I'm sorry I called you on Valentine's Day. I wasn't thinking about what day it was. I just wanted to talk to you." He paused for a few seconds, and she heard him sigh. "And I hate to say it, but I'm glad Hailey was your date."

"You're not that easy a guy to get over, you know."

"Does it make me an asshole if I say I don't want you to get over me?"

"Yeah, it does." Not that it would happen any time soon. "But you're not over me, either, so have fun falling asleep thinking about me in that black dress."

He laughed, which eased her heart a little, but when he spoke again, his voice was heavy. "Would it be easier for you if I didn't call?"

"No," she said honestly. "Losing my boyfriend

hurts like hell, but losing my best friend would just make it worse."

"Yeah, I know what you mean. So…I'll call you soon, then." He was quiet for a second, then softly said, "Good night, Katie."

"Night, Josh." *And happy Valentine's Day,* she thought as she ended the call.

When Katie lay down, tears trickled onto her pillow and she squeezed her eyes shut, hoping to stem the flow. It was so hard to pretend she was okay—that she'd gone through the change in their relationship and his leaving unscathed—but she kept telling herself if she pretended long enough, it would become the truth.

So far that wasn't working out very well, but all she could do was get through one day after another and hope it happened soon.

March

JOSH THREW BACK the blanket and sat up, scrubbing his face with his hands. His sister's couch sucked.

The sun was streaming through the windows, so at least he could stop pretending he was getting any sleep and get up. His gaze fell on the snow globe, which he'd set on the coffee table after Liz had gone to bed. Katie's smile was always the last thing he saw before closing his eyes and the first thing he saw when he opened them in the morning.

After taking a leak and brushing his teeth, Josh

heated a cup of water in the microwave and added the disgusting instant coffee Liz kept on hand. The first sip made him shudder, but he took the mug and went outside, picking up the snow globe on his way to the door. As quietly as he could, he closed the door behind him and lowered himself to the concrete step. There were no comfortable chairs set back on a deep porch to keep the sun out of your eyes. No familiar squeak of wooden boards.

He cradled the snow globe in his hands, then shook it so he could watch the snow slowly drift over their faces. Katie's eyes sparkled with happiness in the photo, and her cheeks and the tip of her nose were so cold they almost matched the red stripe on the Patriots pom-pom hat she'd worn that day. It made him smile, remembering how hoarse she'd been for days after the game from all the screaming she'd done.

He'd missed watching the Super Bowl with her. It had been a month since the big game, but he still couldn't shake off the sense of loss, even if it was a dumb thing to regret. He'd watched every Super Bowl with her since he was nine years old and his dad had declared he was old enough to stay up with his brothers and sister and watch the game. Katie had been twelve and, even though it was a Sunday and a school night, Rosie had brought her to the lodge and let her watch it with them. They hadn't missed one since, until this year. He'd watched it without her in a sports bar in Kansas City, eating a steak that hadn't filled the hole in his gut.

He wasn't sure how long he sat out there, making it snow for him and Katie, but his cup was empty when the door opened behind him and Liz joined him on the step. Her hair was tied back in a messy knot, and her Red Sox T-shirt made him smile. You could take the girl out of New England, but you never took New England out of the girl. It was a tight squeeze on the step, and he shifted over a bit, setting the empty mug on the ground.

"Want a sip of mine?" she asked, offering her steaming mug.

"God, no. One was enough."

"Nasty, isn't it?" She blew on her coffee, then took a sip. "I'm trying to cut back on caffeine, so I only have this in the house. One cup in the morning is all I drink, too. If I had good stuff, I'd drink pots of it."

"Why the hell would you want to cut back on caffeine?"

She shrugged. "The older I get, the more trouble I have sleeping at night. Losing the caffeine helps. And stop trying to hide your snow globe from me. I already saw it."

He'd wrapped his hands around it when she'd come out, but he should have known she wouldn't miss it. He wasn't even sure why he cared. Maybe he didn't want Liz to think he was a sap. Or maybe it was just too personal to share.

"Do you talk to her?"

"I'm not so far gone I sit around talking to a picture in a snow globe."

"No, dumbass. Katie. Do you call her? Talk to her on the phone?"

"Yeah. Like once a week we talk for a few minutes. We email and text. Just because I didn't stay doesn't mean we're not friends anymore."

"You miss her?"

Did he miss Katie? He didn't just miss her. He *ached* for her. He was free to go where he wanted, when he wanted and all he wanted was her. Even during the worst of the slump he'd been in, feeling sorry for himself because they'd all abandoned him to take care of the lodge, he hadn't felt this lonely.

He missed Rosie, too. Hell, he missed all of them. Last week, when Mitch had told him over the phone that Paige was pregnant, he'd heard the emotion in his brother's voice and not being able to see the joy on Mitch's face—not being there to hug him and give him a slap on the back—had twisted his gut until it burned.

He missed *home.*

"Josh?" Liz put her hand on his knee and he realized he'd shaken the snow globe again and was staring at it without even being aware. "Did you ask her to come with you?"

"Yeah. But, you know, she's got the barbershop and her mom and...stuff."

"Did you tell her you love her and wanted her to come with you, or did you make it sound like you wanted your best buddy to come with you on a road trip?"

"I told her I wanted her to come with me."

She sighed. "But you didn't tell her you love her."

"Jesus, Liz. This is a little deep for first thing in the morning on one shitty cup of coffee."

"Fine. Tell me how everybody else is doing. Mitch called you, right?"

He nodded. "Yeah. I'm happy for him and Paige. And I guess Rose and Andy are having a great time scandalizing the town by living in sin after decades of not speaking."

"Have to admit, I never saw that one coming."

"I don't think anybody did. Especially Rosie."

Liz smiled. "I'm happy for her. She deserves it. They're doing okay with the lodge?"

They were doing better than Josh could have hoped. No problems and, according to Rosie, Andy had a real knack for making the guests feel at home. They always asked after Josh, of course, but they hadn't lost any customers. While knowing that put his mind at ease, he had to admit that the fact everything just went on as usual without him made him feel a little...not needed. The fact he'd run the Northern Star involuntarily didn't mean he hadn't poured his heart and soul into that business. He missed it, honestly. Almost as much as he missed Katie.

"Business has been better than anybody expected," he said when he realized Liz was still waiting for an answer. "The snow's good and I guess Andy has a knack for that whole internet thing, which blows my mind. And the guests like him."

"I'm glad you didn't sell it," she said in a quiet voice. "I understood why you wanted to, so I said yes, but it almost broke my heart."

"If they were going to keep it the same as it's been through the family, I might still have done it," he admitted. "But I think it would have broken my heart, too. Stupid old house must mean more to me than I thought."

She was quiet for a minute, drinking her coffee. Then she asked, "Have you heard how Drew's doing? Is his divorce final yet?"

"Yeah. He and I helped Mitch put together some office furniture and he said it was final."

"That's rough. How's he taking it?"

"He's not happy about it, I guess." Josh shrugged. "But he's not locked in a dark room with a bottle of booze, either. Other than that, I don't really know."

"Does he see Mallory at all?"

"I wouldn't know. Why?"

"Just wondering. We spent some time talking at

Mitch's wedding and I was curious about how he's doing, that's all."

"You should ask Rose. I'm sure she knows."

Liz laughed. "Rose knows everything. And I know I have to get ready for work. What are you going to do today?"

"I might sit here on the step all day and wish I had a decent cup of coffee."

"There's a coffee shop a half mile that way." She pointed to the left, then pushed herself to her feet. "Nice day for a walk."

"Your hospitality's as good as your coffee."

"Now you know why nobody suggested *I* run the lodge." She ruffled his hair, which she knew from childhood pissed him off. "You need a trim. Badly."

He knew that. He spent a lot of time trying not to think about it, actually. "I'll get around to it at some point."

Because his ass was starting to hurt from the concrete, Josh stood and picked up the empty coffee cup. As awful as it was, he was going to have another cup. First, though, he was going to tuck the snow globe safely away in his bag. He shook it a final time, tracing the outline of Katie's face as the plastic snow drifted down.

"A second cup?" Liz asked when she emerged from the bathroom, showered and dressed in a waitress uniform. Her hair was in a thick braid, but he noticed she didn't bother with makeup. Probably just sweat it off, anyway. Maybe it was his New England blood, but it was far from chilly in New Mexico.

"Yeah. Even shitty coffee's better than none."

"I told you, there's good coffee up the road."

"I am going to go up the road, I guess. But I'll probably keep going."

Liz paused in the act of grabbing her car keys to look at him. "Time to move on?"

He nodded, and then had to brace himself when she threw herself into his arms. "God, I'm going to miss you."

"Why don't you go home, Liz?" he said, squeezing her tight. "You don't have to live at the lodge. Lauren hasn't sold her house yet. She'd rent it to you and you could be close to Rosie and the rest of the family."

"Whitford hasn't been my home in a long time."

"Hey." He pulled back so he could look directly in her tear-filled eyes. "Whitford will always be your home."

Just like it would always be *his* home. The Northern Star was in his blood just as surely as Katie was in his heart. He knew that now.

"So now where are you heading off to, little brother?"

He pressed a kiss to her forehead, and then grinned. "Gotta go see a barber about a haircut."

Rose was sitting on the front porch, a mug of tea in her hand, when Andy's truck pulled up the drive. It was still too early in the season, really, to be out at the crack of dawn on a March morning, but she was bundled up and hadn't been able to sleep.

While they were definitely into spring conditions out on the trails, they'd had just enough of a snowfall to run the groomer, so Butch and Andy had taken a turn last night. She'd grown accustomed to having him in her bed and she hadn't slept well without him.

After he parked, he walked up the steps and sat in the chair beside hers. "Little chilly to be watching the sunrise on the porch, isn't it?"

"It's worth it," she said. "There's nothing more beautiful or soothing than sitting here drinking tea as it starts to get light."

"You were up all night worrying, weren't you? I was with Butch, Rose. We didn't have any problems."

She leaned her head back against the chair. "It wasn't just worrying about you. I haven't heard from Josh in a couple of days and I'm trying not to call him."

"He needs some space. I know it's hard, especially with him, but you've got to let him run. He'll call when he needs to."

"I thought about calling Liz and checking up on him, but that's sort of the same thing, isn't it?"

"Not sort of, hon." He chuckled and reached over to steal her cup. He took a long sip of her tea, shuddered, and then handed it back. "I think I'm going to go stretch out on the couch for a while. Sitting in that groomer all night didn't do much for my back."

Rose nodded, but her mind wasn't ready to let go of the issue it had spent the night worrying over. "Do you think he'll come home?"

"Honestly? I think he will. But all you can do is be patient."

She swiveled her head against the chair so she could see him. "You've done such a great job with the lodge. Will it bother you if he does come back?"

"Not at all." He reached over and folded her hand in his. "None of this is mine, Rose. I'm proud of the way I've taken care of it, but what holds me here is you. The rest of it belongs to Josh and I'm just watching over it for him. And, if he does come back, I'll still be here, so you two won't be doing it alone."

She felt tears welling up in her eyes and tried to blink them away. "I don't think he's going to come home, Andy. Not for a long time and, when he does, it'll only be for a visit."

"What makes you think that?"

"I don't know. I think he's pulling away. When I talk to him, he sounds more and more distant, and I think he's starting to need me less. To need to be grounded to this place less."

"He'll always need you."

"I just want him to call me so I can stop worrying for a couple more days."

He laughed and squeezed her hand. "You bake when you're worried. I have to say I'm a little conflicted."

"Andrew!" She pulled her hand free so she could slap his arm. "You're so bad."

"Whatever gets me banana bread. I have no shame."

She laced her fingers through his again, her gaze holding his. "I love you."

"I love you, too. Even when you're being a frozen, nervous wreck on the front porch at the butt crack of dawn and all I want to do is sleep."

Rose almost dropped her tea when the phone rang. She'd slipped it into the pocket of her bathrobe and she was so bundled up, it took her two rings to fish it out. She glanced at the caller ID, then sagged in relief. "It's Josh."

"If he's still at Liz's, it's only three in the morning out there."

"Must be important, then," she said, and answered it.

KATIE LOOKED AT the big, old-fashioned clock on the wall and sighed. This day was dragging on, and the fact nobody in Whitford needed a haircut was just making it worse. Every tick of the clock seemed to echo in her head and the old radio on the shelf hadn't worked in about twenty-five years. She probably should have gotten it fixed, but honestly her taste in music and her customers' tastes in music were a couple generations removed. But she'd be willing to suffer even some golden oldies today if it made the time go by.

Of course, every day seemed to drag on since Josh had left, but some days were worse than others. Maybe it was worse because she'd been looking forward to hearing from him and he was a few days overdue to call. She'd known the time would come when the calls would come less frequently. As he made a new life for himself, there would be fewer emails and texts and, when the day came he found a woman he wanted to settle down with, they'd eventually just be old friends who exchanged Christmas cards.

Even worse, his wife—who Katie already hated—would be the one who did the cards and she'd have to suffer seeing Josh's name written in some curly, cute handwriting. Probably with a picture of the happy couple and their fluffy little dog in reindeer antlers on the front.

Okay, she was losing it now.

Desperate for somebody to take her mind off Josh's imaginary wife and dog, she pulled out her phone. School had just let out, so Hailey was no good. The library would be overrun with kids for at least an hour. She tried calling her mom, but there was no answer.

That surprised her, but it probably shouldn't have. Rose had Andy now and she had better things to do than sit around and wait for her daughter to lose her mind and call to chat.

She'd probably get a Christmas card from them, too. All happy and in love, probably in front of the Northern Star's Christmas tree…the one she'd unwrapped Josh under.

Rather than keep dwelling on Christmas cards that wouldn't shove everybody's joy in her face until nine months from now, or unwrapping Josh under the tree, she typed in a text message to her best friend.

Bored. Send me a picture of where you are now.

It was a game they'd been playing since shortly after he'd left, but when Josh didn't respond for way too many annoying ticks on the old clock, she sighed and slipped her phone back in her pocket.

Maybe she should give the floor a good scrubbing. Not just the usual mopping, but a hands-and-knees, toothbrush around the chairs kind of cleaning. Something to work off the boredom before she totally went off the deep end.

She was filling the mop bucket with hot water when her phone chimed and she almost didn't hear it. Turning off the faucet with one hand, she pulled out the phone with the other and looked at the screen.

It was a picture from Josh and she held the phone closer to squint at it. He always had a little trouble framing himself and the background, but she could see that he desperately needed a haircut.

Then she realized he probably knew that, since he was standing next to a barber pole. Behind him, stenciled on a pane of glass, she could make out a few letters. *W-H-I...*

Her heart turned over in her chest and she turned just as the bell over the door jingled. She ran across the shop and threw herself into his arms. "I can't believe you're here!"

"Hell of a long drive from New Mexico for a haircut," he said, squeezing her tight.

"You need one." She pulled back so she could look at him. "Back for a visit already? Has my mom been giving you guilt?"

"No, I'm not back because of Rosie." His face grew serious and she wondered if something was wrong. Maybe he hadn't come back just for a visit. Maybe something had happened and nobody had told her. "I'm back because of you."

"You didn't drive all the way back to Maine to visit me, did you?" Not that she was complaining. She was so damn happy to see him she didn't have words to express it, but she was already thinking about how it would hurt like hell when he left again.

"I'm not visiting. I'm home."

She stared up into his blue eyes, trying to make sense of what he was saying. "For good, you mean? Josh, I'm a little confused. You haven't said anything in your texts or emails about coming back."

"Do you know what you are to me, Katie?"

"I believe you made it clear on the playground when you were in first grade and I was in fourth. Mike Crenshaw made fun of me for playing with you, and you told him I was your best friend and if he didn't like it you'd have Mitch, Ryan and Sean all punch him in the face."

Josh grinned. "I'm no fool. Mike was big for his age."

The memory made Katie smile, but her mind was whirling, trying to understand why he was suddenly here, and why they were reminiscing about elementary school. She wanted to throw herself at him again so he'd wrap his arms around her and she could just *feel* him again.

But it had taken a while for their communication to become mostly normal again and she didn't want to upset that balance. He meant too much to her as a friend to jeopardize that again.

"You're more than just a friend to me," he said, staring intently into her eyes. "You're in all of my memories. The good and the not so good. You've been a part of my life for as long as I can remember, and I think I took that for granted."

"That goes both ways, Josh. We've always taken for granted we'd have each other. I know I never really thought you'd leave, but you did."

"I had to go." He breathed in deeply, regret in his eyes. "But, God, how I've missed you. I've missed your voice and calling you wasn't enough. I wanted to hear your voice every day, but I couldn't because I chose to leave you. I left you behind and I lost that right. I lost *you*."

"You didn't lose me. You were never going to be totally happy here if you didn't get to leave. I know that."

"Because you know me. You *get* me." He laughed, a clipped sound without a lot of humor in it. "I even miss the lodge. How messed up is that?"

"It's not messed up. You never had a chance to figure out what you wanted. It was never your choice." She hated seeing him beat himself up.

"I found what I was looking for and the crazy thing is that you were right there in front of me." He reached down and took her hand as her breath caught in her throat. "I've loved you my whole life, but now I know I'm *in* love with you. Crazy in love with you. I had to go. I had to go find what I really wanted for me and now I know, absolutely, that *you* are what I want. Forever. You're *my* northern star."

"That's how long I've loved you," she whispered. "Forever."

"I love you, Katherine Rose Davis. I always—"

"Wait. Did you just middle name me?"

"Yeah, but not like when Rosie does it. I was just trying to be formal when I propose."

She laughed. "Forget it. Just be you."

He wrapped one arm around her waist and pulled her close, gazing down into her eyes. "Marry me, Katie Davis. I love you and I want you to be my wife."

"Yes," she whispered, and he kissed her until she could barely breathe.

"Let's get married fast so we can get started making babies," he said, his eyes crinkling at the corners. "Awesome babies who'll beat the snot out of Mitch's and Sean's kids in family football games."

"Hell, yeah. And just think, we can tell them all the charming story of how they were each conceived in the barn."

He laughed, shaking his head. "I thought about that, driving home from New Mexico. It's a long drive, so I had plenty of time to think. The office is off the living room and it's downstairs, but at the other end of the house from the guest bedrooms. I think we'll move the office upstairs and claim that space as our bedroom. No screaming, of course, but I won't have to put a pillow over your face, either."

"I like the way you think." She searched his face for any lingering signs of doubt. She didn't see any. "My mom is going to come totally undone."

"She already did, on the phone. I had to call her.

I mean, I left. I didn't feel right just showing up and saying, 'Hey, changed my mind so I want my house and my business back now, thanks,' you know?"

"And she called you a dumbass and cried happy tears."

"Pretty much." Without taking his arm off her waist, he glanced over his shoulder at the clock. "You think the town will protest if you close a little early? I've had twenty-three hundred miles to think about what comes after you saying yes."

"I think Whitford will survive." She looked up at him, her heart almost aching with love and knowing he'd come home to her. "What are you thinking comes after yes?"

He leaned down to whisper in her ear, "What would you say if I told you I've been thinking about bending my best friend and future wife over her kitchen table?"

"I'd say it's about damn time."

* * * * *

*If you liked ALL HE EVER DREAMED,
read on for previews of ALL HE EVER NEEDED
and ALL HE EVER DESIRED, available now.*

*ALL HE EVER NEEDED by Shannon Stacey,
available now.*

CHAPTER ONE

MITCH KOWALSKI WAS doing sixty when he blew past the Welcome to Whitford, Maine sign, and he would have grinned if grinning on a Harley at dusk in a shorty helmet wasn't an invitation to eat his weight in bugs.

He was home again. Or he would be after he passed straight through town and nursed the bike down the long dirt drive that led to the Northern Star Lodge. As eager as he was to get there, though, he eased up on the throttle as the first lights of Main Street came into view.

It had been three years since he'd visited his hometown, but he could have navigated the road with his eyes closed. Past the post office where he'd landed his first real job, then lost it because old man Farr's *Playboy* subscription was a hell of a lot more interesting than sorting electric bills. Then the Whitford General Store & Service Station, owned by Fran and Butch Benoit. Junior year, he'd taken their daughter to the prom and then taken her up against the chalkboard in an empty classroom.

Mitch downshifted and executed a lazy rolling stop at the four-way that passed for the town's major intersection. To the left were two rows of ancient brick buildings that housed the bank and town offices and an assortment of small businesses. To the right, the police department—which had had its fill of the Kowalski boys in their youth—and the library, which had been fertile hunting grounds for a teenage boy looking to charm the smart girls out of their algebra homework.

Yeah, it was good to be home, even if everything was closed up tight for the night. The people of Whitford knew if they had business in town, they'd best get it done before the evening news.

He went straight through the intersection, but he didn't go far before the old diner caught his eye. Or the sign did, rather, being all lit up. Last time he'd passed through, the place had been closed up tight—driven out of business by a bad economy and an owner who didn't care enough to try to save it. But now there was a new name on the sign, a couple of cars in the parking lot and flashing red neon in the window declaring it open.

His stomach rumbled, though he felt it rather than heard it due to the loud pipes on his bike, and he pulled into the parking lot. Josh, his youngest brother, wasn't expecting him—unless the boxes of clothes and other stuff he'd shipped ahead had arrived—and he would have already eaten, anyway.

Rather than go rummaging for leftovers, Mitch decided to grab a quick bite before heading on to the lodge.

The first thing he noticed when he walked through the door was the remodeled fifties decor, with a lot of red vinyl and black-and-white marble. The second thing he noticed was the woman standing behind the counter—a woman he'd never seen before, which was rare in Whitford.

Mitch put her at maybe thirty, seven years younger than him, and it looked good on her. She had a mass of brown hair twisted and clipped up into one of those messy knots that begged to be let loose. Jeans and a Trailside Diner T-shirt hugged sweet curves, and her ring finger was bare of either a gold band or a fresh tan line.

A little plastic rectangle was pinned above the very nice mound of her left breast. Name tags were a rare thing in a town where relationships were formed in playpens and cemented in the kindergarten sandbox, so it caught his attention. By the time he took a seat on a red padded stool at the counter, he could read it. *Paige*.

He deliberately sat with his back to the two other couples in the place in the hope they wouldn't recognize him right off. One, because he'd rather Josh heard he was back in town from him, not the grapevine. And, two, because he was a lot more interested in maybe getting acquainted with Paige than getting reacquainted with whoever was in those booths.

"Coffee, sir?"

"Please." Her eyes were brown, even darker than the coffee she poured into an oversize mug for him. "You're new here."

She gave him a look over her shoulder while setting the carafe back on the warmer. "I've been here every day for almost two years, but I've never seen you before. New's relative, I guess."

He plucked a menu from between the condiment rack and the napkin holder, wondering if the food choices had gotten an update, too, along with the sign and the vinyl. "I had my first taste of ice cream in that booth right over there."

She leaned her hip against the stainless-steel island the coffeemaker sat on and looked him over. "Tall, dark and handsome, with pretty blue eyes. You must be one of Josh's brothers."

Usually a guy didn't like being told he had a *pretty* anything, but he'd learned a long time ago having pretty eyes led to having pretty girls. "I'm the oldest. Mitch."

Her smile lit up her face in a way that elevated her from just pretty to pretty damn hot. "Oh, I've heard some stories about you."

He just bet she had. There was no shortage of stories about him and his brothers, but he couldn't help wondering if she'd heard the one about the backseat of Hailey Genest's dad's Cadillac since it was a Whitford favorite. Rumor had it when old man Genest finally traded the car in for a newer model, it still had the cheap wine stains in the carpet and the gouges from Hailey's fingernails in the leather.

Even though he'd only been seventeen at the time—to Hailey's nineteen—he still heard about those gouges if he got within speaking distance of Mr. Genest. Since Mrs. Genest's looks came off as a little more speculative than condemning, he tended to avoid her altogether. Not easy in a town like Whitford, but he could be quick when he needed to be.

"So you're the one who blows stuff up?" she asked when he didn't offer up any comment about the stories she'd heard, as if there was anything to say. While there might be a little embellishment here and there, most of them were probably true.

"You could say that." Or you could say he was one of the most respected controlled-demolition experts in the country. His education, hard work and safety record never excited people as much as the thought of him getting paid to blow stuff up, though. "You still got meat loaf on the menu?"

"First thing the selectmen told me when I applied for a permit is that you can't have a diner in New England without meat loaf."

"I'll take that, and I'll pay for an extra slab of meat loaf and a bucketload of gravy."

"How about I give you the extras on the house as a welcome-home present?"

"Appreciate it," he said, giving her one of his charming smiles—the one that made his *pretty* eyes sparkle, or so he'd been told. And since he'd been told that by women in the process of letting him slide into second base, he was inclined to believe them.

He could tell by the flush creeping up from the collar of her shirt she wasn't immune to him. Nor was he immune to the subtle sway of her hips as she walked to the pass-through window and handed the order to a young man he was pretty sure was Mike Crenshaw's oldest boy. Gavin, he thought his name was.

Dropping an old casino in the middle of crowded Las Vegas to make way for a grander one was an intense job, so it had been at least a couple of months since Mitch had blown off steam between the sheets. And a six-week cap on the relationship was perfect. He could enjoy the getting-to-know-you sex and the know-you-well-enough-to-push-the-right-buttons sex, but be gone before the I'm-falling-in-love-with-you-Mitch sex.

He checked out the sweet curve of her ass when she bent down to grab a bucket of sugar packets, and he grinned. It was damn good to be home.

HEARING THE STORIES—and, oh boy, were there some good ones—hadn't prepared Paige Sullivan for the reality of Mitch Kowalski taking up a stool in her diner. With his just-long-and-thick-enough-to-tousle dark hair and the blue eyes and easy smile, he could have been a star of the silver screen, not a guy who had just happened in looking for some meat loaf.

And maybe a little company, judging from what she'd heard. Supposedly, he was always in the mood for a little company. Unfortunately for him—and maybe a little for her—all he'd get at the Trailside Diner was the blue plate special.

"So where you from?"

Paige shrugged, not looking up from the sugar holders she was refilling. "I'm from a lot of places originally. Now I'm from Whitford."

"Military brat?"

"Nope. Mom with a…free spirit." Mom with a few loose screws was more accurate, but she wasn't in the habit of sharing her life story with her customers.

"How'd you end up here?"

"That old cliché—my car broke down and I never left." She topped off his coffee, but she was too busy making desserts for table six to stand around at the counter and chat.

As she built strawberry shortcakes, she grew increasingly aware of the fact Mitch was watching her. And not just the occasional glance because she was the only thing moving in his line of sight. No, he was blatantly checking her out. Since she was out of practice being an object of interest, it made her self-conscious, and the fact he was the best-looking guy to pass through the Trailside Diner since she'd opened its doors didn't help any.

No men, she reminded herself. She was fasting. Or abstaining. Or whatever-*ing* word meant she wasn't accepting the unspoken invitation to get horizontal in any man's eyes, no matter what he looked like. No. Men.

Gavin called her name a few minutes after she served up the desserts, and she grabbed the hot plate of meat loaf from the window. Mitch gave her a *very* appreciative smile before picking up his fork.

Ignoring the zinging that smile caused—because she wasn't zinging, dammit—she turned her back on him and started a fresh pot of coffee. Normally she wouldn't so near to closing on a weekday night, but she didn't have enough for one refill each should her customers be in the mood to forgo sleep in favor of caffeine and small talk.

Once the coffee was brewing, Paige pulled a clean bus pan out from under the counter and went from table to table, pulling the ketchup bottles and trying not to think about the man at the counter. She knew Mitch Kowalski had a dangerous job, and he certainly looked the part of the bad boy, in faded blue jeans and a black T-shirt hugging an upper body that screamed of physical labor.

Come to think of it, she knew a lot about the oldest Kowalski. While all the brothers were practically heralded as golden boys around town, there was a special gleam in the eyes of the female population when Mitch's name came up. Right on the heels of the gleam came the details, and if there was one thing she knew about the man, it was that he didn't disappoint.

Using her butt to push through the swinging doors, she took the bus pan of ketchup bottles back to the walk-in cooler. She wouldn't refill them until the morning, but she took a minute, hoping the chill would cool her overheating face. Okay, and maybe her body.

If a seventeen-year-old Mitch could make a young woman dig her fingernails into the leather seat of her dad's new car, just imagine what an experienced, thirtysomething Mitch could do. Not that he'd be doing anything to *her,* since she was abstaining, but *imagining* was an-*ing* word that couldn't really hurt.

The strangest thing about the Mitch Kowalski stories was the lack of animosity. It didn't seem possible a man could romance a healthy percentage of the young women in a small town without leaving a trail of jealousy and broken hearts, but it seemed to her he'd managed. Dreamy-eyed nostalgia was the legacy he'd left behind.

By five minutes of closing, the place was empty except for Mitch and an older couple lingering over their lukewarm mugs of decaf, so she went ahead and turned off the Open sign. Her part-time waitress, Ava, who usually did the closing shift, was sick, so Paige had done the whole shebang, from 6:00 a.m. to 9:00 p.m., and she was ready to collapse into bed.

Mitch met her at the cash register with his bill and cash. "What time's breakfast?"

"Six a.m." At least she managed not to groan out loud in dread of the four-thirty alarm.

He chuckled and shook his head. "Let me rephrase that. How *late* can I get breakfast?"

It hadn't occurred to her she'd be seeing *that* much of him. It was a lot easier to resist temptation when temptation wasn't sitting at her counter, watching her work. "Breakfast all day, but no poached eggs after eleven."

He looked as if he was going to say more, but the couple from table six had figured out it was closing time and were on their way to the register. After giving her a smile that jump-started the forbidden zinging again, he walked out and she focused her attention on cashing out her final customers of the very long day.

When she went to twist the dead bolt on the door

behind them, Mitch was at the edge of the parking lot, getting ready to pull out onto the road on what was a very big bike. The motorcycle rumbling between his legs was a black beast of a machine. While the leather saddlebags hid her view of his thighs, she couldn't miss the way his T-shirt stretched across his broad shoulders.

As he revved the engine and pulled into the street, Mitch turned his head and for a long moment they made eye contact. Then he smiled and hit the throttle, disappearing into the night.

No men. Paige flipped off the outside lights and turned away from his fading headlights. For two years she'd avoided having a man in her life. But temptation had never come in a package like Mitch Kowalski.

MITCH STOOD NEXT to his bike with his arms crossed, his pleasure at being home eclipsed by the condition of the Northern Star Lodge.

How could things have gone so downhill in just three years? The front of the lodge—what he could see by the landscaping lights—looked, if not quite run-down, at least a little shabby. Paint on the porch peeling. Weeds growing around the bushes. One of the spindles on the stair railing was missing. He didn't even want to imagine what the place looked like in the full light of day.

His great-grandfather had built the lodge as a

family getaway back when the Kowalskis were rolling in dough, and it had started its life as a massive New Englander with a deep farmer's porch. It was painted the traditional white, and the shutters, originally black, had been painted a deep green by his mother in an effort to make it look less austere. He could see one of those shutters was missing and several were slightly askew. They all needed painting.

At some point his great-grandfather had added an equally massive addition in an L off the back corner, with the downstairs becoming a large kitchen with a formal dining room, and the upstairs being the servants' quarters.

His son, Grandpa Kowalski, hadn't fared well with the stock market, though, being a lot more of a risk taker than he was a savvy businessman and, when the old family money was gone, along with the big house in the city, he'd reinvented the vacation home as an exclusive gentleman's hunting club, and the Northern Star Lodge was born. The servants' quarters became the family quarters. With the next generation, the hunters eventually gave way to snowmobilers and now Josh ran the place, but the five kids owned it together.

The boards creaked under Mitch's feet as he climbed the steps to the heavy oak front door, which squeaked a little on its hinges. The place was going to hell in a handbasket.

The great room was lit up, and his youngest

brother, Josh, was sprawled on one of the sturdy brown-leather sofas, one leg encased by a glaringly white cast from foot to knee. There was a set of crutches on the floor, lying across the front of the couch. Josh had a beer in one hand and an unopened can sat on the end table next to Mitch's favorite chair.

He sank into it and popped the top. "How'd you know I was coming?"

"Mike Crenshaw saw you walking into the diner on his way home from the VFW. He told his wife, who called Jeanine Sharp, who called Rosie at bingo. She called me."

Rosie Davis was the part-time housekeeper-slash-surrogate mother at the lodge and had been since Sarah Kowalski died of an aneurism when Mitch was twelve.

"You come to babysit me?"

By the look of his baby brother, he could use a nanny. And a shower. Their father had stamped his build on all of his children—all of them, even Liz, pushing six feet and lean—but there were differences. Josh had a rounder face with their mother's nose, and Ryan and Sean a more square jaw and their grandfather's nose. Josh and Mitch had their father's dark hair, while the others were more of a dark-blondish like their mother. Mitch's face was strong, with the Kowalski nose, and he was the best-looking of the bunch, naturally. They all had their father's eyes, too. A brilliant blue that made people, especially women, take a second look.

Not many people would take a second look at Josh right then, though, unless they were trying to figure out if they'd seen his picture hanging in the local post office. His hair was a train wreck and it looked like he hadn't shaved in a couple of days. Worn-out sweatpants with one leg cut off at the knee to accommodate the cast and a T-shirt bearing the stains of what looked like spaghetti sauce didn't help.

"Do I look like a babysitter?" Mitch took a long draw of beer, considering the best way to handle his brother. Head-on didn't tend to work well with Kowalskis. "Heard a rumor there was a hot new waitress in town. Thought I'd check her out."

"Yeah, right. Rosie call you?"

"'Course she did. Your cast probably wasn't even dry yet and she was on the phone. When's the last time you took a shower?"

Josh snorted. "No showers for me. I get to take baths, like a woman, with this damn thing propped up on the side of the tub."

"Got some fruity-smelling bubbles?"

"Screw you. How long you staying this time? Three days? A whole week?"

Tired. His brother looked tired more than anything else, and Mitch felt a pang of worry. His little brother just flat out looked like hell. "Rosie said you were limbing that big oak out front and fell."

"Didn't fall. The ladder slipped." He shrugged and sipped his beer.

"Probably because you had the ladder footed against your toolbox in the back of your pickup."

"No doubt. Didn't have a tall enough ladder."

"Why didn't you call in a tree service?"

"Gee, Mr. Fancy Engineering Degree, why didn't I think of that?"

Rather than rise to the bait of his brother's tone, Mitch drank his beer and waited for Josh to realize he was being an ass. Mitch wasn't the one who'd been stupid enough to foot a ladder in the back of a truck or too stubborn to ask for help, so he wasn't going to sit and take crap where crap wasn't deserved.

"Fine. I should have called a tree service. I didn't. Now my leg's fucked up. Happy?"

"Don't be an asshole." Mitch drained the last of the beer and tossed it into the wastebasket somebody—probably Rosie—had put next to the couch for his brother's substantial collection of empties. "How many of those are from today?"

"Not enough." Josh knocked back the last of his can and crumpled it in his hand before dropping it into the basket with the others.

Mitch wasn't sure what was going on, but whatever Josh's problem was, it wasn't a busted-up leg.

Every time Mitch came home—which, granted, wasn't as often as he should—Josh's attitude seemed to have climbed another rung on the shittiness ladder.

"Why don't you get cleaned up in the morning and I'll take you out for breakfast," Mitch said. "We can sit and watch the new waitress work."

"Paige? She's the owner, not a waitress, and she's not interested."

"She was interested."

"Every single guy in Whitford's taken a shot with her and, I'm telling you, she ain't interested. She's lived here like two years and hasn't gone on a single date that anybody knows about. And in this town, somebody would know."

Mitch thought of the way her gaze kept skittering away from his and how she'd blushed, and decided she'd just been waiting for the right guy to come along. There was no lack of interest on his part and, as long as she understood he was only Mr. Right in the *right now* sense, he was more than willing to break her alleged two-year dry spell. They could have a little fun while he got the Northern Star in order and then he'd kiss her goodbye and go on to the next job with no regrets and no hard feelings. Just like always.

ALL HE EVER DESIRED by Shannon Stacey,
available now.

CHAPTER ONE

Because hectic Monday mornings didn't suck enough all on their own merits, Lauren Carpenter managed to miss her lashes and apply mascara straight to her eyeball. Cursing and blinking, she groped for a tissue.

She wasn't sure why she bothered making herself up, anyway. Over her years working as the entire office staff for the only insurance agent in town, she'd seen communications swing from office visits to phone calls and faxes and then to email. Entire days could go by without anybody but her boss actually stepping foot in the place.

It was the principle, she decided as she mopped up the damage and tried again. She'd long ago given up on giving a crap what anybody thought of her, but it made her feel good to look good. There was a limit, though, and she smiled as she shoved her feet into the battered leather loafers that were even older than Nick. Her feet were usually under her desk, anyway.

Thinking of Nick, she glanced at her alarm clock

and sighed. Morning battle to commence in three... two...

"Ma!" The bellow made her cringe.

She'd asked him not to shout at her from across the house even more times than she'd asked him not to call her Ma. Ma made her think of calico dresses and aprons and churning butter. It also made her feel old, and being the mother of a sixteen-year-old was reminder enough of that, thank you very much.

Lauren left her bedroom and went down the hall, purposely not glancing into the train wreck that was her son's room, fastening small pearl earrings as she walked. "Don't bellow, Nick."

"If I don't, you won't hear me."

He was in the kitchen, rummaging through his backpack at the table while a full bowl of cereal turned into mush on the counter. "You planning to eat your breakfast?"

Shrugging, Nick pulled a crumpled ball of paper out of his bag. "Yeah. You need to sign this."

"What is it?" She carried the bowl of cereal to the table and traded it for the paper. "Eat. The bus comes in five minutes."

When he kept his eyes down and shoved a heaping mound of cereal in his mouth, Lauren's stomach sank. Whatever the paper was, it wasn't good.

Physically, Nick took after Dean, her ex-husband. Nick's hair was darker than her blond and his eyes were a lighter brown. He'd gotten not only his dad's good looks, but his struggles in school, too.

It was a detention notice, assigned due to missing homework. "Nick, you've only had three weeks of school and you're slipping already?"

"I don't like the teacher," he mumbled around a mouthful of cereal.

"You don't have to like the teacher. You do have to do your homework." He shrugged and the nonverbal *whatever* was the straw that broke Monday morning's back. "I know which form I *won't* be signing and that's the driver's ed registration."

"But, Mom—"

"Save it. The bus is coming."

She signed the detention paper while he dumped his bowl in the sink, then watched him ball up the notice and shove it back in his pocket. The faint rumble of the bus came into earshot and he hefted his backpack.

"Walk straight home after detention," she said to the back of his head as he walked toward the front door. "And no video games."

"Uh-huh."

After the door closed behind him—he knew better than to slam it—Lauren leaned against the counter and blew out a breath. Something was going on with her son and she'd be damned if she could put her finger on what. He didn't get a pass because he was a teenager or because of that *boys-will-be-boys* crap, so it was time for an attitude adjustment. And that meant talking to Dean, because if they weren't on the same page when it came to Nick, she may as well find a brick wall to talk to.

Of course, talking to Dean Carpenter was always like talking to a brick wall. Communication wasn't his strong suit. Their son, though, was more receptive if his parents were giving him the same message. Usually.

She'd have to find a few minutes to talk to her ex when he picked up Nick on Friday evening, which meant having an idea what she was going to say before he showed up. And she'd worry about that some other time, because now she had less than ten minutes to get to work.

It took her twelve to drive across Whitford because she had to stop for gas, so Gary Demarest, insurance agent extraordinaire, was already in when she arrived. She'd worked for him since her divorce eight years before, when she'd been looking for a job in town with mother's hours. Demarest Insurance had mostly fit the bill, though Nick got out of school a couple of hours before she left work. When he was younger, the neighbor had kept an eye on him. Now he was mostly on his own, though in a town like Whitford, somebody was always watching.

"I left some notes on your desk," Gary said. He was in great shape for a man in his mid-sixties and prided himself on being a smart dresser, despite the fact that the majority of his clientele wore jeans and T-shirts. "Paige Sullivan's going to be renting out her mobile home, so she needs a price on adjusting the property insurance accordingly. I'll let you know when I get the numbers together, but you can get started on the paperwork if you get a chance."

"No problem." When Gary disappeared into his office, closing the door behind him, Lauren leaned back in her very nice office chair and sighed.

Paige Sullivan was going to rent out her mobile home because she was marrying Mitch Kowalski and they were going to buy a house together. And, of course, thinking of Mitch naturally led her to think of his brother.

Ryan Kowalski. Her *what-if* guy when she let herself indulge in ridiculous fantasy. *What if she'd said yes?*

He'd been in town a few times lately, she knew, helping his brothers straighten out the Northern Star, their family-owned snowmobile lodge. But, as in the past when he'd visited, he stayed close to home and they never got close enough to speak. She wasn't sure whether it was deliberate, but he'd managed not to run into her since he'd graduated from college.

The phone rang before Lauren could give in to the *what-if* fantasy, which was a good thing. With Nick needing an attitude adjustment and Dean to deal with, the last thing she needed was another guy with issues. Her ex-husband's ex–best friend could stay out of sight and out of mind where he belonged.

RYAN KOWALSKI MADE very few mistakes when it came to running his business, but trapping himself in a pickup with an idiot definitely counted as one. "Put the phone on vibrate."

Dill Brophy snorted, just as the phone in his hand sounded another incoming text with the grating, electronic sound of a duck call. For almost five freaking hours he'd been listening to Dill's phone quack, and if he had a shotgun he'd pull over and play an impromptu round of Duck Hunt. Not even a minute later, it quacked again.

Ryan jerked the wheel hard to the left and had the satisfaction of hearing Dill's head thump against the passenger window.

"Ow! What the hell, man?"

"Pothole."

"Matt wants to know if we're almost there yet." *Quack.* "Or if not, can we stop for lunch, because it's after lunchtime."

Ryan put on his blinker and pulled over onto the shoulder. Once Matt Russell had pulled in behind him, he turned to Dill. "Let me see your phone."

Rather than throw it out the window and run over it repeatedly, as he wanted to do, Ryan took it and powered it down. Then he got out of the truck, slamming the door with Kowalski Custom Builders painted down the side, and walked back to the identical vehicle Matt was driving. Well, not totally identical. Ryan's had heated leather seats and a custom sound system. It was nice to be the boss.

Matt lowered the window. "What's up?"

"Give me your phone." Since both guys carried company-provided cell phones, refusing wasn't an option. When he had it, Ryan gave the young carpenter a stern look. "You text while driving one of my trucks again, you're fired."

After he tossed both phones into his door pocket, they got back on the road and Ryan took a deep breath when, not long after, they passed the Welcome to Whitford, Maine sign. Home again. Dammit.

A while back, when his youngest brother, Josh, had busted his leg and the oldest, Mitch, had gone home to give him a hand, the shit had really hit the fan. The Northern Star Lodge—which had gone from gentleman's hunting lodge to snowmobiling lodge under the ownership of several generations of Kowalskis—was in bad shape, both financially and physically. Some rehab needed doing and, since Ryan was a builder, it was his turn to spend a little time in Whitford.

Because he'd be away from his business for who knew how long, he'd left his top guys and most experienced builders down in Massachusetts to keep the jobs going, which was how he'd ended up stuck with two young, less-experienced pinheads to work with.

That wasn't quite fair. They were good kids and they worked hard. If they weren't he wouldn't have them on his jobs. But his current feelings toward them were colored a bit by four and a half hours of the quacking duck and the twinkly chime that sounded when Dill's pregnant wife texted. And she texted a lot.

For a second, he regretted shutting Dill's phone off, but then he told himself that if there was an emergency, she'd call him or the office, looking for her husband. And when they got to the lodge, he'd give the phones back.

As eager as he was to get to the lodge, he didn't want to show up with two hungry guys looking to rummage through Rosie's kitchen, Ryan decided to stop at the Trailside Diner and let them eat before driving the last few minutes to the Northern Star.

Because it wasn't quite two yet, Paige Sullivan— his future sister-in-law—was behind the counter and she smiled when she saw him.

"Ryan! I didn't know you were coming in today."

He leaned across the counter to kiss her cheek. "It was kind of fluid. Had to wrap up some stuff and wait on a granite delivery, then I made a break for it today."

"Does Rosie know?"

"I called her when I hit the road this morning." Rose Davis was housekeeper at the Northern Star Lodge by title, but she'd helped raise the Kowalski kids after their mother died. Ryan knew better than to pop in without giving her enough advance notice to make his favorite dinner. Not that he expected her to, but Rosie liked to fuss. "Is Mitch at the lodge?"

"He's in Miami for a few days. I don't think he expected you until at least next week."

He realized the guys were hovering behind him, obviously waiting for an introduction, so he gestured to each in turn. "This is Dillon Brophy and Matt Russell. They work for me and they'll be helping out at the lodge. This is Paige Sullivan, my brother's fiancée."

Matt and Dill straightened up, smart enough to catch his cue that Paige was as good as a member of the boss's family. Both guys were in their early twenties, but the similarities ended there. Dill was tall—almost as tall as Ryan—and skinny, with sandy hair and an easy smile. Matt was shorter, more muscular, and had the dark and serious thing going on. Ryan watched them each shake Paige's hand, both *very* respectful, before heading off to a table to look over the menu.

"Rosie's just going to eat them up," Paige said, her eyes filled with laughter. "She's always complaining she doesn't have enough people to fuss over anymore."

"They're employees, not grandchildren. She doesn't need to fuss over them and I'll kick their asses if they let her."

The look she gave him was pure skepticism, and he shook his head before joining the guys. They all had cheeseburgers and fries, and Ryan had to admit that, despite the fact he hadn't wanted to stop at the diner, the food hit the spot. The mood was good all around, especially when he told them they could retrieve their phones while he paid. They were out the door before he got all the words out.

"They're worse than kids," he muttered, handing the check and the company credit card to Paige.

"You took their cell phones away? Totally a dadlike move."

"I'm not *that* old." He signed his name to the slip she handed him, then took his card back. "If you talk to Mitch, let him know I'll be around for a while this time."

"I will."

As he turned to leave, he was aware of the door opening and he stopped walking so he wouldn't run into anybody while tucking his card back into his wallet. Then he looked up.

Dirty-blond hair. Dark-chocolate eyes. A body that time and some added pounds had molded into curves any man would take his time savoring. And a familiar face that hit him like one of his brother's wrecking balls.

LAUREN MIGHT HAVE forgotten how to breathe for a few seconds. God, he looked good. Even better than he had in her imagination. Since his brothers had aged well, she shouldn't have been surprised by the still-thick dark hair or the flat stomach and broad shoulders shown off by the Kowalski Custom Builders polo shirt. But part of her wished he'd gone downhill a little. Or a lot, actually.

She'd seen him a couple of times since Josh had broken his leg, but always at a distance. So she hadn't been able to see the blue eyes or the way the years had added character to his face, nor could she have smelled whatever delicious cologne or aftershave he was wearing.

And distance meant not having to do this awkward dance of not knowing what to do or say. They hadn't actually spoken since Nick was a baby, when Ryan had asked her a question that could have changed her life and she'd said no.

He was supposed to stay away. It was unspoken, but understood.

"Hi, Lauren." His voice was deeper. Stronger. "How have you been?"

For a few seconds he looked as if he was trying to figure out how to sum up fifteen or so years in a few words, but then he smiled. But it was the polite smile, not the full, devastating grin, for which she should probably be thankful. "I've been good."

"Good. And how are things at the lodge?"

"Good."

"And Josh's leg?"

"It's good."

"That's…good." Now that they'd established everything was *good,* she'd reached the end of her having-a-clue-what-to-say rope. "I don't have a long lunch break, so I should probably order."

"Of course." He stepped out of her way. "I'll see you…around."

He left before she could say anything else and that was fine, since all she could think to say was "good." And seeing him around would be anything but.

As she sat down, Lauren tried to shake off the nerves that being so close to him seemed to have set to quivering, only to find herself pinned by Paige's all-too-observant stare. She should have made the time to pack a lunch this morning.

"Coffee?"

Lauren pressed a hand to her stomach, cursing the butterflies. "I think I'll have decaf."

"They have that effect on women."

"Coffees?"

"Kowalskis."

Uh-oh. The last thing Lauren needed was the population of Whitford thinking she had a thing for Ryan. "Hectic morning. Nick didn't want to get out of the house and then things at the office were crazy. I've already had more than my fair share of the high-test stuff."

"Mmm-hmm. What are you eating?"

"Grilled cheese on wheat, I guess. With coleslaw instead of fries."

"So, the regular, in other words." Paige rolled her eyes and went to give the order to the cook, but she was gone only a few seconds. "Weren't your ex and Ryan best friends back in high school?"

It was to be expected, Lauren told herself. The woman was marrying a Kowalski, so it was natural people would fill her in on the family details. "Yeah, they were."

They weren't anymore. There hadn't been a fight between the guys, but Dean seemed to think Ryan had gone off to become a big shot and forgotten where he came from. There was some resentment on Dean's part, but it was misplaced. Lauren had never told her ex-husband about Ryan's visit, even though it had been a serious betrayal of the guys' friendship. Ryan had gone away, and every week, then month, and finally year he was gone made it easier to justify not telling Dean.

"And?"

She'd almost forgotten Paige was standing there, no doubt waiting to hear the rest of the story. "And Ryan got his degree and moved to Mass and that was that."

"Oh, come on. It's me!" Paige bent down and

rested her forearms on the counter so they were at the same height. "Mitch thinks there's some kind of history between you two."

"Nope, sorry." It wasn't exactly a lie, but it wasn't exactly the truth, either. It was time to change the subject. "Speaking of Mitch, when are you guys getting married?"

Paige's face lit up and, almost by reflex, she put out her left hand to admire the sparkling ring on her finger. "It hasn't even been two weeks since he asked me."

"From what I've heard, Mitch is in a hurry and you'll be lucky if he doesn't have you kidnapped and put on a plane to Vegas."

"We want to get married at the lodge, but we don't want to do it during the sledding season and he doesn't want to wait until spring."

"That doesn't leave you a lot of time."

"We're thinking about Columbus Day weekend," Paige said. "It falls early this year, so maybe we'll still have some fall foliage."

"It's also not quite three weeks away."

"We don't want anything fancy. He's going to call everybody when he gets home and see if we can make it work. As long as his aunt Mary and uncle Leo can make it from New Hampshire, and his brother Sean and his wife, we'll probably go for it. But he'd like his sister to fly in from New Mexico, too."

"I haven't seen Liz in ages."

"I guess nobody has, except when Sean got out of the army. They had a party for him at Ryan's."

And back to Ryan again. Thankfully the bell dinged and Paige left to pick up Lauren's grilled cheese sandwich, because Lauren could feel the heat creeping into her face. She was going to have to come up with a way to stop doing that or wear more makeup or something. She couldn't blush every time somebody mentioned the man's name.

To make matters worse, it wasn't some leftover attraction to a young Ryan, which was more nostalgia than anything. It's not as if she'd been lusting after him while running around with his best friend. She'd loved Dean and, while she found Ryan attractive, it wasn't until later her subconscious mind had given him the starring role in her sexual fantasies. Probably because he was safely far away so fantasy couldn't intrude on reality.

But right now, grown-up Lauren's body, which hadn't been up against a naked man's in *way* too long, seemed to think the very grown-up Ryan was just the man for the job.

Paige set Lauren's lunch in front of her, then untied her apron. "I hate to run out on you, but I have an appointment to look at a house."

Lauren had been so wrapped up in trying not to think about Ryan Kowalski, she hadn't even noticed that Ava, the second-shift waitress, had shown up.

"I have to inhale this and get back, anyway. When I step out for lunch, it's like Hurricane Gary passed over my desk during the half hour I was gone."

"Don't make any plans for Columbus Day weekend," Paige reminded her as she headed for the door. "I'm not planning on having bridesmaids, but you and Hailey *have* to be at my wedding."

"I wouldn't miss it," Lauren said, and she meant it. But as the door swung closed behind Paige, her undersexed mind coughed up a tantalizing image.

Ryan in a suit. Her in a sexy dress. A few drinks. A slow dance or two…

She shoved a forkful of coleslaw in her mouth and told herself to get over it. There was enough on her plate as it was and she already knew they had almost nothing to say to each other. He was as good as a stranger now and, no matter how her hormones felt about the matter, it was best he stay that way.

It seemed as if he'd been avoiding her for years. Now it was time for her to avoid him. Simple as that.

* * * * *

New York Times bestselling author

DIANA PALMER

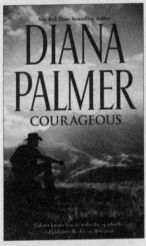

The life of a paid mercenary makes sense to Special Forces officer Winslow Grange. The jungles of South America may make his former job as a ranch manager for his friend Jay Pendleton look like a cakewalk, but it's nothing that the former Green Beret can't handle.

A woman's heart, however—that's dangerous territory. Back in Texas, Grange's biggest problem was avoiding Peg Larson and all the complications being attracted to the daughter of his foreman would entail. Now Grange will need all his training to help General Emilio Machado gain control of the tiny South American nation of Barrera; when Peg arrives unannounced, she's a distraction he can't avoid. She's determined to show Grange she can be useful on and off the battlefield. Once she breaks through his armor, traversing the wilds of the Amazon will prove an easier task than defending himself against her winning charms....

Available wherever books are sold!

Be sure to connect with us at:

Harlequin.com/Newsletters

Facebook.com/HarlequinBooks

Twitter.com/HarlequinBooks

HARLEQUIN® HQN™

™ www.Harlequin.com

PHDP762

**If you build it, love will come…
to Hope's Crossing.**

USA TODAY Bestselling Author

RaeAnne Thayne

Alexandra McKnight prefers a life of long workdays and short-term relationships, and she's found it in Hope's Crossing. A sous-chef at the local ski resort, she's just been offered her dream job at an exclusive new restaurant being built in town. But when it comes to designing the kitchen, Alex finds herself getting up close and personal with construction foreman Sam Delgado….

At first glance, Sam seems perfect for Alex. He's big, tough, gorgeous—and only in town for a few weeks. But when Sam suddenly moves into a house down the road, Alex suspects that the devoted single father of a six-year-old boy wants more from her than she's willing to give. Now it's up to Sam to help Alex see that, no matter what happened in her past, together they can build something more meaningful in Hope's Crossing.

Available wherever books are sold!

Be sure to connect with us at:

Harlequin.com/Newsletters

Facebook.com/HarlequinBooks

Twitter.com/HarlequinBooks

HARLEQUIN® HQN™
www.Harlequin.com

PHRT747

Return to *USA TODAY* bestselling author

CHRISTIE RIDGWAY'S

Crescent Cove, California, where the magic of summer can last forever...

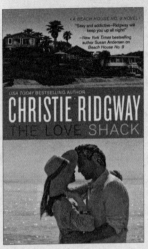

Globe-trotting photojournalist Gage Lowell spent carefree childhood summers in Crescent Cove. Now that he desperately needs some R & R, he books a vacation at Beach House No. 9—ready to soak up some sun and surprise old friend and property manager Skye Alexander. Their long-distance letters got him through a dangerous time he can't otherwise talk about. But when he arrives, the tightly wound beauty isn't exactly happy to see him.

Skye knows any red-blooded woman would be thrilled to spend time with gorgeous, sexy Gage. But she harbors secrets of her own, including that she might just be a little bit in love with him. And she's convinced the restless wanderer won't stay long enough for her to dare share her past—or dream of a future together. Luckily for them both, summer at Crescent Cove has a way of making the impossible happen....

Available wherever books are sold!

Be sure to connect with us at:

Harlequin.com/Newsletters
Facebook.com/HarlequinBooks
Twitter.com/HarlequinBooks

HARLEQUIN® HQN™
www.Harlequin.com

PHCR715

New York Times bestselling author

NORA ROBERTS

will delight with these two classic tales of love meant to be!

BEST LAID PLANS

Abra Wilson had met men like Cody Johnson before—charmers who could make a woman's heart rise and fall, and smile their way out of any situation. The overconfident East Coast architect fits the bill perfectly, and Abra has no plans to fall under his spell…no matter how distracting he might become. Fortunately, Cody has plans of his own that not even Abra will be able to resist!

FROM THIS DAY

When B. J. Clark, manager of the Lakeside Inn, meets the new owner, Taylor Reynolds, she is fully prepared to dislike him. She fears that he plans to transform her lovely, sleepy old hotel into a resort for jet-setters. But when sparks fly between them, B.J. finds herself torn between her professional antagonism and her growing attraction to the man she had sworn to despise.

Available wherever books are sold!

www.Harlequin.com

PSNR168

New Times Bestselling Author

SHERRYL WOODS

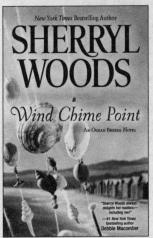

Facing a personal crisis, ambitious and driven Gabriella Castle retreats to the welcoming arms of her family. Everything she's worked for has been yanked out from under her, and she seeks the serenity of her grandmother's home on the North Carolina coast. With difficult decisions to make about her future, the last thing she wants is an unexpected love.

Wade Johnson fell for Gabi the first time he saw her. It's not the only time he's found himself in the role of knight in shining armor, but Gabi isn't looking for a rescuer. To get her to stay, Wade will need a whole lot of patience and gentle persuasion…and maybe the soothing sound of wind chimes on a summer breeze.

Available wherever books are sold.

Be sure to connect with us at:

Harlequin.com/Newsletters

Facebook.com/HarlequinBooks

Twitter.com/HarlequinBooks

MSW1442R

REQUEST YOUR FREE BOOKS!

2 FREE NOVELS
FROM THE ROMANCE COLLECTION
PLUS 2 FREE GIFTS!

YES! Please send me 2 FREE novels from the Romance Collection and my 2 FREE gifts (gifts are worth about $10). After receiving them, if I don't wish to receive any more books, I can return the shipping statement marked "cancel." If I don't cancel, I will receive 4 brand-new novels every month and be billed just $6.24 per book in the U.S. or $6.74 per book in Canada. That's a savings of at least 22% off the cover price. It's quite a bargain! Shipping and handling is just 50¢ per book in the U.S. and 75¢ per book in Canada.* I understand that accepting the 2 free books and gifts places me under no obligation to buy anything. I can always return a shipment and cancel at any time. Even if I never buy another book, the two free books and gifts are mine to keep forever.

194/394 MDN F4XY

Name _____ (PLEASE PRINT)

Address _____ Apt. #

City _____ State/Prov. _____ Zip/Postal Code

Signature (if under 18, a parent or guardian must sign)

Mail to the Harlequin® Reader Service:
IN U.S.A.: P.O. Box 1867, Buffalo, NY 14240-1867
IN CANADA: P.O. Box 609, Fort Erie, Ontario L2A 5X3

Want to try two free books from another line?
Call 1-800-873-8635 or visit www.ReaderService.com.

* Terms and prices subject to change without notice. Prices do not include applicable taxes. Sales tax applicable in N.Y. Canadian residents will be charged applicable taxes. Offer not valid in Quebec. This offer is limited to one order per household. Not valid for current subscribers to the Romance Collection or the Romance/Suspense Collection. All orders subject to credit approval. Credit or debit balances in a customer's account(s) may be offset by any other outstanding balance owed by or to the customer. Please allow 4 to 6 weeks for delivery. Offer available while quantities last.

Your Privacy—The Harlequin® Reader Service is committed to protecting your privacy. Our Privacy Policy is available online at www.ReaderService.com or upon request from the Harlequin Reader Service.

We make a portion of our mailing list available to reputable third parties that offer products we believe may interest you. If you prefer that we not exchange your name with third parties, or if you wish to clarify or modify your communication preferences, please visit us at www.ReaderService.com/consumerschoice or write to us at Harlequin Reader Service Preference Service, P.O. Box 9062, Buffalo, NY 14269. Include your complete name and address.

ROM13R

#1 *New York Times* bestselling author
Linda Lael Miller returns to Stone Creek with
a sweeping tale of two strangers running from
dangerous secrets.

LINDA LAEL MILLER

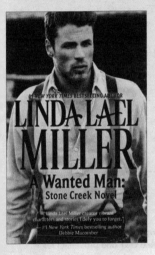

The past has a way of catching up
with folks in Stone Creek, Arizona. But
schoolmarm Lark Morgan and Marshal
Rowdy Rhodes are determined to
hide their secrets—and deny their
instant attraction. That should be easy,
since each suspects the other of living
a lie…

Yet Rowdy and Lark share one truth:
both face real dangers, such as the gang
of train robbers heading their way, men
Ranger Sam O'Ballivan expects Rowdy
to nab. As past and current troubles
collide, Rowdy and Lark must surrender
their pride to the greatest power of
all—undying love.

Available wherever books are sold!

Be sure to connect with us at:

Harlequin.com/Newsletters

Facebook.com/HarlequinBooks

Twitter.com/HarlequinBooks

HARLEQUIN® HQN™

™ www.Harlequin.com

PHLLM722

shannon stacey

77756	ALL HE EVER DESIRED	__ $7.99 U.S.	__ $9.99 CAN.
77755	ALL HE EVER NEEDED	__ $7.99 U.S.	__ $9.99 CAN.
77686	YOURS TO KEEP	__ $7.99 U.S.	__ $9.99 CAN.
77685	UNDENIABLY YOURS	__ $7.99 U.S.	__ $9.99 CAN.
77678	EXCLUSIVELY YOURS	__ $7.99 U.S.	__ $9.99 CAN.

(limited quantities available)

TOTAL AMOUNT	$ _____
POSTAGE & HANDLING	$ _____
($1.00 FOR 1 BOOK, 50¢ for each additional)	
APPLICABLE TAXES*	$ _____
TOTAL PAYABLE	$ _____

(check or money order—please do not send cash)

To order, complete this form and send it, along with a check or money order for the total above, payable to HQN Books, to: **In the U.S.:** 3010 Walden Avenue, P.O. Box 9077, Buffalo, NY 14269-9077; **In Canada:** P.O. Box 636, Fort Erie, Ontario, L2A 5X3.

Name: _____

Address: _____ City: _____

State/Prov.: _____ Zip/Postal Code: _____

Account Number (if applicable): _____

075 CSAS

*New Yor

*Canadian reside   xes.

HILLSBORO PUBLIC LIBRARIES
Hillsboro, OR

HARLEQUIN HQN
www.Harlequin.com

PHSS0513BL

Member of Washington County
COOPERATIVE LIBRARY SERVICES